Turn a Blind Eye

Alaric Bond

Published by Old Salt Press, LLC

www.oldsaltpress.com

ISBN-10: 0-9882360-3-6
ISBN-13: 978-0-9882360-3-5
E.book: 978-0-9882360-4-2

Publisher's Note: This is a work of historical fiction. Certain characters and their actions may have been inspired by historical individuals and events. The characters in the novel however represent the work of the author's imagination. Any resemblance to actual persons living or dead is entirely coincidental.

The cover shows detail from a painting attributed
to George Morland (1763-1804).

By the same author, and published
by Fireship Press
(www.fireshippress.com)

The Fighting Sail Series:

His Majesty's Ship

The Jackass Frigate

True Colours

Cut and Run

The Patriot's Fate

CONTENTS

Acknowledgements

Thanks are due to Mat, Tim, Dee, Rick and Joan for support and advice: Newhaven Local and Maritime Museum for their research facilities, and every member of 'The Shapiro Squad' for keeping me sane through this and other books.

Turn a Blind Eye

Chapter One

She was far smaller than any vessel Griffin had ever served in, let alone commanded. Her single mast appeared tall and the running bowsprit overly long, even while in harbour and fully retracted. That, together with the gaff and boom of the main, as well as two sizeable square sail yards, spoke of a massive area of canvas: possibly too large for the short and slightly stubby hull. Certainly there could be no greater contrast between this and the lumbering East Indiaman he had so recently quitted: the cutter was perfect.

Looking across the span of Newhaven Harbour Griffin could easily imagine the small craft's sail pattern and trace her underwater lines. He knew the keel must, by necessity, be deep and the corresponding draught would make shoal-water work dangerous. Cutters also had a reputation for being dark, damp and dirty. She would be fast, though, of that there could be no question and, if skilfully handled,

1

very manoeuvrable. Griffin's seaman's mind raced and he felt his fingers work with anticipation. He supposed a landsman would equate it to getting to know a strange but powerful horse; one that might prove troublesome and was quite likely to buck its rider at the first opportunity but whom, once mastered, could only satisfy.

He continued to look for several more minutes, before the chill of the autumn afternoon forced him to move on. The harbour was wide at this point; he had the option of walking all the way back to the drawbridge and returning on the other side or taking the ferry that was conveniently moored nearby. The light would be failing before long, and he wanted to have a good look at his new command while there was still the opportunity, so he approached the small boat and a seaman presented himself.

"Want to cross, your honour?" the man asked.

Griffin nodded, and followed him into the ferry. "I'm going to the cutter," he said, with an air of importance, and, because he could not resist, added, "I'm her new commander."

Nothing was said in reply, but Griffin was conscious that he was being examined as the boat set out across the strong current. They had to wait while a heavily laden coal barge passed by, but soon he was climbing the opposite wharf and feeling in his pocket for the fare. The ferryman remained silent as he took the coin then turned his back, as if unwilling to accept that his passenger had ever actually existed.

Griffin went to speak but changed his mind, directing his attention to the cutter instead. Her berth was let in slightly from the run of the river, forming what appeared to be a private harbour. The tide was in full flow and a good deal of debris and flotsam had been washed up and trapped between the side of the vessel and the quay. That current would have to be allowed for when manoeuvring, although the safety provided by such a mooring outweighed many of the disadvantages. He stepped onto the short gangway and looked about. There was no sign of an anchor watch, and as his shoe touched the deck Griffin called out. His voice echoed about the quiet harbour and he looked around in the stillness that seemed to mock him. Then movement from the forward companionway caught his attention.

"What's about there?" The man, who was of an indeterminable age, glared at Griffin in obvious annoyance as he struggled up on deck. He was dressed as a seaman, although the baggy 'petticoat' trousers were unusual, and seemed to place him about thirty years in the past. "You got reason to be aboard, mister?"

Griffin opened his mouth to speak but could not find the exact words; it was hardly the start he had planned.

"'Cause if you ain't, you'd better get off and damned quick," the seaman informed him. "This is a government vessel and those what don't belong ain't welcome."

"I am very glad to hear it," Griffin finally replied, and was about to say more when the cover of the stern hatch flew back with a crack and both men turned to see another figure step up. He was dressed far more smartly, and in a uniform that was almost that of a junior Royal Naval officer.

"This is Mr Davies," the seaman announced, almost smugly. "He'll sort you out."

The officer, who was on deck now, regarded the newcomer cautiously. "Can I be helping you?" His voice was soft, but with an edge and, despite the polite enquiry, not encouraging. "Do you have business aboard?"

"I am your new commanding officer," Griffin replied, self-consciously. He noticed that both men were taken by surprise, and the seaman actually withdrew a step, narrowly avoiding falling backwards down the hatchway.

"Commander Griffin, sir?" The officer appeared to be a good deal older than Griffin, probably in his late forties. He had short, curly and greying hair, blue eyes in a ruddy, weather-beaten face, broad shoulders and a body that looked as if it might be inclined to fat. His uniform was functionally smart – not crisp, as if awaiting inspection and Griffin guessed he would be a solid and dependable seaman. "We weren't expecting you until the morrow, sir." The clear eyes swept down his new commander's civilian clothes.

"I caught an earlier coach," Griffin replied, almost apologetically. "My uniform and other dunnage is expected at any time."

The mate's expression relaxed slightly. "I see, sir. And are you berthing aboard?"

"No." Griffin's first conversation as a captain was definitely not following the intended course; he had hardly anticipated starting with a string of explanations. "I have taken a room in the town, but would welcome a chance to look about."

"Of course, sir." The man stepped forwards and extended his hand. "Forgive me: my name is William Davies, mate of the *Bee*."

Griffin took the horny grip that was firm, but not painful. "Pleased to meet you, Mr Davies; will you accompany me?"

"Be glad to, sir." Davies gave a neutral smile. "Shall we start below?"

Griffin followed the mate down the steep companionway that he knew would lead to the officers' accommodation. "Have you served long?"

"I've been mate for nigh on two years," Davies replied, turning at the bottom of the ladder. "Afore that I was a deputed mariner for three and an ordinary mariner for five, though four of those was in our previous vessel. I was with

4

the colliers afore that, apart from a brief spell with his Majesty."

"So the *Bee* is six years old?" Griffin asked.

Davies considered the matter more slowly. "Must be. Though she still feels like a new'n to me."

Griffin nodded and looked about the tiny chart room. The room was dark, with an overhead of well below five feet that made standing upright impossible.

"Did you not consider applying for command yourself?"

"Oh indeed, sir," Davies answered. "And was considered, though found myself turned over in favour of a better man."

There was a silence that remained awkward for no more than a second before both began to laugh.

"Well, I shall try to justify your description, Mr Davies," Griffin said, still chuckling. "Though I'll admit it now, revenue work is a new skill for me to acquire."

"I take it that this is your first appointment?"

Griffin noted that the mate had missed the customary 'sir', but in such an informal atmosphere as that of the empty chart room he did not feel inclined to correct him.

"Indeed, I have spent some time at the Board of Customs in London, and a month or more sailing with Commander Saunder at Harwich – a busy station, I'd chance."

Davies raised his eyebrows. "You'll find we have our fair share of excitement on this coast, though the Shoreham boat takes most of the prizes."

"Well that is something I intend to change," Griffin said, a little stiffly.

The mate gave a half-smile, "Very good, sir."

Griffin cleared his throat, conscious that he might have committed a faux pas, but unaware of the reason. "And afore that I served with the East India Company," he continued rather lamely.

"Did you, now?" The mate was showing more interest. "I'd imagine that to be a sight apart from what you'll be finding here."

"Which is why I changed," Griffin agreed. "I worked up to second mate, did three full China trips and two to the plantations in New South Wales, but eventually became bored with the merchant life."

"Not enough action?"

Griffin considered for a moment, wondering if he might be giving too much away. But Davies was to be his second-in-command and had an agreeable, trustworthy air about him. "In the main, yes, that is true. I had it in mind to try for the RN, but there seems to be a wealth of officers requiring positions at present, and I have never sat a board. But I also missed England; foreign travel is all very well for a spell, but not for life."

"And are you liking it now?" Davies asked. "Is England all you had hoped?"

"Is anything?" Griffin replied. "The summer was fine though this colder weather is hardly to my taste, and we seemed better served aboard an Indiaman than you are ashore. There is much in the place that I do not understand, but it will do for a trial, and if you can truly show me some action we might make the better of it. Come, let us continue the inspection."

Davies glanced about the tiny space. "Well this, as you can see, is the chart room, though we use it as a general mess." He glanced at Griffin. "In truth, in a vessel this size most of the accommodation has more'n one use. There's none of your John Company luxury in the customs service, I fear."

"I did not expect luxury when I joined, Mr Davies." Griffin replied sharply.

The mate lowered his head briefly. "No, sir. I'm sure not: I was out of line and apologise."

"Very well." The point had been made. "Go on, if you please."

"Me an' Joe Lamport takes our meals in here, Joe's the deputed mariner." Davies continued, his tone now more restrained. "The bo'sun and carpenter do as well, and maybe some of the senior mariners, when we chooses to invite them. Commander Carter, he's your predecessor, he'd often mess in with us also."

"I understand the late commander suffered an unfortunate accident," Griffin chanced.

"That is so." Davies glanced about the small room as if eager for distraction. "Would you care to see your accommodation?"

It was enough, and Griffin looked with interest as the mate opened the light, low door in the bulkhead. He followed him through, noticing as he did how much he had to duck, and that his shoulders actually rubbed at the uprights of the entrance; in anything like bad weather there would be danger enough in simply leaving the cabin.

Inside the area was slightly less than in the chart room and made more cramped by narrowing dramatically towards the stern. The cabin was well lit, however; a central skylight occupied a good portion of the overhead, adding much needed inches to the height. Standing beneath it, Griffin found he was on a level with the upper deck, and could even see much of what was about at the binnacle; it was a feature that might prove to be a valuable asset.

"You have a bed space through here." Davies pulled back a small curtain that hung to one side against the main bulkhead, revealing a recess in which a hanging cot just had room to swing. "And there are the necessary arrangements below," he explained discreetly. Griffin peered through; it was as he had expected; the entire area was considerably smaller than his quarters in the *Gloucester*, and second mate's cabins in Indiamen were not known for being palatial.

"Plenty of locker room," he commented, as if in consolation.

"Yes, sir." Davies raised an eyebrow. "Though they may not all be for your own use. As I said, most accommodation has several uses in *Bee*. Your cabin is also the entrance to the breadroom, such as it is," he added, indicating a large door set to larboard. "An' there is other stores held to starboard and the magazine is below."

Again, Griffin had anticipated as much.

"Commander Carter did not spend much time in here, and rarely slept over," Davies continued. "We became accustomed to shorter trips, especially of late."

"Indeed?"

Again the mate seemed disinclined to meet his eye. "Let us merely say that Mr Carter lost some enthusiasm for his post towards the end."

Griffin considered this for a moment, and was about to ask more when Davies turned and led the way back into the chart room.

"If it is any consolation, you will find the other quarters far less spacious," he said, indicating two small doors to larboard. "Joe and I have berths roughly akin to your sleeping cabin, and the bo'sun and carpenter share little more betwixt them both." He tapped on a single door to starboard. "There's no one else aboard at present, least no officers, only old Gadd, who you saw earlier," he continued, leading Griffin forward. "The rest have been taken as a working party to tidy up Custom House, though most berth aboard a' night time."

Passing the sail locker, they went forward and entered what was obviously the seamen's quarters. The space was divided by the solid bulk of the mast trunk, which looked unusually large to someone used to the proportions of a six-hundred ton ship. A pair of mess tables that hung from the upper beams took up most of the available central deck space and the far bulkhead held a line of ditty bags as well as two small doors, presumably leading to further store-rooms. Light filtered in through the open hatch, and one small skylight. At sea, and in rough weather, it would be quite dark, whatever the hour. Griffin also noticed the smell, which was strong and of stale humanity, only partially concealed by the scent of vinegar.

The seaman encountered earlier was crouching next to a small spirit stove perched, rather precariously, on a larger iron range. He stood up quickly as the two officers entered, but proceeded to shuffle about, still with his back to them, indicating that this was in no way a sign of respect. A line of hooks showed where the crew's hammocks would be slung, and Griffin was quick to note a second, lower bank presumably to allow for additional berths should the need arise.

"How large is the crew?" Griffin asked.

"Twenty-eight mariners, and a lad, sir." Davies had become more formal in the presence of the seaman. "Plus petty officers: a gunner, carpenter, cox'n and bo'sun; though they act as normal hands most of the time. One steward – he and the boy look after victuals – and me an' Mr Lamport. Less than you've been used to, I'd chance, but a cutter's rig is not as hungry for men as an Indiaman, an' we don't fill up like they does in the Navy."

"So there will be fewer to share in seizer money," Griffin added lightly.

"Yes, sir," Davies agreed, although again Griffin had the impression he was being appeased.

"It will still be a mite cramped, I'd chance."

"Tain't as bad as it may look," Davies explained. "With a watch on deck, and few journeys lastin' longer than a week, we don't spend too much time with all below. An' on the long trips Commander Carter always ran two watches, sir," he said, with special emphasis on the last phrase. "The men liked that, an' there was twice as much space for all."

"Mr Carter was quite experienced; a former royal naval officer, is that not so?"

There was a pause. Then the mate replied: "He was indeed, sir: a lieutenant."

"An' as fine a man as ever walked the earth, and better than many who've sailed it." Both looked round to see the seaman staring at them with unusual intensity.

"When the commander wants your view, Gadd, he will request it," Davies snapped. The atmosphere had suddenly chilled. "If there is no duty for you on deck, I shall be sure to find one."

The seaman pulled a sour face and made for the deck ladder, muttering to himself. Davies waited until he had gone before turning to Griffin.

"Don't mind him, sir; he's nothing but an old fool. But you may be hearing stories of the commander and I'd be slow in believing them, were I you."

"Do you mean how he died... Surely it was a simple accident? A fall from a horse, or so I was informed."

"That's about it," Davies conceded. "Though some will be pleased to tell you different. And they'll have just as many opinions of Mr Carter; about who he knew an' who he didn't. I'd give them a wide berth as well." The mate's expression softened. "But that's folk for you. One thing's certain, none of us is going to learn more now; neither can we put matters straight; you can be assured of that."

"By straight, you mean..?"

"Let them be, at least until you have the chance to judge properly. Things might not be as they seem, an' I'd be sorry if you were to set off on the wrong tack."

"I rarely listen to tattletale," Griffin said.

"Then you'll be wise, sir. This is your first command and, without wishing no disrespect, you are just as new to the service. An' to England, if it comes to it. I dare say things is different in London, and John Company."

It was an uncommonly direct speech considering the circumstances, although the look in Davies' eye was enough to tell Griffin that no offence or insubordination had been intended; the mate was simply offering him advice, and with the best of motives.

"Very well," Griffin said, after considering the matter for a moment. "I take what you say, but you cannot but expect me to be surprised."

Davies inclined his head slightly. "Aye, it must all sound strange to someone new to the area and not acquainted with the way we lives."

If the mate intended this as a form of explanation, he failed and Griffin was left even more confused. However, intuition told him that little would be gained by pressing the matter further. "We may speak of this again," he said.

"Indeed, sir." Davies replied, relaxing slightly. "Perhaps when you have had the chance to sight the lay of the land?" The blue eyes were just as clear, even in the half-light, and in one Griffin thought he might have caught a faint twinkle. "And you will always have my support, sir." The mate continued. "Never fear anything less."

* * *

11

It was beginning to grow dark by the time Griffin finally quitted the *Bee* and started back on the long walk to his lodgings, in the town proper. On his way he passed the kings' warehouse that sat slightly back from the legal quay, where any imported goods would be unloaded and judged. He had barely looked at the place before, when heading for the cutter, but Davies' words worried him and now he gave it far more consideration. Good solid brickwork, no windows and two stout doors with heavy, serviceable locks; it would take much to penetrate such a structure. He moved on, uneasily aware that a few hours ago he had given no thought at all to the security of the building. And there had been no misgivings about Newhaven, or the area thereabouts. The town's inhabitants seemed a rosy enough bunch; the ferryman was perhaps a trifle sour, although that could be excused. Naturally it all seemed very different from life in the Company's service, but there was little wrong in that.

There was little wrong with his career in the Honourable East India Company either; in the last eleven years he had learned as much as the average sea officer, and earned quite a bit more. The men he worked alongside were mixed, some becoming solid friends, at least for the duration of the cruise, while others had inclined themselves to the role of passenger. And there had also been more than a few plain bad eggs for variety. But that was to be expected, and might be found anywhere. No, the reasons for him quitting his former life were rather more complicated.

Firstly, he had become an orphan. His mother and father had died within a few months of the other but, as he had been on a Far Eastern trip at the time, both events had appeared to be simultaneous. His only sibling, a sister, had moved to Ireland with her husband two years before, and

Griffin had suddenly realised that he had few family and hardly any friends actually living in England.

This had disconcerted him, although it was strange that it did because his homeland had never been especially important; the reverse in fact. As soon as he was able Griffin began to travel and throughout his career with the East India Company had spent most of his life afloat.

Afloat: he supposed the word summed it up. He had drifted through the previous years with few ties and little knowledge of his home and country; now he felt the need to get to know the place a little better. And, in the brief time he had spent on land, there had been many surprises.

The cost of food was one; some items were exorbitantly expensive while others seemed unobtainable, and the number of laws and petty regulations appeared vast to a man used to a simpler regime. There was also an undeniable culture of favours. This was hardly novel – indeed, he had benefited from it more than once in the past; but the practice was no longer a preserve of the rich or influential classes. Everyone did it; from street-side merchants to government officials. On ordering his uniform, the tailor had told him of the problems in raising enough broadcloth; a suitable coin proved extremely effective in reducing the delay. While in other matters, from obtaining clean sheets in a lodging house to arranging for a ship to be provisioned ahead of schedule, money, or some other favour, always seemed to be required to ensure an agreeable outcome.

But then almost all of Europe was at war and, even when in India or the East, he had been affected to some extent by the general lack of security, so he should not be shocked to find his home country altered. Still, the change saddened him; it was as if England had lost honour, and her people were reduced to the barter and bargaining of what he considered to be less civilised countries.

Finally there was a more subtle reason for his change of life. Griffin had never credited himself with the gift of insight but he could see, all too easily, how his future lay. Men in the Honourable East India Company either progressed or failed and success, the only outcome he would permit himself to anticipate, was cast in one universal mould. He had risen from apprentice to fifth officer, and then on to second. Another prosperous trip and he would be a first, before maybe taking a ship himself. Further advancement would inevitably follow; larger vessels with more important cargoes and richer passengers until he had accumulated enough to retire on. This would likely come by the time he reached fifty. Along the way that same course dictated that a number of things would be acquired, the first probably being a wife, one he would court at home, abroad, or even, clandestinely, aboard ship. He would also assume a cynical, almost distrustful nature – that was pretty much obligatory when in the Company's employ. And then there would come the liking, which would swiftly grow to dependence, on wine, spirits, tobacco or some other drug that was far stronger.

None of this was inevitable; he might deviate in some way: break from the rut, even strike out on a totally different path. But insight told him that the longer he took to make a change, the harder, and less satisfactory the outcome would be. And so, almost a year from making the decision, he had finally taken the step from a solid and safe position with an established private company, to the risk, danger and doubtless excitement of being an officer in his Majesty's customs service.

The choice had actually been relatively easy, so much so that he wondered if it were to be a change at all. The Royal Navy was the other option, but one he quickly discounted. At present the amount of officers of junior or intermediate rank was particularly high, and if the rumours of demobilisation were true, it was a position hardly likely to improve. He might try for a place as master's mate, or even midshipman, but would be dependent on time, or an act of luck, before he could sit his board and have the chance of passing for lieutenant. Even then, with no helpful family member or acquaintance of influence at the Admiralty, the prospects for employment at such a rank were small, and probably limited to land-based roles such as regulating work. He might eventually get to sea, and even retire a commander, but that was no great achievement, and the possibilities of a happy marriage seemed about as small as with the Company.

But in the customs service he was in a far better position. His late father's brother, a singularly remote individual that Griffin had only met on three occasions, held a reasonable position at the Treasury, and had arrange for Griffin to take up a post as commander. It was regrettable that, so soon after proving himself an ally, Uncle James had just as swiftly died, but at least he did so after Griffin was safely installed in his new profession.

Since then, there had been precious little chance to make much of it; the spell at London had been brief, and that at Harwich only long enough to establish that the sailing of a cutter was very different to that of a six-hundred ton merchant. The next few days would tell him more and, with only a hint of doubt instilled by his new second-in-command, Griffin remained optimistic.

He was approaching Newhaven itself now; the dim streets held only a few passers-by but no one failed to meet his eye or seemed in any way different from those he had seen in London or Harwich. In the far distance he could see the iron drawbridge that spanned the river while nearer, and directly ahead, a young girl emerged from a doorway, her arms filled with laundry.

She turned directly in front of him and seemed about to start off in the same direction when her pile tipped to one side. Griffin stepped forward, catching several sheets and a towel on their way to the ground. The girl's cry of surprise soon turned to laughter as the two of them struggled with the damp linen, catching further pieces as they started to fall, but ultimately keeping all from the dirt. Eventually order was restored, and both were holding manageable amounts. They grinned at each other, then the girl lowered her pile as if to accept Griffin's on top. He shook his head.

"We are sharing the same course," he said. "And it would be foolish not to do likewise with your washing."

She looked up and he noticed almost with a shock, the beauty of her pale features. Most of her auburn hair was pressed inside a small round cap which also covered much of her forehead, but even in the evening light there was no disguising the deep brown of her eyes, the red of her lips or the white teeth that shone through her smile.

"It's kind of you, sir, but I have a way to go."

"And I also, though neither of us will make much headway if we discuss matters further." He set off at a fair pace, and was pleased to note that she was soon beside him. Griffin found the rhythm of their steps comforting; he had been alone for most of his time in England and even this slight company was welcome. After a while he felt the girl's eyes on him, and he turned to look at her.

"Yours is a new face," she said.

Griffin smiled. "I arrived only this afternoon, but will be staying a while I fancy. Have you lived here long?"

"Oh, I grew up in Newhaven; my father has the inn on the other side of the bridge, and Matthew, that's my brother, is part-owner of a fisher smack."

"Then we share much," Griffin laughed. "If the inn you talk of is The Star than I also live there, and I also make my living from the sea."

"You don't seem like a fisherman," she replied, clearly surprised.

"A seaman," Griffin corrected. "Eleven years with John Company."

She paused, then they both continued at a slower step. "So you will have travelled," she said, her voice tinged with awe. "Seen places far off, I mean."

"A sight more than Newhaven, that is certain."

"Oh, I would so love to do what you have done!" Her voice brimmed with envy, and Griffin felt gratified that he had pleased her in some way. "I'd do anything to get out of here, to be gone: to be in another town, another country altogether." The longing in her voice was undeniable.

"Newhaven seems a fair enough place," Griffin said cautiously.

"It is," she replied. "Until you gets to know it."

"I have not been here long, of course." Then he remembered the mate's words, and added, "tell me what is so very wrong."

"Oh, take no notice of me: it is not so very dreadful." They were back to a faster walking pace again, and approaching the drawbridge. "Least no worse than others hereabouts."

"Is it the war?" He fumbled in his pocket for a coin to pay the toll, then led the way across the bridge. "Are you short of provisions? Or work?"

"We have all we need," she replied, smiling briefly at the bridge keeper. "More of some things, less of others, though all-in-all we make do right enough. And there is no lack of work, not since the war took most of the younger men and several trades-folk. Some round here have a boat,

17

or access to one; they can live well enough as fishermen. The rest are left with a difficult choice; there are usually places for farm workers or the like..."

"And the other option?" he asked, after a moment.

"Or they can join one of the gangs in the area," she said, in a rush. "Work as free traders, and earn more in one night than they would all week elsewhere."

He stiffened slightly, but she was already well into her speech.

"There's little risk and hardly any discomfort, so a good few have chosen that line."

"I am certain of it," he said, his tone deliberately neutral. "But you say little risk; surely they must fear capture? Prison or impressment must be the least of their worries: some may hang."

Her head lowered momentarily, and he thought his words must have upset her. For a second he considered tempering them, but she had begun to speak again.

"A few are caught, to be sure, and yes, the penalties can be harsh. But many about here share the proceeds of their work, and have an interest in seeing it continue. And some of those administer the law."

That also should hardly have shocked him: the point had been rammed home often enough during his time at the Board of Customs, and later at Harwich. Smuggling required finance to purchase the contraband goods; those participating would either be a cooperative, with many taking an equal share and risk, or one man with sufficient funds to stake the purchase alone. That person, usually known as a venturer, was all too often a pillar of the community: a doctor, a member of the gentry, even a minister of religion or a magistrate. And when the law was administered by the local populace, with judge and jury being every bit as culpable as those in the dock, crime was liable to go unpunished.

"So, do you wish for the smuggling to cease?" he asked.

She paused at the end of the bridge and thought for a moment. "I would wish for another course, perhaps. But in truth the free traders are just part of the problem."

Griffin waited, hoping she would continue, although the girl, it seemed, had had a change of heart. He glanced in her direction, but her gaze remained fixed into the middle distance, and he noticed she had coloured slightly.

"What then?" he tried eventually, and this time she did turn to him.

"I have spoken too much already." Her tone was clipped and, although looking at his face, she avoided his eyes. "An' me not knowing you from Adam. You're to stay a while, you say? It is best that you draw your own conclusions, rather than listen to those of others."

They only had to cross the road now to reach the inn; all too soon their conversation would end even if, for a number of reasons, Griffin very much wanted it to continue. She paused as they reached the front door and something of this must have shown in his face, as hers suddenly broke into a delightful smile.

"But I am thanking you for your help," she said, using an expression he had heard several times during his brief spell in Sussex. Then, balancing her load on one arm, she carefully reached for his. The pile of clothes tottered, but was soon secured. Griffin opened the door and held it for her, as she squeezed inside. He followed, but even as he entered the hall she was disappearing down a narrow staircase at the far end. For a moment he thought she might turn back, and was disappointed when she did not. The hall was empty and his upstairs room seemed a long way off. But they were still in the same house and, despite all he had heard that day, Griffin found he was unaccountably optimistic.

* * *

"Stuffed up, pumped up and still wet behind the ears," Gadd pronounced, before taking another gulp of his tea, a drink that had been stiffened with a fair measure of spirit. "Nothing like the man Commander Carter was. And did I mention he's from John Company? What good will that be in a revenue cruiser?"

"Might come in handy when we comes to a rummage," Fuller mused. At something over forty he was one of the senior members of the cutter's crew and, like many of the others, had served in the Royal Navy. "Them Indiamen are usually stuffed full of booty that we don't get close to; like as not he'll know all the old hidey holes."

Gadd pursed his lips. "Well, he's hardly going to be understanding much about a fore an' aft rig, that's for sure."

Fuller sipped at his own tea, which contained nothing more potent than a little cow's milk. "We don't know that; why not wait 'til he takes her out?" he said, after considering. "And with a bit of luck, that time won't be too far off. The old lady hasn't seen proper salt water for several weeks now; I'm feared the shock might sink her."

"Ask me, we're doing very well where we are." Forsyth was a northerner who had also swapped his berth in a man-of-war for what he had assumed to be a quieter life. "With all that's been going on the last few months, I'd say it were the safest place."

"Safest place ain't always the best." Fuller again. "*Bee's* already missed one moon. There must have been twenty runs sent home in that time, and the longer we're here, the harder they will be to crack when we do come back."

Wooderson shook his head. "It ain't the free traders that bother me, it's that Horsebridge lot, together with them what deals ashore." Wooderson knew more about the subject than anyone else and his views were usually respected. He was by far the oldest and had forsaken the more lucrative world of the smuggler and turned gamekeeper with the revenue service. Consequently he was known as a ten-shilling man, a sobriquet derived from the mariners' weekly pay. "They're wrong 'uns, and no mistake, though their punishment will come, by the grace of God. 'Pride goeth before destruction, and a haughty spirit before a fall': Proverbs sixteen, verse eighteen," he added slickly. Wooderson's conversion had been complete, and was in no way confined to his attitude to smuggling.

The cutter lurched slightly, then a call from above heralded the arrival of six more men who began to file down into the berth, bringing with them a fresh draught of evening air. The newcomers, who had mainly been employed painting the Custom House stables, grizzled and moaned as they made themselves at home after the day's labour.

"Blimey, Gadd, you might have kept that oven burning," one said, as he rubbed his hands together then blew on his fingers theatrically. "What you been doin' all day, while honest men were workin'?"

"He'd only just got it lit when I comes in," Fuller told them glumly. "Cold as a mother-in-law's kiss it were, an' there's no sign of supper neither."

The room seemed to have grown darker as the newcomers found places to sit, and the smells of turpentine and linseed mingled oddly with those of damp canvas, wood smoke and unwashed bodies. But despite what had been said, they were warm enough; in fact, with the cutter at rest, the fire now burning, a tarpaulin over the hatch and any other likely source of fresh air firmly sealed up, all knew their cramped quarters would soon be hot and airless, just as they liked it.

"I've been entertaining the new cap'n," Gadd told them self-importantly.

"That right?" one of the recent arrivals asked. "What's he like then?"

"Green as grass, an' no understandin' of revenue craft."

"You don't know that," Fuller corrected. "He's an experienced seaman, by all accounts, and as for sailing cutters we have yet to find that out."

"Well it ain't a seaman we needs, it's a fair-sized ship," Calver, one of the new men, said. "Something with a bit of clout to give them big buggers a decent seeing to."

"He's right," another agreed. "But what did we expect when Pitt's lot started handin' out privateer papers? That one we ran up with just after Christmas was the size of a bleedin' frigate."

"It ain't the ships, nor the free traders that's our problem." Wooderson had returned to his original theme. "Nor any boy of a captain come to that. It's what goes on shore-side: that's the true evil."

The rest grew quiet as the older man continued.

"When the law is set by a gang of cut-throats, an' God-fearin' folk can't walk peacefully in the street, that's when you have cause to worry. Until the Warrens and their cronies is sorted proper, it won't make no difference if they send us a ship-of-the-line with Admiral Howe to command."

There was a murmur of reluctant agreement.

"You never could stand a bit of honest smuggling," Fuller said, fumbling for his tobacco. "If it weren't for the free traders, we'd all be out of a berth and probably back in the RN."

"Or gaol," Forsyth added, philosophically.

"It's gone far beyond that, an' you knows it," Wooderson replied unabashed. "What we got on land is an army of criminals, and unless they're accounted for, there's no knowing what's to happen. 'The earth is given into the hand of the wicked': Job nine, verse twenty-four."

"So what do we do about it?" Forsyth asked.

"I'm prepared to give the new cap'n a fair crack," a fresh voice, Colclough, spoke up. "But can't say I hold out much hope. Best he can do is keep us out of trouble, and hi'self come to that." He paused and took a sip of his tea before adding reflectively, "that's where Mr Carter went wrong."

"He tried to sort the Warrens and their Horsebridge gang out. Nothing wrong with that," Wooderson said.

"Oh, he tried... but wasn't very successful," Gadd replied. "You know how he died, I suppose?"

"That's just a tale put about to frighten children," Fuller said swiftly. "An' it seems to have worked in your case."

There was a smattering of laughter and Gadd began to sulk. "Well, story or not, he still wound up dead," he grumbled.

"So what would you have this new man do?" Colclough asked. "Take the Warrens on, or end up as bent as all the rest at Custom House?"

"I just want a bit of peace," Gadd replied. "An' if it don't come soon, I'll be back to the Navy."

"He's got a point," Forsyth agreed. "Fighting Frenchman ain't exactly a quiet life, but at least you know who your enemy is."

* * *

That evening Griffin sat in the parlour at The Star, having just eaten a substantial portion of beef and kidney pie that had been topped off with one of the finest currant duffs he could remember. He felt full with food, beer – a local brew that was strong, dark and very bitter – and company. The latter was a borrowed pleasure; he sat alone, although the room was reasonably crowded and the buzz of nearby conversations gave it a warm and friendly feel. Griffin drained his tankard and considered ordering more: he felt in need of an early night, but there was still a chance that the girl might appear. A movement from behind caught his attention and he turned towards the door, but was disappointed to see three uniformed figures enter the room instead.

They were dragoon guard officers, he knew the uniform, and they carried themselves with the casual authority of professional soldiers. Griffin had encountered several members of the local volunteer militia when at Harwich and had not been impressed; the strutting attitude of some, together with their garish uniforms and overuse of military terms, made them appear like something from a caricature. Salutes were stiff and often unnecessary and none seemed to be able to make even the slightest move without the action being likened to a march. But these men were very different, and he watched with interest as they approached the landlord, who had clearly been summoned especially to look after them.

"What can I get for you gentlemen?" he asked, wiping his hands on a cloth and smiling professionally.

"We'll take beer, Mr Ward," the older and more senior replied in a relaxed, almost offhand manner.

"No wine, major?" the landlord asked. "Or we have some spirits: maybe a little port?" Griffin noticed he did not offer brandy.

"Listen to the cove," one of the juniors, who sported a magnificent set of side whiskers, simpered. "'We have some spirits...' Why I suspect there to be Crowling gin enough in your cellars to float the fleet to France." The second gave a high-pitched nasal laugh that was both loud and grating.

"Beer, sir," the major said resolutely. "It is the only drink you serve that we cannot expect to be smuggled."

The landlord went through a pantomime of shock and amazement, but none of the dragoons took notice. The whiskered one even turned his back, and addressed the room in general.

"Any other of you fine and loyal Englishmen adverse to a spot of foreign liqueur?"

There was no response, although all conversation had long since dwindled to nothing more than the occasional whisper.

"Maybe join us in a bottle or two," he continued, slapping his gloves against his hand as he swaggered. "Why, the major here would be happy to change his habit were it to our benefit."

Griffin watched intently. His initial assessment had been wrong; professional they may be, and their dusty uniforms were certainly not for show, but these men shared other characteristics of their amateur colleagues.

"Why don't we sit and yarn?" the officer continued. "I'm sure a lot could be learned that we might find of interest."

The drinkers regarded them with a silent hostility that seemed to amuse, and even encourage, the younger man.

"I thought not, though I am certain that, if persuaded, you might relent."

"Perchance that is what they require," the second, who was no older, smirked. "A bit of persuasion, and there is no telling what we might learn. Sure the pitch cap would work as well on these shores as any other."

"Leave them, Weston," the senior officer replied. "You ain't in Ireland now: neither do we behave so to our own folk. Drink this, and we will be on our way; there is still several miles to cover before Lewes."

The young officer laughed off the rebuke, and accepted the tankard that was handed to him. Conversations started again, but remained guarded. Then, when the officers had finished, and seemed about to depart, the silence returned again.

"We'll leave you to your pleasures, gentlemen," the senior officer said, in an affable enough voice. "But don't think we are not aware what goes on hereabouts." The man surveyed them briefly. "You may possibly continue a while longer, but we have our eyes on you, and it will take more than a group of London coxcombs to keep us at bay, of that you may be certain."

Chapter Two

Griffin had woken with first light and climbed out of bed while still half-asleep. There was much to do that day; he was to call on the Collector of Customs at nine, and hoped to meet with the rest of his crew, and maybe take *Bee* out for a trial sail afterwards. But first there was another matter with which to attend, and that filled him with almost as much excitement as the rest.

The parcels, along with the rest of his luggage and a few personal possessions, had been delivered while he was in the cruiser the previous afternoon, and he had purposefully waited until the morning before opening them. Of course he had seen most before; there had been a number of fittings, and he was no stranger to naval uniform, but still his fingers flustered with the cord and he felt a growing sense of anticipation as he opened the largest package.

It was the jacket; he had guessed as much from the size and weight. He removed the protective paper and held the garment up, looking at it approvingly. A plain blue lapel-coat, slightly longer and heavier than those he had been accustomed to in the East India Company, and also a little more ornate. There was a fair amount of gold lace, as well as nine large gilt buttons set in three groups to signify his rank. Those buttons, along with the smaller sets on each cuff and the jacket skirt, had been the only part of the uniform provided by the Treasury; the bill for the remainder had fallen squarely on his shoulders but, as he examined the garment more closely, he judged the expense worthwhile.

The remaining brown paper parcels contained two kerseymere waistcoats and five pairs of cotton trousers; three of white for ceremonial wear and summer use, and two of blue for winter. He also had a fine pair of black leather boots, a bicorn hat, and a plain leather sword belt, as well as a sword that he had known when ordering might be more suitable for wear rather than actual use.

Griffin draped the jacket back down on the bed with care, then slipped off his night shirt. He could send for hot water but that would use up precious time, and he had bathed in far worse conditions. An enamel jug stood in a basin on his night stand. In it there was sufficient water for a sponge bath, with even some left for shaving lather afterwards, although much of the latter had to be wiped on the coarse towel as there was no fresh for rinsing. By the time he was finished he felt clean and ready for breakfast. He dressed quickly in shirt and trousers and was just selecting his shoes from the day before, rather than the leather boots that were bound to be stiff, when he remembered the girl.

She had not been present all the previous evening. After the departure of the dragoons the other occupants of the parlour had also dispersed, and Griffin took the early night he had been considering. However, she certainly lived and presumably worked at the inn, which meant there was a fair chance he might meet her again. The idea warmed him; this posting might be different from his expectations, but not all aspects were bad.

His jacket was still lying in splendour on the bed. Griffin considered wearing it but rejected the idea; such finery would look ostentatious at breakfast; he could just as easily instil a bad impression as a good, and leaving it, along with the sword and hat, he opened the door and left the room.

The parlour was empty and Griffin realised that, despite his preparations, it was still relatively early. He stared at the long case clock that was ticking solidly in the corner; not yet seven: most working men would be about, but obviously not overnight guests at The Star. The remains of last night's fire were glowing, and he seated himself at a table nearby just as a young boy came in whistling through his teeth and with a bundle of logs held against his chest. The lad jumped slightly on seeing him, then dashed from the room, still carrying the wood. There was silence for a moment, and Griffin felt uncomfortable. It was his first morning at the inn, and after spending so much time at sea and abroad, he was unused to British protocol. So much about his home country was alien to him; he may even have committed some social blunder by appearing before everyone else. Then the lad returned, this time bringing with him the girl from the afternoon before, and Griffin's spirits rose.

"Good morning, I suppose you'll be wanting some breakfast," she told him with mock severity.

"If the time will not trouble you?"

"No, the hour is fine, but I'm afraid your meal may be lonely. Those that work have already eaten; we don't bother laying a fire for them. As for the gentlemen, five are staying here at present and none will rise until gone nine. Oh and then there's Mr Jarvis, but we'll be lucky to see him afore noon."

The boy had been raking out the fire and spreading fresh kindling while they were talking and the flames soon woke up the cold room.

"Well, if I have to eat alone, I insist you join me," Griffin said. She looked doubtful, but he hooked the nearest chair with his foot and pulled it closer. "Come, it is my first morning in Newhaven; you have nothing better to do, and would not disappoint me."

"Oh I have plenty to keep me occupied, thanking you," she replied, her tone excessively prim and proper. Then their eyes met and they both giggled softly. "But I'll gladly bring you yours," she continued. "And we may even talk a little whilst you eats."

* * *

It was important that his boat left that day, even though Matthew Ward had spent more than half the night at sea, and felt he could have slept for a week, given the chance. A fisher left in harbour for no apparent reason was liable to attract comment, even if the preventive men were not exactly sharp at present. He was still several hours behind the others, but that could easily be explained by a problem with tackle, or blamed on Nettle or Romsey, his crew, if need be. There was a light, if fitful wind just off the quarter that would serve to take him up river and, as a natural seaman, Ward felt as comfortable in the smack's stern holding the well-worn tiller as anywhere.

They approached the revenue cutter as the lazy autumnal sun was starting to gain height; she was still apparently asleep, although a faint pencil of smoke could be made out from her flue. Ward considered the craft with a fascination made of both curiosity and fear. Certainly there were few vessels afloat that could not be caught by her, least of all his own ponderous boat. With an area of sail far larger than many of twice her tonnage, she was without doubt a dangerous enemy. A row of light cannon stared out at him as he passed silently by; there were seven a side. They might not be of the latest pattern when compared with the latest Navy pieces, but each would fire six pounds of iron shot; a single broadside could sink most fishing craft, and do serious damage to anything larger. Had he met with her last night, there would have been little choice other than to be taken. They were carrying over fifty tubs of gin, and a dozen more of brandy, together with two crates of gloves and a bolt of silk, the latter being a special order for the minister's wife. All was now safely stowed in his hide not a mile from the harbour mouth, but even the sighting of the silent vessel that was now so close would have wrecked everything.

Matthew smiled quietly to himself. In reality there had been little chance of him being spotted, and none whatsoever of meeting with the revenue cutter. Jones, the local riding officer who kept watch on all the likely beaches, was known to be in Lancing during the late afternoon; he could never have made it back as far as the Tide Mills by the time they landed. And as for the proud vessel they were now leaving behind in their wake, she was of no threat to him; and if his luck held out, never would be.

He and Joe Lamport had been friends since they had shared all too brief a time in Mrs Casey's schoolroom. They had even fished together for a couple of years, until Joe got married and decided that the guaranteed ten shillings a week the revenue paid was better terms for a man with responsibilities. Since then he had worked his way up to deputed mariner aboard the *Bee*. It wasn't a particularly senior position; third-in-command of a bum boat, as Joe liked to call it, but he and Matthew stayed in close touch, and their friendship was fruitful to both parties.

Joe could not always tell where the cruiser would be patrolling; mostly the *Bee*'s movements were at the whim of her commander and, occasionally, Dobson, the collector. However, he certainly knew when she would be staying in harbour for a spell, and that information was just as vital to someone in Matthew's position. Knowing they had only the landsharks to contend with was very much a bonus, and well worth the occasional guinea he slipped his friend. And Joe had a small family now, so the arrangement suited both parties admirably.

Of late there had been little to report, however; the *Bee* had remained idle since the death of her commander and Matthew, together with all the free traders in the area, had enjoyed a succession of clear runs. But that golden time may well have ended; rumour was a fresh man had been appointed, so news of the cutter's movements would start to resume its former importance. Not that Matthew begrudged what he paid his friend; whether the cutter was active or not, it gave far better value than the unofficial tax the Warrens put on his using one of their designated beaches.

The family and their associates, commonly known as the Horsebridge gang, had held total control over all operations for the past year or more. Not a tub could be run, or a bale of wool traded without their say, and a sizeable cut off the profit. That was something Matthew could tolerate, but their influence ran further, and far beyond any mere smuggling enterprise. The recent reduction in taxation on some items, tea being the main, had meant that free trading was not quite the lucrative enterprise it once had been. The days of vast profits for little risk were fast disappearing, and might even be gone entirely if the rumoured peace with France ever did come about. Unfortunately the gang had built themselves up during the glory days, and now had a large and powerful organisation to maintain. Of late they had been broadening their efforts; not content with the smuggling they undertook themselves, and taking a cut from Matthew and other independent operators, they had begun to put pressure on businesses in the area. William Catt, at the Tide Mills, was certainly cooperating, grinding any grain they had on demand, and even deducting one sack of flour out of every eighty milled for the Warrens' use. If peace did come, or an enlightened government decided that punitive taxes were no longer the best way to raise revenue, the Horsebridge gang would be without their main source of income, and must extend these other methods in order to survive. Should that happen the power they had accumulated, together with the clandestine nature of their operation, would be extremely hard to combat; far easier to seize a ship-load of brandy or disrupt a major landing than catch a bunch of roughnecks putting pressure on a tailor or terrorising local farmers and landowners.

But there was still a reasonable living to be made on many smuggled items. Gin was taxed at twenty shillings to the gallon and brandy could not even be legally purchased despite the demand. When coupled with the silks, lace, oil, hair powder and all else down to hats and playing cards that carried sizeable levies, the profit was sufficient, even with the Warrens exacting a cut. Matthew Ward paid his dues, as did others of the smuggling community, but of late whatever he gave was never quite enough. Already most of the local traders were skimming their profits to the bone to keep the Horsebridge gang off their backs, and there were others who had actually gone out of business because their demands had been too high.

Matthew had considered relocating; when the smack was finally paid for he might still move east, to be nearer Flushing, or west, where the beaches were a little more welcoming, and trade convenient with Guernsey. But even then he would have had to go a fair distance; Stanton Warren and his lot held the area for a good twenty miles, and Matthew wasn't sure he wanted to make such a significant change. He had been brought up in Newhaven, understood its ways and knew the waters; besides he didn't see why a bunch of priggers should drive him from his home town.

They were long past the revenue cutter now and the smack's mainsail was starting to flap slightly with the vagaries of a land breeze. Nettle drew the sheet in and some of the boat's speed returned, although a more solid wind would be found on leaving harbour. Then they could stay out a spell, and maybe set the trawl; a few fish in the hold would make for cover were he to be investigated, although Matthew wasn't expecting trouble and didn't want to tire himself unnecessarily. A new man might have been appointed to the cutter, and was even expected that morning, but he couldn't see him putting to sea on his first day. Meanwhile he was due to meet up with his Dutch supplier at two; allow an hour for the changeover, and three more to get back into home waters, and they should be reaching the beach at the Tide Mills just after dusk. It was the ideal time to his mind – light enough for communication with the shore without the need of fires or snout lanterns, with darkness near to rescue them if they did meet with any opposition. If all went well though, as things had done of late, they should be clean away, with the booty stowed, by eight. Then sleep, glorious sleep, and probably another late start tomorrow. The wind caught them and his boat began to take on speed. It was just as he had predicted; so much so, in fact, that he was starting to grow arrogant, and that was a dangerous condition for one in his profession.

* * *

Griffin sat in an ante-room off the collector's office at Newhaven's Custom House. He was dressed in all his finery, his new jacket apparently ablaze with gold lace, the only uniform hat he possessed tucked carefully under one arm, and the sword's pinchbeck glowing like bullion. However, at that moment he could not have cared less about his appearance. In the past two hours he seemed to have gone through a number of emotions, ranging from elation to utter despondency, and that was not allowing for the fair amount of confusion and outright astonishment which had also shown a hand.

The girl, and he had yet to learn her name, had been as good as her word, and served an excellent meal of eggs, cold ham and soft bread with a pot of tea that was certainly the best he had tasted since leaving the Company's service. And they had spoken long and hard, laughed a little and even teased each other with cautious gentleness. That she was as interested in him as he was her could not have been in doubt, and for all his misgivings about Newhaven, it suddenly became the best posting in the world and he could not have wished to be anywhere else. Then, when the meal was finished and he could not put off the time any longer, he left and returned to his room, where the full glory of his revenue uniform awaited him. He pulled on the jacket and fastened the sword belt with true excitement; not only was he wearing it for the first time, but she would see it and be impressed: of that he was certain.

He had been right. More so; he seemed to have created a stir throughout the entire building. The inn was fully awake by the time he swaggered heavily down the stairs, and clumped through in his fresh leather boots. Even the sound on the bare floorboards was enough to make all in the crowded hallway turn, and he fancied a good few must have looked in wonder and amazement. But others had been differently affected; some instantly turned away as if slighted, and not a few simply stared at him in clear and open loathing.

He supposed it was hardly surprising; in an area where smuggling was known to employ a good proportion of the population, a customs officer could expect little else. But it was the girl's impression that affected him the most. He was almost clear of the hallway, and actually pausing, disappointed that she had not been there to witness his departure, when he finally saw her.

She came up the cellar stairs carrying a tray loaded with clean crockery. The boy was following, and she was saying something to him, not looking clearly where she was going when she and Griffin all but collided. Her body swerved and she muttered something in apology before looking up and into his face. He noted her changing expressions as they formed, one of surprise, which turned into disappointment, sorrow and then apparent disgust. The tray trembled, and she appeared to maintain her hold only with great effort, before letting out a single gasp of shock and turning, almost knocking her follower over.

To Griffin the world seemed to have stopped; certainly he had little thought for the crowd that still milled about him. He had called out once, although now was not sure what he had said, but the girl was clearly intent on leaving, and as fast as she could. Dodging through the busy hallway, she pushed through the mob, her head down. He stood for several seconds after she had gone, and even when he did move it was slowly and as if without willing it.

Throughout his journey to Custom House, he had been as if in a trance. The streets were crowded on the western side of town, and several people pushed into him as he went. A few may even have intended to barge him out of spite or bravado, but Griffin could not have cared less. And now that he had arrived, had already met some of the staff, and was about to be interviewed by his immediate superior, his mind was certainly not on matters that should concern him. The door to his left opened suddenly, and he turned to see a short, balding man peer out.

"Commander Griffin? Would you step this way?"

Griffin stood and brushed himself down briefly before following the man through the open door. The next few minutes were likely to be of extreme importance to his future career, and yet all he could think about was the past half hour.

* * *

"'Ere he comes now," Gadd said looking up. He was perched on the cascabel of one of *Bee*'s six-pounder long guns, and had been involved in an intricate piece of splicing: a task Gadd particularly enjoyed. Forsyth, who was helping him to renew one of the boat falls, glanced across, and both watched their new commander stride down the path towards them. The sun caught the gold of his uniform and sword, and with his new boots squeaking with every step he certainly drew the eye.

"There's a coxcomb, if ever I saw one," Forsyth murmured.

"Couldn't tell him from a whore-monger's dog yesterday," Gadd grumbled. "Better give Davies the nod."

But the mate, who was below, under an open skylight, had heard and was already stamping up the deck ladder. With the new commander appointed, the *Bee*'s crew had finally been released from other work ashore and allowed to return to their normal duties. No vessel can stay in harbour for long without routine maintenance, and they were setting her to rights. Consequently, everywhere was in a mess; one party was currently at work with sand and holystones so that half the deck shone white and burnished, while the rest looked like it had been lifted straight out of a stable. The boatswain and two others were in the process of airing the studding sails, which now hung from fore and back stays like so much washing, and Harry, the ship's boy, was polishing what brass they had with a generous application of brick dust and spit.

"The bugger told me he were seeing the collector 's'morning," Davies muttered, as Griffin drew closer. "When Dobson gets a visitor, it's usually cause for a meal. Thought we'd be free of him till long after noon, and pr'aps even the morrow."

"Maybe they didn't get along," Gadd mused; he was enjoying the mate's discomfort and wasn't afraid to show it. "Reckon we've landed ourselves a lively one there, and that won't please old Dobbers."

Davies glared at him, before summoning the hands. "Come on, he won't be afraid of a bit of mess; it's not as if we we're 'avin' a party. Form up, and let's meet him proper."

The men duly laid down their work, and formed an orderly line just as Griffin reached the gangplank.

"Probably used to side boys and whistles," Forsyth whispered.

"Probably used to a bit of civil silence," Davies replied sharply. Then they all held their breaths as their new commander made his first official visit to the *Bee*.

* * *

Griffin glanced at the men as he stepped from the gangplank and on to the crowded deck. They seemed respectful enough, although evidently his visit had interrupted them in the middle of morning duties. Davies was there, dressed in red shirt and duck trousers like most of the men. The rig was excusable in the circumstances, and Griffin felt mildly guilty about catching them all on the hop, especially when he himself was considerably over-dressed. He stood for a moment, uncertain as to what was expected of him before common sense took over.

"Very good, men, we shall meet properly when I read myself in. But I can see you are busy and have no wish to interrupt your labours." He turned to the mate. "Mr Davies, we shall have the topmast up and the 'sprit extended as soon as all current work has been completed. The tide will be with us presently, I fancy?"

"Suitable in an hour, sir."

"Capital, then what say we take the *Bee* on a short cruise?" He regarded the crew and was pleased to note a general air of approval; they seemed ready to get back to sea, and after the morning he had just experienced, he was of the same mind.

He nodded to Davies and made for the aft ladder, his sword knocking against his leg as he lowered himself down. The chart room was empty, although doors to two of the other cabins had been left ajar and the remains of someone's breakfast lay uncleared on the table. He walked through to his own quarters and shut that door firmly behind him. Noise from the deck came through the opened skylight; he reached up and closed it, before unhooking his sword and belt and throwing both onto one of the two upholstered lockers that ran to either side and were the only seating provided. His heavy jacket followed, then he slumped himself down opposite and drew a sigh.

His first inkling of trouble had come the previous afternoon, when he had spoken with Davies. The girl's behaviour had also been disconcerting, while the meeting he had just experienced with Dobson just about put the seal on things. The man was supposed to be in overall command; Treasury representative; King's representative, when it came down to it. He was in charge of all customs matters in the sector, from the landguard: riding officers, coast, land and tide-waiters, searchers and gaugers, to Griffin himself. Of all at Newhaven, Dobson should know what Griffin was starting to suspect, and be capable of acting; he not only had the position, but also the power. A word from him could raise the militia, bring the dragoons riding down from Lewes, or even organise an unofficial hot press, rounding up any rabble that might be too clever for the local assizes to convict, for service in a King's ship. The collector set an example for the entire customs service, both in the town and its surrounding area; Griffin had been hoping for a senior he could trust, honour and respect and was deeply disappointed.

Instead he had found an elderly, ineffectual man who might be better employed in any number of genteel professions. One who clearly valued small talk and prevarication above plain speaking, and was more interested in his damned pottery collection and where he would take lunch than addressing the concerns that Griffin had attempted to raise. Clearly Dobson was content to let matters rest, for fear of causing a nuisance in the mending, and his staff seemed happy following the lead their master set. It was not a good start.

Griffin was unclear of the actual size and nature of the problem, but it was evident that a good deal of smuggling was being tolerated on every level; why, the collector had even offered him a mid-morning glass of brandy! But this seemed far worse than an occasional bottle exchanged with foreign fisherman; he was starting to suspect that something far more ambitious was afoot. And, more worryingly still, there appeared to be a further and more subtle underlying culture; one that all but saturated the entire area, even affecting those not involved with any supposedly 'free trade'. From what Griffin could gather, major crimes were regularly being committed on a wide scale and nothing was being done to address the situation.

Talks of a truce with France were filling the newspapers at present, and rumour had it that Hawkesbury was actually speaking to that fellow Bonaparte. Addington might have taken power on the promise of peace, but the country was still at war and, as far as Griffin was concerned, was liable to remain so for a good while yet. Consequently, the land-based forces had other matters than smuggling with which to concern themselves; it was up to the revenue service, and the preventive men who ran it, to see that their jobs were being done properly. Taxes must be collected, and smugglers arrested – anything else was tantamount to aiding the enemy. He supposed that in any local community some degree of latitude could be expected when it came to minor felonies, but that should not mean that those appointed to enforce the law should fail to do so or, as Griffin was starting to suspect, be actively involved in aiding the criminals.

Dobson had announced himself quite content for Griffin to rummage any passing ships: East Indiamen on their way to the Downs, or an occasional independent merchant, but any with local connections were to be given an extraordinarily wide latitude. When Griffin challenged him on the subject, the collector had grown defensive; of course he was not condoning smuggling, but the occasional undeclared ship's store might be excused. Griffin had not been a customs official long, and his experience was suitably limited, but even in the short time he had been in Newhaven he could tell the problem was on a far larger scale than that.

Then he remembered his predecessor, a man who, by the sound of things, had harboured similar thoughts, and probably from the comfort of the very same locker that now supported him. When Griffin broached the subject the collector made it clear that Carter's death had been very much his own fault: "placing his nose where it were not required," were the actual words used. Well, so be it; Griffin was no hero, and had little intention of becoming one, but when he accepted a task he liked to see it finished, and the idea of leaving anything half-done was as repugnant to him as devolving all responsibility in the first place. He was damned if he would overlook smuggling on any level, and was determined to arrest any and all at the first opportunity. His actions might not be approved of by those at Custom House, but right was on his side, and he was not afraid of a bunch of criminals, even if everyone else was. First, though, he must see that the crew and vessel under his command were suitable for the job.

If they performed well, or at least showed the likelihood of doing so, things might not be so bad. As the commander of a revenue cutter he would enjoy what was pretty much a free hand while at sea, and that was where his responsibilities truly lay. With a sound craft, and men to match there was still much that could be achieved and let those on shore worry about the consequences.

Chapter Three

Four hours later, bareheaded and wearing a watch coat over his shirt and trousers, Griffin stood holding *Bee*'s starboard running backstay and swaying easily with the gentle motion of the waves. They were clear of the harbour and making good progress through the roadstead, even though the cutter was sailing under a solitary foresail.

"Set mains'l, sir?" Davies asked, and Griffin nodded. There was little point in putting the moment off any longer. The cutter was still very visible from the shore but to continue under a reduced rig would only look strange and excite comment amongst the crew. He watched the hands, or mariners as the revenue would have them called, as they manhandled the huge sail, cranking it up, way above his head.

"And you may set the jib as well, Mr Davies," he said. The increased pressure from forward would do something to balance that of the main, and give a fairer indication of the speed *Bee* was capable of. The wind was sitting comfortably in the north east so there was also a choice of square and studding sails to play with, should he become bored.

But he soon realised that such a state would be a rarity in *Bee*. As the oversized sails were sheeted home her forefoot dug into the swell and the hull appeared to come alive. A cloud of spray began to steam over her prow, soaking all on deck as the speed increased, until she was positively vibrating with power.

"Just what the old girl needed," Davies informed him, his eyes alight and left knee bent to accommodate the slight list to starboard. "Bit of a blow, and we'll all be the better for it."

"How long since she was at sea?" Griffin had to shout to make himself heard.

"Must be two months or more," the mate replied.

Griffin noticed that Davies was going to add something, but obviously changed his mind. Two months, that would tie in with the time Carter died; it was a long spell for any government vessel to remain inactive. Even without a commander, revenue cutters frequently put to sea with the mate in charge, so why hadn't Davies taken her out? The collector should have insisted on it. Then his mind came back to Dobson. No, he would have been more than happy to see *Bee* lie idle, and was probably quite cross that Griffin had even been appointed; the more so now that he looked likely to spoil what had become a quiet life for all at Custom House.

"We'll jibe, and head west for a spell if you please, Mr Davies."

The mate touched his forehead in the seamen's manner and bellowed to the crew. Griffin watched as they brought the cutter round, the boom swung across and was braced up as she swiftly took up on the opposite tack. With such momentum the manoeuvre was smooth and appeared easy, but Griffin could guess that, badly handled, she might be an absolute mule and her rig, though powerful, would damage only too easily.

They stayed on the new course for no more than twenty minutes before Griffin turned them to the south. The sun had grown surprisingly hot, and he felt its warmth on his back; this was turning into a pleasurable experience, the day itself having improved greatly. He glanced behind and was surprised to see the land so distant; they had covered a good few miles in a remarkably short time.

The general atmosphere was also lighter; the crew had woken up with the speed and motion and were far more alert. Most had lost that faintly glum expression that Griffin had been aware of in the brief time he had been aboard. He noticed the helmsman, his face a picture of contented concentration as he watched the luff of the mainsail while tapping his fingers on the tiller boom in time with the motion of the waves, presumably to anticipate the rogue seventh. The man was gently flexing his body as she rolled, and appeared in total harmony with the craft. Such a hand was an asset to any vessel, although his presence would make what he had to do now that much harder, and the seaman looked almost annoyed as his captain approached and asked his name.

"Forsyth, sir."

"Very good, Forsyth; I shall take the helm for a spell."

The man's eyes opened wide, but he held the tiller steady while his captain moved into position, then raised both hands in the air to show the others he had relinquished control and went to shelter in the lee of the weather bulwark.

Griffin could have wished for less of an expert audience; Davies was also watching him, as were most of the crew but, if he were really to get the feel of his command, it would be necessary to conn her in all weathers and conditions. And if, in the process, he made a fool of himself, it may as well be now.

He flexed the tiller, which was far firmer than he had anticipated, although the hull responded to the slightest movement. The wind was constant and easily judged; he was not keeping to any set course, and there was a clear path ahead: ideal conditions, in fact. He pressed the wooden beam to bring her onto a broad reach and noticed how the sails were magically adjusted to account for the change in course. There had been no orders, the only clue the trimmers had been given was his movement at the tiller; that and an innate feel for the vessel. It was gratifying to realise he had inherited a crew of true seamen.

"Deck there, sail ho, deep on the starboard bow."

They were in the Channel proper now, so any sighting should not be a surprise.

"Looks to be a big one," the lookout continued. "Probably an Indiaman, or a liner."

That was also not unusual, but Griffin felt inclined to take a closer look.

"Very well, let's make for her. You can take in the jib, Mr Davies, and set tops'l and t'gallant. Forsyth, you have the helm."

The northerner regained the tiller with an air of proprietorship and soon *Bee* was running with the wind just off her taffrail, her square sails board tight and mainsail boom released as they bore down on the sighting.

"There's another in company," the masthead called again. "Just standing off her, and smaller. Looks like the 'ound," he added, in a tone of disappointment.

The *Hound* was the Shoreham-based cutter; Griffin had run into her mate, John Butler, some weeks back while he had been at the Board of Customs. He was a pleasant enough fellow, and happy to pass on a good deal of advice, much of which Griffin appreciated. But Butler had also been disparaging of the Newhaven operation, and at the time Griffin had wondered slightly at his attitude. Now he was beginning to understand it a little better.

"If the *Hound's* got to her first there's little point in us joining," Davies muttered. Certainly the crew of one cutter was sufficient to rummage the average deep-sea merchant, even if there was likely to be a deal of contraband aboard. In all of Griffin's home-bound trips, most of the officers and a good many men had been keen to turn their wages into illicit goods. Consequently silk, spices, porcelain and other precious items were constantly trickling into Britain by this route, with those involved reckoning on at least a fivefold profit on the deal, as long as they weren't caught. Some were, of course, but the preventive men were usually satisfied with a little, and content to let the rest pass by. There were even a few who noticed nothing at all, apart from a discrete envelope passed to them by the second officer. Griffin was aware that such things went on, and had even been involved in the past, to the extent of a bolt of silk for his sister's wedding dress and a dollop of tea for his father. At the time, some cloth and forty pounds of dry goods hardly constituted a serious offence and he reconciled the breach very easily; from his new position, it was doubtful that he could see matters in quite the same light.

"Very well," Griffin said. "But we may as well take her a little further. Do you think she will take stuns'ls?"

Davies looked up at the rig, then back at his commander. "I'd say them not worth the setting, sir," he said at length. "M'be the lower, but anything above will only bring the prow down, forcing her to plough, and would be bound to cause strain elsewhere for no gain in speed."

Griffin accepted what was probably good advice and again was reassured by the competence around him.

"Then re-set the jib and we'll take her deeper. Starboard the helm and take her sou' sou' east, if you please."

Once more the cutter performed well, her hull setting at an angle that was both exhilarating, and mildly disconcerting. But there was no doubting her speed; he could have asked for the log to be run, but Griffin was experienced enough to know they must be making at least nine knots, and he felt that, given time, he would coax even more from his new command. Davies was staring at the vast expanse of canvas with a contented smile. Griffin looked about; the other hands appeared equally satisfied, and then he realised that he also was grinning like a lad. But in such conditions, and with a perfectly suited craft, it was hard to be anything but exhilarated. He remembered that morning's interview with Dobson, and how his uniform had upset the girl: both matters that now appeared trite and insignificant. Even the fact that Newhaven was apparently in the grip of villains seemed unimportant; he had command of one of the most stimulating vessels ever designed, and that was more than sufficient to outweigh a few minor annoyances.

"Sail ho; sail fine on the starboard bow." The lookout's voice was calm; this would not be an invasion fleet, or even a stray French frigate. "She's a smack – trawler, by the looks," the man continued.

"One of the local fishing fleet?" Griffin asked, and Davies shrugged.

"Might be, sir," he conceded. "But then she may not be trawling at all. Be better off further to the east, that's if she's a going for cod."

"So what else would they be about?"

Davies paused. "Probably nothing, sir."

Griffin had the distinct impression the mate knew, but wasn't going to say, and was suddenly suspicious. "Likely nothing, as you say," his voice was level and low. The run out to sea had been freeing in more ways than one; it was probably his first experience since arriving that had not held some form of hidden agenda. "But I think we might take a closer look," he added, and was gratified by Davies' change of expression. If the mate was cautious about that boat, then he was determined to find out why.

"And I take your advice about the upper stun'sls, Mr Davies," Griffin continued, his words chosen carefully. "But think we may try the lower on her." The mate flashed another look at him before roaring out the order. The studding, or stun sails, provided extra canvas, and thus pressure, to either side of the cutter's square sails. They would be difficult to set, three men per yard needed to rig the extension booms and send them out, while others below were required to actually set the sails and trim them. And for the dubious addition of what might be no more than a fraction of a knot, it was doubtful if the effort was worthwhile. But even if Davies was right, Griffin remained in charge, and intended to demonstrate the fact from the start. No harm would come from the men getting a bit of practice aloft; one of his intentions for today's sail was to give the *Bee* and her crew a thorough workout, and he was determined to exploit the exercise to the full.

"Smack looks to be turning eastwards and setting a jib; she's no trawl set," the lookout called down. Now that was a surprise; Griffin had anticipated the boat simply heaving to when a government vessel was seen charging down upon them. Some of the crew obviously shared his feelings; comments were exchanged amongst them and even Davies was looking mildly confused.

Griffin grabbed the deck telescope and clambered up to the minute platform atop the tiller head. He focussed the glass forward and swept the horizon, centring on the flash of white that marked the vessel's position. She had indeed altered course by several points, and was now heading east south east. Making a run for it, by all accounts, although a stumpy little smack would have little chance against the *Bee* in these conditions. However to catch her he must also turn, and that would mean taking in those damned studding sails.

He gave the order, and closed his mind to the reaction of Davies and the men about him. The extra canvas had only just been set, yet now they must take it in. And all in pursuit of a simple fisherman that even the ship's boy knew was not worthy of a second glance. But now that he had started Griffin was determined to see the task through, and felt he must close on the smack if it was the last thing he did.

The studding sails were cleared with credible speed and *Bee* turned to larboard on a course that would intercept the hapless fishing boat within a few miles. "Hoist colours and pennant." Griffin had returned to the binnacle and was throwing all caution aside. This was now an official chase; the rig of a revenue cutter was distinctive; no private vessel was allowed such a length of bowsprit and, consequently, as large an area of sail, so the crew of the smack would already know *Bee* for what she was. But the coloured bunting streaming in the wind would also tell them this was no social call. The cutter was in pursuit; they were on government business: and the other boat was now, officially, the quarry.

"Changing course, close hauled to larboard, heading eastwards," the lookout called. As much could be seen from the deck; the fisher was clearly intending to drag this out for as long as possible.

"Keep her in chase, if you please, Mr Davies."

The mate growled a command and Forsyth pressed the helm across. *Bee*'s head came round as the sails were braced, and soon they were powering through the waves with the unfortunate smack firmly in their sights. Griffin looked about; the crew seemed as intent on the prize as any, but he could detect a distinct lack of enthusiasm, some might even say bewilderment as to why so much effort was being wasted.

"Closing on her fast, sir," Davies said. "Should be in hailing distance in no time."

"What do you see there?" Griffin shouted up to the masthead.

"Nothin' to note, sir," the lookout replied. "Thought there might have been a couple more sails to starboard, but them's well below now."

"Anything beyond the chase?" Griffin bellowed back.

"No, sir. I can see a fair way past, and it's clear water."

Griffin closed the glass with a snap. He had hoped to find a supply ship, either French or Dutch: coopers, they were called; large hulls, often ship-rigged, they were always stuffed full of all types of contraband, and available to any with the money to purchase, be they friend or enemy. Taking such a prize would surely have been the ideal start to his career, but even if that wasn't to be, he remained reasonably certain the trawler was up to no good, and a brush with the law might well bring it into line.

"Clear away a for'ard piece, larboard battery," he said, then added, in a softer voice, "remind me of the gunner's name."

"Blackman," Davies whispered. "Used to be quarter gunner in a frigate."

The chase could be seen clearly now; she was no more than two miles off, and still trying vainly to escape, although *Bee* was gaining on her with every second.

"Mr Blackman, I want a shot across their bows as soon as we are in reliable range. Make it as close as you wish."

A seaman at the forecastle touched his forehead in respect. "Do you want a swivel, sir?" he called.

The six smaller guns mounted on either bulwark fired a shot weighing less than a pound and would not make the impression Griffin was looking for.

"No, a carriage piece." He wanted all to know he meant business. "And load with round shot, if you please."

The gunner appeared surprised, but the smack should have spilled her wind by now. Griffin was well within his rights, and could even sink her if he chose. The cutter continued to close, and now they could see three men on the trawler's deck adjusting their sails to get the very best from the wind; clearly they were hoping for a miracle.

"Keep an eye," Griffin shouted. "Anything goes over the side, I wanted it spotted and marked."

At Davies' word, two men collected what looked like a bundle of junk and strode forward to the cutter's prow. The buoys were crudely made from wood and feathers, with inflated pigs' bladders to give buoyancy and bricks for weight. In theory they would keep pace with any item the smack's crew chose to discard, making its eventual retrieval easier. But there was no jettisoning of cargo and they were now well into the range of Blackman's six pounder.

"As you please," Griffin shouted. For a moment the gunner sighted down the long gun's barrel, then stood to one side and pressed his slow match into the touch hole. There was a brief pause then, with a ring that seemed to echo about the small craft, the cannon fired. Griffin moved to avoid the smoke and watched as the round shot skipped twice, a good thirty feet in front of the chase. Nothing happened for several seconds and Griffin was starting to contemplate another shot when, with a total lack of urgency, her head was turned into the wind, and the smack started to wallow in the water.

"She's struck, sir," Davies said, a trifle melodramatically. Griffin nodded; the scent of burnt gunpowder was strong.

"Clear away the quarter boat, I'm going aboard."

"Galley away!" Davies roared and Griffin cursed silently under his breath. Of course, quarter boats were called galleys and seamen, mariners: why the revenue service needed their own particular brand of jargon was beyond him. But he had to either get used to it, or look the fool for as long as he served. Some things translated perfectly however; in any language a vessel that ran when chased was likely to be hiding something and he was determined to find out what.

* * *

Joe Lamport stood at *Bee*'s prow, watching while the new commander clambered awkwardly into the boat. He had barely exchanged a dozen words with the man but felt he knew enough already to judge, and Commander Griffin did not come off well in his estimation. He was clearly as keen as mustard; there was no surprise in that: Lamport supposed it was to be expected when a new officer took command. The fact that he was a reasonably skilled seaman was neither in his favour nor against; Lamport had worked with captains who could hand, reef and steer and others that didn't know a backstay from a bagnio, and either could be trouble. He had also shown himself independent enough to ignore that old fool Davies' advice, which might not be such a good point. But something far worse about Griffin worried the petty officer a great deal more.

Matthew Ward's boat was lying in the water not fifty yards away from where he stood. Lamport had no real fear; Matt and he went way back, and he could be trusted for keeping his name clear. Besides, Lamport had no material connection with either him or the boat. But the tenaciousness that the new commander had already exhibited did not augur well for the two men's future. With one child born and another on the way, Lamport needed the money Matt passed to him. Were it to stop, he would have to look for an alternative source of additional income; that or chuck in his lot with the revenue service entirely.

He might take to free trading himself; that was always an option. Knowing much about how the preventive force worked gave him a distinct advantage, and he wouldn't be the first to have gone to the other side, traffic between smugglers and his Majesty's customs being extremely brisk, and in either direction. But Lamport didn't see himself as a free trader; neither did he particularly want to give up what had become a secure position. Something must be done to gain that extra money, however, and in reality he was left with only one other choice. Of them all it was actually the least attractive, but became more likely the longer he thought about it.

The Horsebridge gang was every bit as eager for information as Matthew Ward, and would pay far more handsomely than his friend. Lamport had been approached on several occasions, but never at the right time: either there was nothing of value to report, or he would have been implicated as the source. He told himself that, with a bit of effort, he might settle both problems, and it need not be intelligence of any great value. Besides, he would only do it the once, just to tide them over until the baby came: after that the Warrens could chase rainbows, for all he cared.

* * *

They had come quite a distance and the chop of the Channel became obvious as soon as *Bee* heaved to. The small boat was made for such conditions, however, with a broad beam and deep set thwarts that brought the weight comfortably low. Griffin scrambled aboard and settled himself in the stern sheets feeling relatively secure while Gadd, at the bow, shoved off. He had considered sending Davies, or at least bringing him with him. The mate must have boarded a thousand such vessels, and his local knowledge might come in useful. But there was something about the way this particular smack had tried to avoid arrest that intrigued Griffin; he particularly wanted to carry out the inspection, and did not feel the need for an audience. Besides he already sensed the mate had been allowed too great a leeway, and he wished to make his mark as captain without always relying on the older man's help or advice.

The men began to pull for the smack, which lay hove to, her sails flapping in the strong breeze. Her name, *Free Spirit*, stood out plainly on her counter, and Griffin wondered if some less-than-subtle irony was intended there; it would certainly be in keeping with the casual acceptance smuggling had acquired in the area. One of the mariners called out as they approached, and there was a reply that Griffin could not quite hear, although the tone was derisory. He was still wearing the watch coat, but had thought to bring his hat and, rather than the decorated sword, a simple boarding cutlass hung from his waist. He considered drawing it now as he stood to climb up onto the smack, but rejected the idea. Holding a heavy sword would only make the awkward manoeuvre more ungainly, and Griffin had long ago learnt that carrying a weapon is usually threat enough; drawing it only raises the stakes, and might even mean having to use the thing.

Always, in the past, he had followed someone more experienced but this time he would be first aboard; it was the way of things, and something else he must get used to. The boat was being held against the side by two mariners, and Griffin noted that no member of the smack's crew had thought to lower man ropes or even a fall to help him. He pulled himself up, and over the high bulwark, glancing to right and left as he swung his leg across and finally stood uncertainly on the more stable deck.

"Good afternoon, captain," he said, instinctively addressing the better turned out of the three men who regarded him. He was young, probably in his early twenties, although life at sea can play tricks with age. And he also appeared vaguely familiar, although Griffin was equally certain he had never set eyes on him before. "My name is Griffin: his Majesty's customs. I have reason to detain your vessel."

"Oh yes?" the young man asked. "And why would that be?"

"You did not heave to when you saw us in pursuit," Griffin continued, avoiding a direct answer. "A customs vessel with pennant flying, yet you took to your heels; an explanation is in order."

"We have better things to do with our time than wander about the seas," the lad answered, to the obvious amusement of his crew.

Griffin's glance swept about the boat; she was a trawler, and her nets were set, ready for launch, although it was the afternoon, and they had clearly not been used.

"And what exactly have you been about? I see no sign of honest work, so must assume the opposite."

The younger man indicated the rolled net that lay toward the stern. "We have been attending our trawl; the lift line had separated: Jamie and Pete here have been reeving a new one. Till that be done there was nothing we could do; and now that it has, you come along and delay us the more."

It was a likely enough story but still did not explain the smack's attempt to avoid them. Griffin moved towards the fishing gear and examined it. The nets were definitely worn, and had seen good service, whereas the lifting line appeared brand new. All the equipment was dry, however, and might not have been used for several days. He looked down at the trawl weights; they were also used, and heavily scraped as was to be expected. But a closer look revealed a fine layer of rust on one, which spoke of a reasonable period since it was last hauled, as well as poor maintenance on behalf of the fishermen. He glanced about; the rest of the boat appeared in order: he guessed that a thorough rummage might bring forth an odd bottle of spirit, but the captain would simply explain that away as ship's stores, a story that would undoubtedly be believed by a genial magistrate. Had the boat been in contact with a supply ship her deck would likely have been crowded with booty, there being little need for subtle concealment. Griffin knew that for a run to be successful it must be as large as possible; if the smack really was up to no good they would have caught her with half a cargo as easily as a full load.

"Very well, then I shall not detain you further." He turned from the gear fully intending to leave, but paused. The whole thing just did not add up; why had they even put to sea with a broken, or worn, lifting line? And there was no need to run from the sight of a revenue cutter unless the captain had an ulterior motive. Quite what could that motive have been? Why would he have wanted to waste time, and several sea miles? Griffin's thoughts started to race; he knew something was amiss but, just as surely, that it had little to do with this fishing boat; instinct told him that a far larger vessel must be involved, and somewhere a good distance from where they currently lay.

And then it hit him; he had been unaccountably stupid: missed an obvious point that the rawest recruit should have spotted. Griffin felt his face flush and it was with effort that he finished the interview with any degree of sense.

"I would however caution you that to fail to stop for his Majesty's customs is an offence in itself." The words were coming out like clockwork, but Griffin's mind was elsewhere. Both palms were starting to sweat and his heartbeat had increased, although neither had anything to do with the humiliation of a wasted journey.

The young man relaxed and a smug smile appeared; he even said something that might have been mildly sarcastic, but Griffin had no ear for it, or anything else aboard the fishing boat. How could he have been so foolish when all the evidence was right there before him: the chase; the attitude of the fishermen; even how Davies and the others in *Bee* had behaved... The fact that when they had first spotted the smack a nice juicy cooper had been just over the horizon was as obvious to him now as if her topsails had actually been in sight. He had been led astray, duped into a wild-goose chase when there was far more attractive game so near at hand. But a chance remained that he might still find it, if time and fortune were on his side.

Without further word he jumped down into the boat and was shouting at the crew long before anyone had settled. In no time the galley was heading back to *Bee*, but they could not row hard enough for Griffin. Neither did the huge sails that filled with impressive speed carry the cutter anything like as fast as he wished, as she set off once more. The wind remained strong and obligingly in their favour, although it would still be a long journey and possibly fruitless.

This was his first time out as a captain and so far things had not gone well. His agitation mounted as he realised just how close he would come to compounding the mess further. What the crew must be thinking of him was all too easy to guess and, if his current theory proved groundless, he would be confirmed a laughing stock. But that need not concern him now: they were committed, he was committed, and *Bee* set off once more at high speed, in apparent pursuit of an invisible quarry, on an entirely empty sea.

Chapter Four

The girl, whose name was Sophie, had indeed been shocked by Griffin's uniform. It had come as a surprise mainly because the role of customs official was the last she would have guessed for him. She held no love for the revenue service, but neither was there any real hatred. Her father and brother were heavily involved in illicit goods, indeed the entire family's livelihood depended on income from free trading, but that placed no obligation on her to despise all preventive men, any more than a poacher must actively dislike the gamekeeper who came after him. Besides, if any of her menfolk could have picked for themselves they would probably have opted for a different trade. Choices were few, though, and no other offered anything like the profit of smuggling, albeit at such a risk.

The Star acted as both a storage depot and contact point. Customers could come and place an order for just about anything that was either unavailable on the British market, or so heavily taxed as to make it a luxury. The orders were fulfilled, either from stock or in due course, and her father collected the money like any other man of business. But that was not solely the reason that Sophie had looked so aghast, nor why little had been forthcoming from her for the rest of the morning, and all of the afternoon. That single image of Griffin striding through the hallway had hurt her in a way she had not expected. For even if she was not obliged to actively hate him, he must certainly be avoided in future.

They had only spoken a couple of times, and nothing significant had been said, but already she harboured a warmth for the man. There had been no one significant in her life since Jack was lost, well over three years ago. That was time enough and she had wondered, not so very vaguely, if Griffin might take his place. He was no oil painting, and his manner could be quite direct, even brash, but there was something else about him; a touch of naïvety perhaps, that should not make her want to love him, but inevitably did.

In any case, she felt drawn; and had truly thought he might have been the one to finally banish the melancholy that threatened to become part of her personality. And then there he was, unexpectedly vivid in the morning light. With sword and brave uniform, blithely walking through the crowded hall, blissfully unaware of the number, so horribly close, who would be quite prepared to kill, maim or torture him without a second thought or moment of regret. Many might even have craved the chance, and not a few were already experienced in that area.

Her father had noticed her change of mood but, like so many men, had come to the wrong conclusion. However by now he may also have discovered the man's profession, and Sophie was worried about what he might do. To evict a guest without good reason could only invite suspicion, and yet Griffin could not be allowed to remain. Being the local hub of the Horsebridge gang's organisation meant that deliveries came regularly, and not all during daylight hours, or from recognised merchants. Besides, they were expecting some of the Warrens' men at any time. They called, on an irregular basis, just to check that all was running smoothly and to their benefit. There was money waiting for them to collect, so she knew the next visit was imminent; Griffin must be gone before then: that or be taken under control.

'Squaring' they called it, and a regular bribe, either in money, booty or the withholding of delicate information, had been successful with other members of the customs service. But if, as she feared, he failed to respond to such an approach, it could only end badly, just as it had for his predecessor. And for reasons that she still remained unsure of, that was the last thing Sophie wanted.

* * *

In the smack, Matthew Ward was subdued. He had watched the customs men go, and even joined the derisory laughter as their boat pulled away. The other two were still joking together, making fun of the stuck-up prig who had dared to detain them, but Ward had grown more thoughtful. Commander Griffin was a new face, and clearly one to be wary of even if he had missed a fine opportunity to forward his career. There were thirty-seven guineas hidden in *Spirit*'s beakhead, covered by nothing more than a few sheets of tarpaulin. A decent rummage by an experienced officer would have found them in minutes leaving him with a deal of explaining to do.

But Ward knew that experience was quickly earned with practice and, rather than share in the other's ridicule, he remained concerned by what he had seen. There had been something in the commander's eye, a look that worried him, despite the bullion that was missed. Even the way he left, without threat or insult, almost as if he had read his mind, was concerning. In fact, the more he thought about it, the greater his feeling of disquiet grew.

The revenue cutter was heading away and at speed; already she had covered a fair distance, and, as further sail was set, her captain clearly had a positive course in mind. It might be nothing more than a jolly jape; a new broom in the customs service who delighted in thrashing his little cruiser to the fullest extent. Ward had not spoken with Joe Lamport for a while; maybe he would give slightly better news. A few weeks down the line Commander Griffin could turn every bit as compliant as others in the service; that or dead like the fool who had come before him. But Ward thought not; something inside said they had chanced upon a sharpie, and things may get more difficult from now on.

* * *

The horizon would not stay empty for long, of that Griffin was certain. He could go below to the chart room and calculate the distance they had already run; a few minutes reckoning, with rough estimates for speed and travel, would come up with a course, but he felt his mind was adequately attuned without resorting to mathematics, and shouted out a heading as soon as they had gathered steerage way. Davies was looking at him oddly; well, he would have to get used to *Bee*'s new captain's moods although, should this prove futile, as Griffin was secretly fearing, he might not stay a commander in the customs service for many more days.

To be safe, he decided to say nothing of his plan; doing so would admit his previous error and then compound the crime further if no trace of a supply ship was found. As far as Davies and the others aboard *Bee* were concerned, this was still a testing cruise, a brief day's sail to get the feel of craft and crew. And if they, in turn, discovered their captain to be an odd cove, subject to strange moods and acts of whim, then he would not have lessened his position greatly. Far better that, than a fool who missed the obvious and failed to act when an opportunity presented.

The deck was small and much too crowded for pacing, but still he felt an urge for movement that was quite irresistible. Men were clearing *Bee*'s bilges using the twin elm-tree pumps that stood amidships. After several hours of high-speed sailing the fact that there was now sea water in her was not to be surprised at, but Griffin found himself watching the physical activity with a curious envy.

He glanced up at the sails yet again; all were trimmed board tight and, with the wind comfortably on her quarter, *Bee* was travelling at a good speed. But much time had been lost and, as the minutes steadily rolled by, he wondered just how long he could keep up the chase. There had to be a point when he would admit defeat; a considerable journey remained before they raised Newhaven, and the bar was impassable for several hours of every day. He must allow for that, if he didn't want them hovering about the roadstead for most of the evening.

There was a watch in his pocket and he longed to look at it, but that would only convey his anxiety, and the crew were probably already concerned by their new captain, and his reasonless actions. A call came from the masthead, but it was only to report a passing packet boat, and still *Bee* sailed on, her prow set against a horizon that remained as void as ever, and was now indisputably starting to dim.

"We shall have to see her back to port afore long, sir," Davies chanced.

Griffin glanced at him; the man's expression was concerned, as well it might be, but did not convey ridicule or pity. In fact the mate seemed supportive, even though he knew nothing of Griffin, or his wild theories.

"Keep her steady for now, if you please," he replied. "I'm aware of the tide, and will do all to return in time."

Davies seemed to understand. "We can stay out all night if it pleases you," he said quietly. "To be honest it would make a change, and the lads won't be any the worse for a bit of evening activity."

Griffin was grateful. If this did turn out to be a waste of their time, there would be little recrimination from his second-in-command. And yes, that sky was certainly starting to grow dark; perhaps it was better to call it off, and set course for home. Even now a proper heading must be calculated: it would take too long to simply turn to the north, and gradually creep along the shore to find their berth.

"Very well," he said finally. "I think we might call an end to the day." Even if he had been correct, and there had been a cooper, they were obviously too late to find it.

"As you like, sir," Davies replied unemotionally, but the voice of the masthead lookout cut in to any further conversation.

"Deck there, sail dead ahead!"

Griffin felt his weariness drain away as Davies looked at him with renewed respect. They waited expectantly, but nothing further came. Both men were dying to ask for more, but little would be achieved by bullying; the man was obviously trying to make out the sighting.

"Looks like another fisher, sir," he said eventually. "A bigger one this time, an' right on our bow, heading for shore."

That just about summed up the mixture of emotions Griffin had experienced throughout the day. At the first call he thought he might have struck gold, but to hear they had effectively been chasing one more smack made him want to scream with disappointment. Davies had taken the deck glass forward and was standing at the prow, waiting for the image to appear, while Griffin told himself that at least there had been something at the end of their chase. For all the crew knew it might even have been his objective; he could close with the fisher, inspect if he so wished, and then high-tail it for home, and hopefully still have the water to see *Bee* into harbour. He shifted his weight from foot to foot, desperate for a chance to take some exercise while telling himself that he had joined the customs service for a bit more excitement, and really could not complain.

"Wait," the lookout called again. "She must have sighted us, and is going about. Putting up more sail as well."

Griffin's senses pricked; she was heading in the opposite direction, and at full speed by the sound of it – the same behaviour as the last fisherman. But however hard the smack may have tried, she was no match for the *Bee* and within minutes the sighting was visible from her deck. Griffin took a step forward and stared intently as the vessel gathered shape and form. Davies joined him shortly afterwards with the deck glass. "I believe she's a local boat, sir," he said stiffly, passing the telescope across. "Belongs to a family, name of Warren."

Griffin could not have cared less about the ownership, but there was something in the mate's expression that made him question.

"Fisherman?"

Davies raised an eyebrow. "So they say."

"Strange that she should run as soon as we are sighted."

The mate grunted, but added nothing; clearly he did not think it strange at all.

"Do you think her worthy of inspection?"

This time Davies gave a half-smile. "Probably, and for a number of reasons. The Warren lot are well known in these parts. It's my guess she's met up with a cooper: they hover about this coast quite often. With the size of organisation the Warrens run it might even be a regular routine; one drop a week, to keep their coffers topped up."

Griffin felt mildly gratified that his instincts had been correct, but Davies was continuing.

"And considering her original course, I'd say she were on her way back, so chances are she'll be filled to the gun'les with all manner of fine things."

"Then we must stop her."

Davies gave a start, before controlling himself with obvious effort. "If that's what you wish, sir."

After the initial shock, the mate's face was giving nothing away as Griffin examined it in the falling light. "How could we do anything else?" he asked. "They are smugglers: it is our duty."

"Duty, sir, yes," Davies agreed. "Though there may be more than one way of skinning a rabbit, if you don't mind my saying."

"Whatever do you mean by that?" Griffin snapped. It had been a long day and he was getting just a little tired of enigmatic talk.

"Well, the Warren family are pretty important round here." Davies was apparently impervious to any frustration on his captain's part. "It isn't that their deeds are unknown to authority, but we have to play things a little careful when they run such a large organisation, and we are pitifully few."

"Do we not have support from the militia?" Griffin demanded. "And the dragoons if need be? Surely there is military in abundance hereabouts, and I may call in the Navy, should the need arise. Just why is everyone so afeared of a bunch of rogues running goods?"

"It ain't as easy as that, sir." Davies' voice had fallen, almost to a whisper. "You have to know the situation, before you may judge. An' taking one of their craft might not be the best of moves, not until you fully realise with whom you are dealing."

Griffin pondered. Despite his protests, he did have some understanding of what the mate was trying to tell him. He was, as he kept reminding himself, new to the area, the service in general and, when it came done to it, the country of his birth. Doubtless there would be many subtleties to learn and allowances to make in due course. It had also become obvious that England itself had succumbed to a culture of bribery and corruption. Even his present position could be squarely attributed to favouritism, which was little better. But still he could not see how ignoring smugglers caught red-handed could be excused or justified; it was the very nature of their business as officers of the revenue, and such an opportunity could not be ignored, if only for their own esteem.

"Maybe so," he said at length. "But I'll not let a boat filled with contraband pass me by."

"Very good, sir," Davies replied, and even went to say more, before finally deciding against it.

* * *

"You're home early, Matt; not in the suds, I trust?"

Ward pushed past his sister and into the small, private room at the back of the inn. "In the suds? I'll say – bloody preventive men ran me down."

Sophie raised her hand to her mouth. "They snagged you?" she asked.

Ward shook his head; there was a pot of tea on the side of the stove, and he looked about for a mug.

"No, nothing like that. Ran into the new man in the cruiser when I was headin' to meet with Frans. Fortunately he were still a good way off, so I was able to lead them away. But I think I was smoked; last I sees they are heading right for the hovering ground, and I didn't like the cut of that new commander's jib."

"He's stayin' here," Sophie confessed and Ward, who was in the process of filling a mug from the pot, almost dropped both.

"He's what?"

"We didn't realise," Sophie told him hurriedly. "He signed in with just his surname: there was no uniform or nothing."

"Does Dad know?"

She shook her head. "I think not, and only found out myself this morning when he left."

Ward sighed. "Well, he'll have to be got rid of. An' the sooner the better. He's got a look about him I don't like. That Carter man were bad enough, but this could be a good deal worse."

Sophie had also noticed a certain look about Griffin. "I can tell him his room is taken," she chanced.

"No," he said, lowering the mug. "I mean what I say; we can't afford to have him around."

* * *

The fishing boat had all sail set but *Bee* was gaining steadily and soon would have her in range. Even such a well-found smack had no chance of evading a vessel with *Bee*'s sailing qualities, but the very fact that she was trying confirmed Griffin's instincts. The nervous energy already expended had left him all but exhausted, and it was with effort that he refrained from sitting down on the near-by hatch cover. A commander could not give in to such human frailties; this had to be seen through to the very end.

Colours and pennant had been ordered again and, as she was continuing to run, there was cause enough to stop, board and even impound the vessel should he so wish. Davies' words had made their mark, however. Despite his bluster, Griffin was conscious that his command of *Bee* had lasted barely a day and the total time he had spent in the customs service was less than three months. It could well be that arresting a vessel with a strong local connection was high-handed, but if his job was to uphold laws which were being broken quite blatantly, then surely he had little choice.

"What do you see there?" he shouted up at the lookout. There was still a measure in him that remained in doubt, and it would cost nothing to be certain.

"We're closing fast, sir," came the assured reply, and Griffin had to hold back an angry retort.

"Masthead! A proper report, if you please."

There was a pause while the lookout scanned the horizon, then he replied in a slightly crestfallen tone: "Sail beyond, sir. Brig, carrying topsails, t'gallants and stays. She's close hauled an' heading to intercept the chase."

"Distance?"

Another pause before the shameful reply: "Hull up, sir; an' will be in sight of the deck at any time."

It was inexcusable, as all on board the cutter were well aware. Whatever might be the centre of attention, a lookout's duty was to scan the entire horizon. But this could be dealt with later, and Griffin was reasonably certain the man would be particularly attentive for the remainder of his trick. He looked towards the western horizon. There was no sign, but he must remember that *Bee*'s masthead was lower than that of an Indiaman; whatever it was could not be so very far off.

That she was a brig made the situation more curious. There were Royal Navy ships a plenty in the area; many were frigates and larger, although a variety of small unrated craft frequently plied the Channel. It might also be a merchant; traders of various nationalities were common in what was one of the busiest seaways in the world. A deep-sea fisher was another option; one who had a government licence to move outside home waters and 'go foreign' as the expression had it. But the final consideration interested him most; the sighting could easily be the supply ship he had originally hoped to intercept. And the fact that she was heading back to rescue what was probably a recent customer would seem to confirm this.

"Gaining steadily," the lookout reported in a tone intended to be both efficient and conciliatory, adding: "nothing new in sight," almost as an afterthought.

"Yes, a cooper, by God!" Davies exclaimed, peering through the deck glass. He turned to Griffin. "Seen her a couple of times when Mr Carter had command, but never got the chance to inspect. Dutch, by the look of her, and well-armed, I'd say. Most carry nine or twelve pounders, and they'll be enough aboard to use them."

Griffin walked to the starboard side and looked forward. Nine or twelve pounders: he certainly hadn't expected that degree of fire-power, although, now that it had been pointed out to him, it would seem to be an obvious precaution for any merchant carrying valuable cargo. That being the case he could not risk his fragile command anywhere within the brig's range, and the two vessels were closing at speed.

Not for the first time that day Griffin cursed himself for the fool he was. It was one thing to have guessed the smack had been heading for a supply ship, quite another to be able to fight her. Why had he assumed that a ship carrying a deal of merchandise would be equipped with few, if any, guns? The only advantage *Bee* possessed was her speed, and at that moment he failed to see how he could use such an asset.

The fishing smack was considerably closer now. Even under all possible sail her barge-like hull was making poor progress, and she was already within range of Griffin's broadside. Should he fire now, attempt to disable her, or continue to chase, board and risk closing with the brig? About him, the hands were chattering happily; it would seem that the frustration and confusion of the last hour or so was long forgotten. Confidence in their captain had clearly been totally restored, and they were looking forward to a successful encounter. He could only hope himself worthy of such trust.

"Keep her as she is," he said, returning to the binnacle. Davies looked at him quizzically, and Griffin tried to adopt an attitude of unconcern. They might speculate but there was no knowing the brig's weaponry, she may be completely unarmed and even poorly crewed, although a sixth sense warned him that such a case was unlikely. Therefore he must keep her at arm's length although, at the rate at which the two vessels were closing, that was not going to be easy.

The smugglers were clearly not intending to surrender. Griffin might open fire, but it would be a shallow victory, and one he could hardly glory in. Such an action might also disable the smack, in which case a tow would be required; something that would be hard to organise without coming dangerously close to the guns of the oncoming Dutchman. No, to successfully take the fishing boat he must board and sail her off; that was the only method that might achieve a capture, whilst escaping the attentions of the larger vessel.

He must be careful, however; *Bee* had speed and reasonable fire-power for her size, but there was no disguising the fact that her scantlings and frame were light. Should he allow the brig into range, and were she to be armed with anything heavier than swivels, a cutter would not come off well; in fact even one important hit on *Bee*'s fragile hull might well account for her totally.

Chapter Five

The sun was dropping in the sky and evening approached, although Griffin no longer worried about getting back into harbour. The smack lay barely a quarter of a mile to leeward, with the Dutchman less than two miles beyond. It would be close, and he was starting to doubt whether it was even possible. The brig was still making directly for them but could turn and present her broadside at any moment. It was still long range, but he had yet to actually catch the smack and, were the Dutch to open fire and disable the cutter, her capture would be a certainty.

He closed his mind to the thought and what would be made of his defeat. Both the smugglers and the Batavian Republic would delight in taking one of his Majesty's revenue cutters into their service, and it would definitely be a spectacular beginning to his customs career. But still he wanted to press closer, if only to prove to the crew, and himself, that he would not run at the first obstacle. And there was also the added incentive of that fishing smack. She may be owned by a powerful family, but he was now quite determined that the boat should not escape. The Warrens apparently represented a force in the area, and were obviously used to getting their own way. So be it, but he had accepted a role that directly conflicted with them and their interests. Since he was a child, Griffin had made a point of standing up to bullies and he was not going to change now. Besides, if he really did want to stamp his mark on the area, he guessed there would be few better opportunities than the present one.

"Shall I order us about, sir?"

Griffin knew the mate had been watching the situation every bit as closely, and may well represent the voice of reason, but still he was not to be moved.

"No, Mr Davies," he said deliberately, and in a voice loud enough for all close by to hear. "We have not come this far just to watch them escape. Clear away the guns, if you please."

* * *

Gadd was cursing quietly to himself; this new man was just a little too keen for his liking. The broadside cannon were being loaded and he and four others were looking after numbers one and two, the furthest forward.

"We was only supposed to be out for a trial sail," he grumbled as Calver and Colclough took the strain and ran the starboard gun forward. "So far he's stretched every piece of canvas and line on board, rummaged one smack and looks likely to do damage to a second, while making us a present to the Dutch into the bargain."

Fuller was also annoyed, but that had more to do with handling the cannon. When he had served in the Royal Navy five men would have been considered the very minimum to serve even light pieces such as theirs, especially as none were dedicated gunners. But in a revenue cutter they were expected to serve both starboard and larboard guns, as well as handle a complex and oversize sailing rig, man the swivel guns and, if need be, indulge in a little hand-to-hand combat. At the end of what had turned out to be a tiring day, he was actually in agreement with Gadd: a rare occasion in itself.

"Them square heads can do serious injury, given half the chance," Gadd continued. "And even if we do gets away, the tide'll be against us back at Newhaven. Likelihood is it'll be mornin' afore we're safely back over the bar."

"Worse things have happened than being up all night," Wooderson said, as he and Colclough finished attending to the starboard gun. The twine wrapping about the apron covering the touch hole was loosened and the lead cover removed.

"This one'll still be warm," he muttered, as they turned their attention to the larboard piece that had been fired only a short time ago. Calver and Colclough ran her in then Gadd set to, sponging out the barrel. Fuller passed the small paper cartridge that contained two pounds of cylinder powder, which was inserted down the barrel, and Gadd rammed it home, following with a wad made of junk, while Wooderson selected a round shot from the nearby garland. The ball came next, and was held in position by another wad, while Fuller collected the priming horn as Colclough and Calver heaved the gun back into the firing position. Then, peering down the touch hole, Fuller inserted his priming spike to puncture the canvas cartridge before tapping a good measure of fine meal powder suspended in spirit from the horn into the hole. Harry, the ship's boy, had already placed shallow tubs at regular intervals down the deck. Each held a length of burning slow match, and it was a sign of the falling light that the red glow was reflecting eerily about the inside, making the bins look as if they contained hot coals.

"And then he wants us to seize a Warren boat – that's pretty chancy in my mind." Gadd was still whining on. "Them Horsebridge lot don't appreciate folk interferin' with their business. If *Bee* had merely taken a squint afore wandering off home we might have got away with it. We could all be drinkin' at The Buckle tonight, but with this new Johnnie fixing for a fight..."

"Well, something has to be done," Wooderson interrupted, glancing at Colclough for support. "We can moan all we wants about the gangs, and how free traders have taken over the area, but it ain't gonna stop unless someone stands up to them."

"Carter stood up to them," Gadd reminded them. "An' look what happened to him."

"He fell from his horse," Wooderson countered. "It were an accident."

"That's not what I hears. He was murdered, a rope stretched across the road. And when they brought him down, they did for him."

"That is nought but tattle-tale." Colclough spoke with calm assurance. "Go on spreading such stories and you're as good as working for the Warrens yourself."

"Well I didn't join the gobblers to end up a prisoner of the Dutch," Gadd sulked.

"We're none of us ending up prisoners of no one," Wooderson said firmly. "Least not unless we tells ourselves we are. The Warrens are a problem, but it's not one that's going to go away without someone addressing it."

"There's too many of them," Gadd protested. "And no one rightly knows who is a member and who's not. I'm afraid of no man, but how can you fight an enemy that can't be seen?"

"I can see that boat out there," Wooderson said firmly. "An' I knows exactly what they're about. You want an opportunity to make a stand, well there it is. 'Who will rise up for me against the evildoers? Who will stand up for me against the workers of iniquity?': Psalm ninety-four."

"Aye, this new man might be a touch on the eager side," Fuller agreed, after a respectful pause. "But that don't make him wrong in my mind. Ask me, them Warrens need a bit of opposition; someone has to take the lead, and if he is prepared to, I'll follow."

* * *

"Very well, Mr Blackman, you may open fire whenever you wish."

The gunner, who had taken over the forward starboard six pounder, raised his hand in acknowledgement. The smack was now less than fifty yards off their starboard bow, but *Bee* had a good four knots on her, and would soon be passing. Even from that distance it was clear she was well laden, her deck being neatly stacked with half-ankers of spirit and indeterminable bales which, so convinced were they of their safety, the crew had not even bothered to jettison. Meanwhile the brig was less than a mile away, and they were certainly within range of her guns. She had not yawed, and remained heading for them, sailing close hauled and stubbing the Channel waves with her bluff bows as she inched closer.

"Do you think she will strike?" Griffin asked, looking at the smack once more. Davies shook his head.

"No, that's not the sort of thing a Warren craft does. We're gonna have to board her."

"I had thought as much." Griffin turned towards him and added in a softer tone, "I shall go."

Davies looked surprised. "That would normally be my privilege, sir," he said. He had been slightly offended when Griffin boarded the last smack, now he was wondering if the new captain really trusted him.

"Indeed, Mr Davies, and I am sorry to be depriving you. But I am very much the newcomer, yet you have sailed *Bee* for many a year. She will need an experienced man at the conn."

The mate pursed his lips but accepted the point. Griffin continued.

"Assuming they do not defer to our shot, I intend to steer for them, pass as close as possible, then board. What crew will she be carrying?"

"No more than five," Davies replied. "None of them will be Warrens, but all as keen as mustard, you can be sure of that."

"Then I shall take six; you will need the rest to work *Bee* back."

That also was beyond doubt. As soon as the boarders had left it would be up to Davies to see the cutter round, before heading off close hauled, away from the Dutch brig and on towards safety.

"I should be obliged if you could select some likely men," Griffin said. "I have yet to fully acquaint myself with the crew."

"Very good, sir." Davies caught the eye of Lamport, the deputed mariner, who had moved back from his usual position. "See to it, will you, Joe?"

The petty officer touched his hat briefly, before beginning to single out likely candidates.

"We want volunteers, mind," Griffin added in a voice intended to carry, and Lamport touched his hat once more.

"Jibe as soon as we are clear," Griffin continued. "Then come back as close as you can make." With fore and aft sails, *Bee* could bear several points nearer to the wind than the square rigged brig. "Take no notice of us; we shall survive or not. Should the Dutch disable you, use the guns by all means, but do not hold out too much of a fight."

"What about yourself, sir?"

"I shall endeavour to overpower the crew, and turn for home. With luck we should both be on course for Newhaven within fifteen minutes."

"Very good, sir," Davies agreed, although both men knew that such a time frame could also see a very different outcome.

Blackman's gun spoke suddenly, making all on board jump, while the bright flash contrasted painfully with the darkening sky and left a few blinking and rubbing at their eyes. The ball landed with a splash well past the smack's hull, as Griffin ordered *Bee* round to close on her. She bore down on the vessel's stern and the two were about to collide when the helm was put across. The action came almost simultaneously with a cry from the smaller vessel, but Griffin ignored it; were it to be a call to arms or surrender, it would make no difference; they were so near to the Dutchman that there was only one course of action.

He glanced down *Bee*'s starboard side and noticed how the six men had divided into two groups of three and were poised, ready to board. One of them was Lamport, the deputed mariner; obviously he had included himself in the boarding party, which was commendable. And another was Gadd, the grumpy mariner he had first met only the previous afternoon: it was a surprise to see him; Griffin would not have put him down as being one who would readily volunteer. The rest he did not know, but they seemed a worthy enough bunch. Then, even before he had fully realised it, there was a brief cheer and the cutter began to scrape along the smack's rubbing board.

Griffin drew his cutlass, and braced himself. The smack was slightly lower, and there were numerous places suitable to board, but still he was tense. Then the moment was right, and Griffin jumped.

He landed on the stern, about six feet from the nearest of the smack's crew, and almost alongside the first of *Bee*'s boarding party. One – Griffin didn't know the man's name –

was quick, and had the solitary smuggler at the point of his cutlass even as he set foot on the deck.

"Very good," Griffin shouted, and moved forward, stepping past the rows of neatly stacked spirit tubs. He had yet to learn the identity of most of *Bee*'s crew, but would remember that man's face, and be sure to credit him later. Amidships the second group had also landed successfully, although they were facing stronger opposition. Three of the smugglers were coming for them with swords and, as Griffin stepped forward to join the fray, there was the flash and bang of a pistol.

He raised his sword and struck down, catching one man square on the shoulder and forcing him to drop something that fell to the deck with a clatter. From one side he noticed Lamport, and the rest of *Bee*'s boarders, join the fight, but another of his men had tripped, and seemed to be wounded. A smuggler came into view, this time carrying what looked like a filleting knife; Griffin was able to keep him at bay with his cutlass, while Gadd knocked him down from behind with the hilt of his own sword.

Griffin looked his thanks, but there was no time for more; this could not last long: even as they fought, the fishing smack was sailing nearer to the Dutch brig. Then he glanced about and realised with both surprise and relief that there was actually no more opposition: they had control.

"You," he said, pointing desperately at a member of his crew. "See to the for'ard sheets." He noticed that Lamport had secured the uninjured members of the smack's crew next to the mainmast. "Which of our men can steer?" he bellowed.

"Conway's the best, sir," the petty officer replied, and a man raised his hand.

"Very well: Conway, take the tiller." Griffin pointed at a man who was peering at the wounded smugglers. "Keep control of those; get them with the others if you can, and don't take your eyes away for a second. If they give trouble, deal with them in any way you feel fit. The rest, follow me." So saying he made for the main sheets. "Jibe upon my word," he shouted, and received a few grunts of confirmation from the others. Then: "Up helm!"

The smack's deck tilted and she began a tight turn; one of the cutter's men stumbled as they fumbled with the lines. For a moment she wallowed, before the large mainsail caught the wind and swung across. Griffin began to sheet it home and was just looking to see how those on the fore had managed when the whistle of shot passing overhead distracted him. A crack came from above, and the gaff was snapped cleanly in two. Canvas drooped about the deck, covering the helmsman, who threw it off like so much unwanted bed linen, and the boat began to slow.

Griffin turned back; the brig was broadside on with smoke drifting lazily from her guns. She was less than six hundred yards off but even under fore alone, the smack was drawing away. They would not be out of range before the Dutchman's guns spoke again though, and the next broadside may finish them.

"Keep her as close to the wind as you can make," he shouted to the helmsman. Looking forward he could see *Bee*: she must have turned almost as soon as the boarding party left and was now stoically dipping her stem into the waves less than a cable ahead. But even as he watched she luffed up and slowed also, clearly intending to allow the wounded smack to forereach on her. He swore silently under his breath; this was not the time to play hero: Davies should be making what speed he could and leave them to their fate. Then he noticed a figure at *Bee*'s taffrail holding a line.

"You at the fore," he shouted, his frustration at not knowing all their names giving his voice an extra edge. "Be ready to take a tow from the cruiser."

A wave from forward told him that he had been heard; Lamport was there, and obviously had the matter under control, and Gadd was supporting him. They were creeping very steadily up to the cutter, and Griffin could see it was Davies himself who was proposing to throw the heaving line. It came when they were less than twenty feet off, and the brig was due to fire again. The weighted end dropped neatly across the smack's prow, and Gadd had pulled the single hawser in and secured it even as the enemy's guns spoke once more.

Griffin lowered himself instinctively, but they had made some distance since the last broadside; either that or the gunners were not so lucky, as all the shots missed or fell short. Then the hull of the smack gave a jerk as *Bee* took up the strain, and soon both vessels were back on the wind, the tow wrenching the tiny hull of the fishing smack forward at speed.

The fore crew had their sail trimmed tight while the helmsman kept her as true as possible, and gradually the brig began to disappear into the fast falling darkness. Griffin drew a deep sigh; his hands were shaking and he felt an unaccountable desire to laugh. But it was over, and for some reason they had carried it off. He had arrested his first smuggler within a day of taking up his duties, and hopefully made a mark on the area he was to control. The crew of the smack was sitting discontentedly forward. They might be members of a large gang but none appeared particularly powerful now. And if he had taken them, he told himself, he could take the others; it would only be a question of when, and how.

Chapter Six

"We have matters to discuss with the landlord," the man told Sophie.

"Very good, sir," she replied and fled from the hallway, relieved to be able to go so quickly. Heading into the back room she looked about, but seeing no one, moved on and outside, into the small yard. Again, no sign of Father; for a moment the dread of having to return to those men without him dismayed her. She shouted once, but her voice rang about the seemingly empty building to no reply. Then an idea came, and she ran down to the stables beyond the yard.

"There are men in the hall," she said, her voice unnecessarily breathless as she saw him standing next to Clive, the ostler.

"Men?" Her father smiled. "Why, Soph, that is a rare event to be sure..."

"You must come," she said. "They wish to speak with you."

"And who are they?" His face cleared as he realised his daughter was genuinely upset.

"I – I am not sure, I have never seen them before." It was hard to convey feelings that had no foundation, but were purely the product of instinct, and having Clive grinning like an oaf as witness was no help at all. Thankfully the older man apparently understood, and ambled out of the stables.

"You say you've never seen them afore?" her father asked, as she hurried next to him.

"No... Yes... I don't think so," she blustered. "One of them is familiar, the other I don't know, but they seem important."

Her father paused and looked at her quizzically. It sounded like some of the Horsebridge gang, and yet members came in on a regular basis; why was the girl behaving so strangely this time?

"I think one of them may be a Warren," she said finally, and in a voice that was barely more than a whisper.

"What, a Warren here in person?" her father gasped, and she nodded, equally appalled.

* * *

Griffin woke in his room at The Star and had to think for several seconds before he remembered where he was, and how he had come to be there. The events of the previous night were hazy, due in part to all that had gone on and the three large glasses of Hollands he had downed in his room before finally finding his bed.

They had taken nearly two hours to beat back to Newhaven, under assistance from *Bee*, and only felt reasonably secure when they came under the protection of the shore battery just outside the harbour entrance. The tide was against them, and they had to wait for a further hour and a half until there was enough water for the fishing smack to make it over the bar, followed some time later by the cutter. Then there had been the inevitable confusion on shore; the guard was raised, along with one of the landwaiters, who had been summoned from his supper. Clearly the elderly man had dined well and was close to being in his cups, although news of Griffin's exploits soon sobered him up and he looked with astonishment as the haul was unloaded at the legal quay. There were one hundred and eighty half-ankers, each holding three and a half gallons of over-proof spirit, as well as a bolt of lawn lace and four packages of silk fabric. Griffin was also surprised to find a number of more personal items that might well be specific orders: a painting, three pieces of expensive porcelain and a life-size statue of a naked goddess that caused a good deal of comment and speculation from the cutter's crew.

The prisoners and wounded had already been landed by boat, but there was still a good deal of paperwork to complete in addition to the inventory. In all it took several hours and then Griffin had to wake the boy at his lodgings when he did finally make it home. He remembered his room being unusually cold and, with no food inside him other than some hastily eaten biscuit and cheese while they had been waiting for the tide, the raw spirit seemed unusually attractive. He regretted it now, of course. The previous night's excitement alone would have been enough to give him a headache; as it was, he could barely open his eyes fully. He rose slowly from the bed and moved across to the jug of water, where a decent sluice did much to restore him. After a brief wash he decided against a shave as being too demanding, and dressed hurriedly in shirt, trousers and uniform jacket. His watch told him that there would be no chance of a breakfast, although what he really craved more than anything else was coffee. In an establishment like The Star, that should be readily available at any hour but, as he heaved the heavy jacket over his shoulders, the doubts began.

Memories of the stir his uniform had created only the previous morning were still fresh in his mind. He might leave his jacket behind, but by now most of the other guests would know his profession and he was beginning to understand that it was not a popular one. For a moment he weighed the prospect of fresh strong coffee with a confrontation and decided instead to head straight for Custom House, and take his chances there.

His sword was still in the cutter; he had left it there the previous night without a thought, but as he strode through the parlour entrance he noticed its absence and felt extremely vulnerable. His step increased and he avoided the eyes of three heavily built men who stood, as if on guard in the hallway. As he looked away, Griffin noticed the landlord, seated at a table by the parlour entrance. The man was deep in conversation with two others, and all three looked up and straight at him as he passed by. With both a headache and an empty stomach he was not at his best, but there was something in their stare that struck Griffin deep inside. If he believed in such things he would call it a premonition, and not one he particularly welcomed. He walked on, inwardly admonishing himself for the fool that he was, although there remained little doubt in his mind that he had been the subject of their conversation.

Outside, the chill of the early autumn morning helped to clear his head and he struck out for the drawbridge. His right arm was paining him at the shoulder, probably from the rigours of boarding that smack last night and he supposed he should congratulate himself that this was the extent of his injuries. Whilst serving with the East India Company there had only been a few times when he was called upon to exert physical violence, and one of those was more in a directional capacity, when pirates had tried to board his ship off Canton. Firing a cannon, or rather ordering one to be fired, was different from hand-to-hand combat. Last night had been very real; almost personal and, thinking about it now and how it might have gone, he was appalled. For such an event to occur so early in his customs career also made him wonder if he had made the right choice. Then he almost laughed out loud at his own doubt. He had left the Company's service in order to break away from the mind-numbing routine that was threatening to engulf him. Yet now that his previous life had been exchanged for something that actually promised adventure, he was regretting it.

The thought cheered him and his pace quickened as he turned onto the road that led to Custom House. There was also a deep glow of self-satisfaction from what was undoubtedly a good job well done and as he reached the oak front door he was in a far better frame of mind. The collector and his staff were bound to be pleased, especially as he had been attached to the area for so short a time; in fact, he was quite looking forward to being acclaimed as the hero of the hour.

* * *

And so he was, to some extent at least. The boy on the door stared at him with frank amazement while Griffin was shown directly through to the collector's empty office where he sat on his own in front of the great man's desk. A large pot of coffee appeared unrequested almost straight afterwards, and Griffin helped himself to a cup.

But as he drank it down he became uncomfortably aware of the sound of voices that filtered through from the next room. Two men were deep in a loud, but indiscernible, conversation. One, whose tone was slightly higher, grew increasingly heated, but the other kept repeating what sounded like the same phrase that Griffin, try as he might, could not decipher. Eventually curiosity got the better of him, and he placed his empty cup down, stood up, and moved nearer to the wall. The conversation had stopped, however, and he was left standing far away from his seat, and cup, when Dobson suddenly erupted into his office. He was followed by a short, slight man wearing an old fashioned wig and carrying an urgent look on his weasel face, who all but pushed past the corpulent figure of the collector in his eagerness to get to Griffin first.

"Ah, Commander; capital performance, sir, capital," Dobson said, almost absent-mindedly, as he blocked the smaller man's progress and shook Griffin's hand. "You will know Mr Dwyer, I assume?"

"We have not been introduced," Griffin replied, regarding the newcomer warily. Dwyer was quite a bit younger than Dobson; probably no more than thirty, and easily the shortest man in the room. His suit, though of a good cut, seemed to have been styled for someone older, and he carried an ornate silver-mounted cane that appeared to be purely for decorative effect. Griffin noticed that he held himself strangely erect, as if straining to claim the very last inch of his height, while the slightly mottled complexion spoke of recent physical exertion.

"Mr Dwyer, my Comptroller and deputy: Commander Griffin," Dobson grunted. "My apologies: I had thought the two of you were acquainted."

"I am very pleased to meet you, sir," Griffin said, bowing slightly. Dwyer merely inclined his head in response, and muttered something that could almost have been a snarl.

"Well, it seems that you have been busy, Commander," Dobson said, waving Griffin back to his seat, while settling himself down behind the large, polished desk. There was one other chair, but before Dwyer could claim it, the collector addressed him. "Thank you, Mr Dwyer, I think we can spare you. I am certain there are other matters that demand your attention."

The younger man froze before glaring hard at Griffin then looking back at the collector.

"I said, thank you, Mr Dwyer," Dobson repeated with emphasis and he remained motionless until the man reluctantly left the room. The door closed loudly and there was a silence afterwards that lasted for several seconds.

"Well, we have had an assessment of the goods seized," the collector said eventually, holding up a paper that Griffin recognised from the night before. "And it amounts to several thousand pounds." He paused and considered. "Mind you, that does not allow for the value of the boat, although I fancy there is some dispute as to the exact ownership." The man set a smile upon his fat face. "But it will still look fine in the weekly report to the board; being utterly frank, I was starting to run out of things to say."

Griffin thought this a strange statement, considering the degree of smuggling prevalent in the area.

"And of course, you and your men will be entitled to shares of the seizure money when it is finally decided."

That was something that he had not considered. As commander of the cutter Griffin's portion would be almost half the value, a considerable sum, and far more than he could earn on a two-year trip in an Indiaman, that was for sure. The men would benefit as well: his men, as he must now think of them. Davies would be entitled to a healthy chunk and Lamport a lesser one with the ordinary mariners sharing what remained; again, a sizeable figure. He doubted if he could have wished for a better start to his time at Newhaven.

"Mind, you must not expect the money to be available for some while; the wheels of the claims court grind exceedingly slow, to be sure, and allowances must be made for repairs to the cutter, together with our own expenses here, of course." There was something in Dobson's words that did not ring true, although in his current mood Griffin was prepared to accept them, as well as the delay; after all, only a few minutes ago he had forgotten that any money was even coming to him.

"The goods will be sent up to London in a coaster; they are not suitable for an open auction hereabouts. Normally such a charge would be escorted through each sector by the cruiser responsible for that area, but what say I make a special concession in your instance?"

Dobson may have been trying to look benignly at Griffin, but the expression came across as that of an elderly lion anticipating his lunch. "A spell in London would be welcomed by your men, I am certain, and you and your officers might also enjoy the capital. So why not accompany them for the entire journey in *Bee*?"

Griffin was about to agree when something made him stop. London, with all its delights, did sound attractive and such a trip could probably be stretched out for several days. But he had spent some time in the City only so very recently, and a break now would naturally take him away from his new posting. Besides, his headache was not so great that he could ignore an inner warning that Dobson might have an ulterior motive. Then he caught a look in the collector's eye and knew that he was right.

"Thank you, sir, but I would prefer to remain in Newhaven."

Dobson's expression seemed to change from one of calculated manipulation to astonishment. "Indeed, I am more used to young officers straining for a chance to get away," he flustered, arranging the papers on his desk as if his current interview was suddenly a distraction from proper work. "Why, such an invitation would normally be appreciated and accepted with gratitude; it is surprising."

"I meant no disrespect, sir." Griffin swallowed. "But I am especially new to the station, and wish to acquaint myself as soon as is possible."

Dobson looked down. "Very well then, the usual arrangements can be made. Or maybe the collector at Shoreham will provide an escort; it will make a change for me to ask him for a favour. As I remember he has a prisoner to transport to the Fleet, so I dare say he will have no trouble finding a more appreciative officer willing to take the trip." The man's glance returned to Griffin, and he appeared to assess him afresh. "So, to get back to last night's exploits; one of the biggest hauls we have made in many a month, and highly commendable, highly commendable. Mind, we can expect some reaction from the Warren family; you will have heard of them, no doubt?"

"I have, sir."

"Quite a direct bunch, I may say, and influential with the lower classes."

Griffin said nothing. He might have misjudged Dobson; the trip to London could have been nothing more than a way of keeping him safe until the Warrens' anger died down. He thought not, though; there was an undeniable air about the man, and his deputy, that bothered him.

"Indeed, they can be most disagreeable, but are not as powerful as they may care to pretend." The last sentence was spoken especially loudly, as if Dobson were addressing someone who was not in the room, then he continued in a softer, more confidential tone. "We are not unaware of their activities, and do all we can to keep them in check, don't you know? Should you encounter any unpleasantness I trust you will report it to me, so that the appropriate action may be taken."

Griffin said he would, although the man did not inspire confidence: either in himself or any action he might take.

"Excellent. Well, I am sure you will wish to meet with your men and share the good news of the seizure money. I must say, you have made a brave start to your time here at Newhaven, Commander. I expect to hear great things from you in the future."

Griffin stood, as it was clear the interview was drawing to an end. The morning sun was just breaking through, casting a strong beam that lit up the line of porcelain jars that stood on a shelf to one side of the room. Griffin was shaking the collector's hand once more and half-listening to further platitudes when it happened. They had turned together, and Dobson was showing him to the door, talking all the while, when Griffin's eyes fell again upon the row of china pots. There were five, and they seemed oddly spaced; almost squashed together. Then Griffin realised there had only been four the previous day. And, now that his attention had been drawn to them, he was equally certain that the larger one on the end was part of the cutter's haul; booty from the smack, and last seen on the legal quay only a matter of hours ago.

* * *

"Yes, Mr Ward," the visitor said deliberately. "It is a regrettable situation."

He was sitting at his own table, in his own parlour, which was housed inside his own inn, but still the landlord felt uncomfortable in the presence of the two men.

"And one that should be addressed extremely swiftly," the man, who was actually no older than Ward's son, continued. "Unless we wish for a repeat of last night's tragedy."

"I could ask him to vacate his room," the landlord chanced. Both men's eyes became fixed on him.

"And how would that help?" William Warren asked. He was Stanton Warren's youngest, and carried himself with all the assurance that a favoured member of such an important family was entitled to. "Do you think such a problem will disappear because he has not a bed for the night?"

"Or will it maybe make him more suspicious," the second man, who was older and a good deal heavier, asked. "Surely a dangerous state for any revenue officer?"

The landlord shook his head; he had not followed the thought through, but was reluctant to suggest a more permanent solution. He had only spoken with Mr Griffin – Commander Griffin, he supposed he should think of him – a couple of times, and held no affection for the man. But still, he felt a natural reluctance to any method the two opposite him might be contemplating.

"With what our friend will be earning from last night, he could buy his own house," the second continued. Ward did not know his name, and they had not been introduced. "And if he is allowed to continue, maybe even an inn as fine as yours." The cold dark eyes swept about the room as if he himself were sizing it up with a view to purchase.

"Yes, I suppose he could," the landlord agreed. "And maybe buy mine; in truth it is nought but a millstone about my neck." He smiled hopefully, but met only dead stares in return. "Well, what do you want of me?" Ward asked finally, taking the initiative. "I can keep him in sight, and advise you of his moves, though that may be of no great benefit. And I have to take in my stock; the cellars are almost empty. You promised more wine, and I need other stores: tobacco, spirit, and there are outstanding orders that should have been fulfilled from last night's run."

"We cannot see you with empty cellars, Mr Ward," Warren replied.

"An empty cellar is an insult to business," the second man agreed.

"You will get your wine, and everything else, very shortly."

The landlord thanked them, even though he felt little comfort from the reassurance.

"You may even get more than you require: what do you think, Mr Brady?" Warren asked his companion.

"Oh, a good deal more," the older man agreed.

And now both were smiling, although their slick, unpleasant expressions owed nothing to humour.

"Much more than you have ever held before, I am thinking."

"A few pipes of wine, spirit and maybe a pound or two of tobacco," the landlord said. "I need little else."

Warren turned to his friend. "I think we can do better than that."

Brady nodded. "Yes, Mr Ward has storage a plenty and, by his own admission, is in need of goods."

The landlord shifted uncomfortably. None of the Horsebridge lot was easy to deal with. They might have been named after the local hamlet their gang operated from, but the family actually came from Nutley, a village far further north. And most, this Brady included judging by his accent and fashionable clothing, were Londoners; as hard and bent as used doornails, and just about as easy to work with.

"This is a very public building; I cannot store more than I need, you must see that."

Both men's expressions hardened again and the landlord thought he might have overstepped the mark. Then he noticed their attention was set in the far distance, and following something. Turning, he saw the Griffin man walking through the hallway. He came almost past their table, and dressed in full uniform, as bold as you like. They were all silent until he had gone by and for a few moments afterwards. Then the landlord spoke again.

"You can see how it is," he said. "I have a preventive officer living at my inn, and you want me to store booty for you."

"Oh yes, we can see exactly how it is," Brady assured him. "The man has shown he is not afraid to act, and yet we cannot deal with him in a similar manner to his predecessor."

"You cannot?" Ward asked, his tone a mixture of relief and disappointment.

"Of course not." Warren shook his head. "We are hardly animals, Mr Ward. One customs man dies, it is an unfortunate accident: regrettable, but unlikely to attract attention."

"But two men die," Brady said, taking up the thread. "And there may be considerably more interest."

"So what am I to do?" the landlord asked, almost in desperation.

"Whatsoever you will, Mr Ward." Warren gave a cheeky grin and the older man longed to modify it with the back of his hand. "Keep him as a tenant, or throw him out; that is your choice. You may even decide to opt for something a little more permanent, but that will also be a decision only you can make."

"And be responsible for," Brady reminded him.

"You want me to deal with him?" The surprise in his voice was evident.

"You are in a better position." Warren began to examine his fingernails, which were well chewed, although free from any hint of manual labour. "But whatever your choice, make it swiftly," he warned. "We will not accept the loss of any more goods, and you will be receiving a large delivery on the evening of Saturday next. Be sure that in all areas you are ready to receive it."

* * *

Griffin bounded down the path to where *Bee* lay moored, his boots fairly ringing on the hard ground. The sun was definitely hotter now, but there was a slight breeze, and he wanted above anything else to set sail and quit the shore with all its problems. Of course he knew that to be impossible; the tide was still making and there would not be sufficient water for several hours. Besides, the cutter had performed well last night and his men could be excused for wanting a restful day after all they had done.

He mounted the short gangplank and stepped on deck. Gadd was there, as he had been when Griffin first boarded *Bee*, but this time his greeting was very different. With the knowledge of shared experiences the man's face actually broke into what might be regarded as a genial expression and he even went so far as to drop the lines he had been splicing to knuckle his forehead.

"How is it with you, Gadd?" Griffin enquired.

"Well enough, thanking you, sir," he muttered. "Though I don't think you can say the same about them Horsebridge priggers."

"No doubt the assizes will deal with them in due course."

"Aye, sir. But it ain't them that should worry us: it's those what's left."

"That's enough, Gadd." The mate's voice broke in and Griffin turned to notice Davies standing next to the tiller. "There's no need to spread more gloom and despondency; we got all we need."

"Only stating the truth like I knows it," Gadd replied, sullenly.

"You fought well last night," Griffin told him. "And if there's something to be said, I'm prepared to hear it."

Faced with the sudden attention of his two most senior officers, the mariner paused for a second and began to fiddle with his knife, opening and closing the blade and fid as if they were part of a complex mechanism.

"It ain't for me to say, really, but that Warren lot have friends here abouts."

"So I believe," Griffin replied. "And that is a concern to you?"

"It is to us all, your honour; and rightly."

Davies cleared his throat. "Some of the men are a mite worried, sir," he said. "There have been threats in the past, and it is well known that the Warrens don't take opposition lightly."

"Has anything been said since last night?"

The mate shook his head. "No, sir. But two of the lads may well have run."

"Run?" Griffin was startled. Desertion from the customs service was almost unheard of. Pay and conditions were better, and the average lower deck seaman enjoyed a far wider degree of latitude than in the Royal Navy.

"They both have families, sir." Davies seemed almost embarrassed to admit the fact. "My guess is they'll be on the road to London by now, or at least out of the county."

"Bankhead's one," Gadd told him. "He has kin in Ireland, an' he told me he would be making to join them."

The name meant nothing to Griffin, although the loss of an experienced man certainly did. His eyes returned to the mariner. "Gadd, I know you not to be a coward, and am quite certain that this gang is powerful, but we must uphold the law."

"With respect, sir, you're not from round here and don't know what they're capable of. I'll face any man in a scrap, all will tell you that, and some might say you got to stand up to them. That all sounds fine and dandy, but when you does, you gets to worrying: they got so many in their control, and there's no knowing what they might do."

Davies said nothing, and it was clear that Gadd was speaking from the heart.

"In that case, I had better talk to the men," Griffin said.

"I was doin' that very thing afore you came aboard, sir," Davies told him. "They're below now: would you care to join them?"

* * *

Griffin perched, more or less comfortably, on top of the bread bin, while about him the thirty or so members of his crew sat at their mess benches. It was awkward; this was their space and world and he did not belong; neither did he know them. Never during his career in the East India Company had he ever spoken with the hands in such an intimate manner, or even heard of it being done. But things were bound to be different in the revenue service, and everyone accepted there was a more informal order of command in smaller craft.

Griffin felt slightly guilty as he gazed back at those under him. There was the undeniable feeling that he had acted rashly in some way; placed them in danger due to his own enthusiasm and lack of understanding. He supposed that Davies had tried to tell him, but he had not listened; well, he would listen now, but first he had to speak.

"Before we begin I must pass on what I trust you will regard as good news," he said. They waited respectfully. "I have just been with the collector who tells me the haul last night was substantial; you can all expect seizure money, and it will be generous." The news brought a good reaction; there were murmurings and comments from amongst the men, and one was even heard to give a short chuckle. Then the silence returned, and the men went back to waiting expectantly.

"But I hear that some have concerns, and I wanted to speak with you all to see if these may be addressed." Griffin had not prepared himself for such an interview; indeed the entire experience was both novel and unexpected. "The main subject being, I believe, the Warren family."

There was a general nodding of heads, and a few whispered 'yes'.

"Very well, then we shall have to see what can be done. It would seem that their influence is wide."

"They control all of the local businesses, and most of the farms, sir." Lamport, the deputed mariner, spoke up. "There is also the feeling that they have power over local magistrates, though that is not so easy to prove."

"It's a fact, Joe," one of them said, and there was a general murmur of agreement.

"An' nae jury is likely tae convict 'em," another added in a broad Scots accent. "Of 'at ye can be certain."

"So be it," Griffin said, striving to retain some control. "And you are afeared to cross them?" There was a sudden cooling in the atmosphere and he added hastily: "I can understand why that should be."

"Many who have done so in the past have come to no good," the first voice stated. "As Joe says, their influence is wide; there ain't many places they don't have control."

"How many of you are berthed ashore?" A few arms were raised. "And do you feel safe in the *Bee*?"

"As safe as anywhere, sir." An older man spoke this time. "None of us is afraid of going on land, or wants to hide in the barkie, but there's some what have families."

Griffin paused. This was a situation he had hardly expected and was certainly not why he joined the customs service: or accepted the posting to Newhaven for that matter. Without a doubt he had stirred up something he knew little of, and now it was up to him to settle matters. In his mind there was only one way that it could be done.

"Well, I can make no promises, but will do all I can to see that this situation is resolved."

"With respect, sir; there is little you can do on your own." It was the older man who spoke again, and he had such natural authority that Griffin was happy to listen. "What Mac says is right; the Warrens have a finger in every pie. Those who ain't a working for them are customers, or depend on the gang for their livelihood. Even members of the militia are caught up so deep they can't see a way out."

"There was a landing not three month back," someone else confirmed. "The local men just stood by and watched."

"An' 'en they ran th' whole lot doon th' main causey." The Scotsman was speaking again. "Fifty horses, thaur waur, an' aw th' carts frae miles abit waur 'ta'en tae move it."

"Well we need not be dependent on the militia," Griffin said, when the muttering had died down. "There are dragoons based nearby that Mr Dobson can call upon."

"We cannot trust them at Custom House," a voice from the back declared, to general agreement.

"That Dwyer is the worst," another agreed. "He's as thick with the Warrens as anyone, an' has old Dobbers wrapped about his little finger; you don't want to trust either of them, your honour."

"Then I won't," Griffin replied crisply. "And shall call in the dragoons myself if need be." He had their attention now, and continued quickly: "As for the assizes, we can bring in magistrates from out of the area, or send important cases to London for trial." He paused and looked at them; their faces stared back in solemn concentration. All were taking his word seriously, and he had never felt so responsible for a group of men in his life.

"But something must be done," he said. "This will not go away of its own accord, neither can we hope to placate or quieten the situation. We have to take the Warren gang on head first, seize their goods whenever possible and report any other misdemeanours as soon as they are apparent. All of you may speak to me at any time and I will listen. If you feel your families are in danger then I shall endeavour to protect them. Advise me if there is anything you require and I will try to obtain it. We will not be spending much time in Newhaven; I expect to have the *Bee* out whenever possible and, while she is at sea, we will be very much on the hunt for free traders: whoever owns them, and wherever they might be from."

Griffin paused, still considering the row of faces opposite. Some were dubious, others appeared thoughtful, but the vast majority seemed to have accepted what he said and even looked hopeful. He scratched at his chin; no, this was certainly not what he had expected, and he wondered quite how such a situation had arisen so quickly. His words might have been well received, but he was still uncertain if even he truly believed them. It was fine to speak of cracking a band of local villains, but he had no experience of such a task. And how could he realistically expect to offer protection to families ashore when he and their menfolk were likely to be many miles out at sea? But now that he had committed himself, he was determined to see it through to the end, and would do, wherever that end might lead.

Chapter Seven

All had been in agreement with *Bee* sailing on the afternoon's tide and Griffin was certain it was the best move they could make. He watched as the cutter was singled up to her stern hawser. A hand at the prow had a line looped about the forward bollard, and was paying out carefully, allowing her bow to swing gently round in the current while the foresail flapped, unsheeted, in the light breeze. It was a delicate operation to carry out in the crowded harbour, and one Griffin was prepared to leave to Davies and the other more experienced members of the crew.

This was the second time he had witnessed the cutter leave her berth, and for all the rest of them knew he would remain content to play the captain forever. But in reality Griffin was watching intently from his position by the taffrail as he intended to take her out himself on the next and all subsequent occasions. In fact, so caught up was he in the manoeuvre that it took two or three calls from the quayside to attract his attention.

"Ahoy there, the *Bee!*"

He turned and looked down over the bulwark to see a middle aged man with a heavy thatch of dark red hair waving at him.

"Name's Jones, I ride for the revenue. Permission to come aboard, sir?"

"Belay for'ard!" Griffin shouted to the seaman at the bow, and the cutter halted, her bowsprit pointing dramatically out across the river, before being hauled back against the tide to her berth.

"That will do, nicely," Jones called back, with more than a hint of a Welsh accent. "I can make it from there."

The newcomer was wearing the uniform tunic of a customs officer under an open, nondescript greatcoat, and seemed quite willing to leap the three or four feet to the entry ladder without waiting for *Bee* to be brought hard alongside. Davies came aft to look just as he sprang, and laughed when the heavy body landed squarely on the rungs and clambered up and through the entry port with commendable speed.

"Neatly done, Jackie," the mate said, grinning broadly and shaking him by the hand. "Step back and meet the Commander."

Griffin waited while the riding officer approached; he was bareheaded and wore grey britches tucked into worn black riding boots, and was probably older than he had first guessed. Well in his fifties, Griffin decided: quite an age for the type of work he undertook, and yet the smile that seemed permanently attached to his face was that of a far younger man.

"Jack Jones, sir; I'm mighty pleased to be meeting you."

They shook hands and as Griffin introduced himself he was struck by the crystal blue eyes, so very similar to Davies'.

"Welcome aboard, Mr Jones; I am afraid you have just caught us and we cannot miss the tide."

"Do you propose to stay out long, sir?"

It was a question that would normally have gone unanswered; the lack of pattern and general unpredictability of a revenue cutter's actions being one of her key strengths.

"It may be a while, Mr Jones," Griffin started, cautiously.

"Come with us, Jackie," Davies broke in, his exuberance at meeting with the man overpowering usual protocol. "We can drop you off in the galley later. How's about it?"

The last words were directed to Griffin and a hurried 'sir' was added as the mate realised quite how forward he had been.

"Very good, Mr Jones." Davies had already earned a measure of leniency and in truth Griffin was rather interested to speak at length with another member of the local revenue service. "If you care to join us, I am sure we would be glad of your company."

* * *

The sun had grown unusually hot for the time of year, and did much to lift their spirits, while a strengthening breeze and the prospect of being at sea brought an atmosphere close to cheerfulness aboard the cutter. They cleared the harbour without incident and headed east, and soon Davies was conning them as close to the beach as the falling tide would allow, while Jones began to point out areas known to be used by the free traders.

"That will be the Tide Mills," he said, indicating a series of rather stark, industrial buildings set just inland behind a shingle beach, to the east of Newhaven Harbour. "You see, in earlier times the river ran parallel with the coast for several miles, and only found an outfall under Seaford Head."

"That's what made Seaford such a major port in the past," Davies agreed. "Hard to believe it now; the place is no more than a backwater."

Jones waited for Davies to finish, so that he could get back to his story. There were few things the Welshman liked more than telling a good tale. "When the river changed course, the old harbour just silted up."

"And Seaford was left high and dry," Davies agreed, to the riding officer's mild annoyance.

"So how recently was the present harbour established?" Griffin asked. He was amused to note that the mate, whom he had assumed to be Sussex born and bred, was speaking with a slight Welsh lilt in the presence of a true son of the valleys.

"Not more than fifty years ago," Jones replied quickly. "But see, before then there was another outfall just about here, and the waterway is still in evidence; you will have noted its mouth, just within the current harbour."

Griffin had, as well as the considerable number of grain barges that used it.

"It takes a fair measure of water with every tide, so they set a mill across, and now we has our own tide mill."

"Just like at Chichester," Davies added. "Though far bigger; some say it is the largest in the world."

"Well, it makes jobs for many," Jones said, claiming the story once more. "And a lot of money for rather less, but the energy's predictable, and as free as the tides that create it."

"They got five grinding wheels running near enough twenty hours a day," Davies told them. "Though the word is old Bill Catt wants to more'n double them."

"And he will, like as not." Jones again. "Say what you wish about him, he gets things done. They built a new granary only a year or so back, and that was to replace Kale House, which everyone said would always be too large for what they needed."

"Do the mills themselves get used for smuggling?" Griffin asked.

"On occasion," Jones replied. "Mr Catt – that's the owner – he runs a tight ship, but cannot be everywhere. We have the Horsebridge gang hereabout, an' they are no respecter of anyone, or anything. I'd chance if you took a careful look in the Tide Mills storehouses you'd find a fair bit that didn't want to be there."

"The beach is certainly a regular spot for landings," Davies continued. "There must be a dozen hides in the area; and the new road takes you up as far as Croydon in no time," he added.

Yet again Griffin felt his frustration grow; it all seemed maddeningly casual. Something of his thoughts must have been communicated to the riding officer, who gave a cheerful grin.

"Of course we don't know exactly where they are," he said. "And haven't the manpower to dig up the whole beach. But we do keep watch, and they knows it. If we can't stop them, at least we do our damnedest to make their work more difficult."

They had passed the Tide Mills now, and the coast was starting to rise up once more to the steep cliffs that were so much a landmark of the area.

"We'll carry on to the Cuckmere," Davies said, indicating the next break, which was a good few miles further east.

"That's a far better beach for a run," the riding officer told him with strange enthusiasm. "Beautiful, it is. They got a clear road straight to town, and plenty of places along the way who will store if they brings in too much."

"I've known times where they've been all but queuing up to get in," Davies agreed, and Jones also seemed quite content at the thought.

"But if you are aware you can act, surely?" Griffin asked, the exasperation in his voice now quite evident. He instinctively liked the riding officer, but was well aware that his position was open to corruption.

"Oh, I can act right enough, and would, were I to be fully awake to the time and place," Jones replied steadily. "Organising the militia takes time, however, and is about as secret as a sneeze in chapel. Were we to have the intelligence, there's nothing I would like better than an all-out fight. To be sure, it would be preferable to sitting and watching from the rise."

"They come in considerable numbers, then?" Griffin asked.

"Oh yes, a decent landing will use upwards of an 'undred men, fifty to do the shiftin', and fifty batsmen, for protection. I can't do much to stop them on my own, and by the time I've gone for help, they're on the road for London or safe and in their beds."

"And what of the boats: do they use their own?"

"The Horsebridge gang got several," the mate cut in. "Most are small stuff, like the one we caught last night."

"I heard about that." Jones beamed. "Not a popular move, I'm thinkin'. Make those Warren boyos sit up an' think though."

"Then there are three big ones," Davies continued. "Two based in Boulogne and a third at Rye. They're all two-hundred tonners, and carry nine-pounder broadsides."

"But surely that's illegal?" Griffin questioned. The mate shook his head.

"Can't do much about the French craft, and the Rye boat's licensed as a privateer. Mind, if any were stopped they might get into trouble, more'n half the crew being British. But we ain't gonna do much about them in *Bee*. It would take the Royal Navy, and even they'd need a good day, as all can out sail your average frigate."

"They don't beach round here, surely?"

"No." Jones took up the story. "Not the depth, see? They stands a good way off and the fishermen fetch in the booty. That or they sows a crop; a line of ankers that hold a few gallons of spirit a piece: they're tied together and dumped over the side. A boat can tow them in, or they can be sunk to an anchor and collected afterwards. I bet if we got our creeping irons out now we might even come across something but again it's knowing where to look, isn't it?"

"An' if they're carrying cloth, or dry goods, they might just ship them in a smack." Davies again. "Most can beach here lovely; it's fine sand from now on, apart from some rock near Seaford Cliff. They can come in and be gone within the hour. A lot of the smaller traders do that for the spirit as well: flaskers, they calls them."

Griffin was taking this in; it was all very different from his experience at Harwich, and came across as casual to the point of being lax. "The ones that are not connected with the Horsebridge gang," he asked. "They are tolerated?"

"The small traders?" the mate replied. "Yes, the Warrens don't mind at all. The market's pretty large, no chance of sating it with a couple of fisher boats. An' Stanton Warren makes sure he gets his cut out of what they bring as well."

"In what way?" Griffin asked; his original question had been misinterpreted, but he was content to hear the rest of Davies' answer.

The mate shrugged. "They takes a skim from every landing on what is considered one of their shores, just to keep the name known. There's no risk to them, so they're more than happy."

"It's a bit like a tax, see?" Jones explained with heavy irony. "Old man Warren's quite the man of business."

"But our enemy all the same," Griffin grunted.

"Oh yes, and as bad as anything you'll find the other side of the Channel." Davies lowered his voice and added, "ask me, the Warrens are our real target; the small operators don't account for much."

Nothing was said for a moment, but Davies and the riding officer exchanged glances. Clearly they were deciding whether or not Griffin could be trusted; then the mate took the plunge.

"I have to say, sir; as far as we are concerned, a few boats of contraband don't make no difference to no one. They rarely export, not being big enough to carry wool, and most haven't the funds to buy large quantities of bullion. Some might try to up their loads, but they lack the supply chain, and can really only sell to local people."

"But the Warrens, now they're a different story." Jones had picked up the story again and gave the impression he was not going to let it go for a while. "Most of their runs are well-financed: they buy gold in London, and sells it to the French for a premium. Tea's not as popular as it once was, but they still got plenty of City houses with regular orders, and as far as spirit and tobacco is concerned, people are falling over themselves to buy. They also got the resources to dilute the 'bove spirit tubs, so a haul of over-proof will be worth twice as much once it's let down with water and caramel."

The tide was falling quickly now and, unbidden, Forsyth at the tiller brought the cutter to larboard to maintain deep water.

"So you would say we should concentrate our efforts on the Horsebridge gang?" Griffin asked.

"I would, had we the force." Davies hesitated. "They are more powerful than us in every way, and certainly receive more respect, even if it be earned through fear."

"They have so many more at their command," Jones agreed. "And it's manpower they ain't afraid to use. You wouldn't get no small-time smuggler threatening all and sundry; Newhaven was a fair place till they showed their faces."

"Do you know who they are?"

"Some... the Warrens obviously, but they're as slick as a barrel of wet fish. A few of the others are quite prominent as well," Jones conceded. "There are several who actually live in the town. They keep an eye on things, and tell the family if anyone looks like stepping out of line and will have known about you long since. Not much that can be done about it, though. On the face of it, all stick to the straight an' narrow, and if we do catch them out, they're just hauled up to the local court."

"A jury will never convict a Horsebridge man," Davies explained. "Neither would a bench of magistrates, come to that. And whoever peached on them in the first place is liable to find his ears nailed to the Custom House door."

"Pleasant," Griffin reflected.

"Aye," Davies agreed. "Just the kind you want marrying your daughter."

* * *

The crash was sudden and unexpected. It came as a dramatic contrast to the pleasant murmur of afternoon conversation, breaking into the congenial atmosphere like a shouted profanity. Everyone in the parlour jumped and two, who sat nearest to the window, stood up. Sophie, sitting in the far corner, also rose, dropping her needlepoint to the floor and upsetting the cat that had been fast asleep on her lap.

"What in the devil's name...?" her father said as he entered the room, but Sophie was already half-way to the window. One of the upper panes had been broken, and there was an ominous house brick lying in the centre of the wooden floor. She bent and picked it up as her father joined her.

"The Warrens?" he said, staring over her shoulder at the brick.

"I should say so," she replied. The shock, together with a draught of colder air that came in through the smashed window made her shiver. The innkeeper turned and left without another word. He would be going out into the street, she supposed. It was mid-afternoon, and the town must be quite crowded; someone might have seen something, even if the perpetrator had gone.

Nothing would be said, of course, she knew that even as the sound of the front door slamming came to her. No one would have noticed a thing out of place, and whichever member of the Horsebridge gang had been sent to carry out such a senseless and cowardly attack, they would have been able to saunter away at their own speed.

And it was senseless: The Star must be one of the more important bases to the Warrens. Not only did it act as a major storehouse and shop front, the inn was frequently called upon to provide free food and accommodation for their associates.

From what her father had said that morning's interview had not gone especially badly. They had a problem with the Griffin man staying, but it would be addressed, and breaking a window in the middle of their afternoon trade was hardly going to solve matters, or make them in any way less obvious.

But then the Warrens were not known for their tact or understanding. The Star was under their control, and if anything happened to threaten that situation, Sophie supposed they were bound to react. The men nearest the window seemed to have recovered, and were staring into their tankards as if convinced they were brim-full with broken glass. She would pour them fresh pints, and call Mr James in to fit a new pane. They were fortunate it was a warm afternoon; a sweep of the floor, and everything should be back to normal again. The inn made enough to pay for such damage, and her brother was starting to bring a bit more in now that his own business was flourishing. But a feeling of dread stayed with her when she went to the hearth for the brush and shovel and, as she started to sweep the glass into a manageable pile, she still shivered.

* * *

That afternoon was spent with the cutter anchored off the Cuckmere, while Griffin, Davies and Jones paced about the beach. The riding officer showed them a break in the shingle bar that smugglers used when beaching their boats and they discovered tracks made by a landing, probably less than a couple of nights back. Griffin asked a lot of questions, but little new was learned and, as they sat in the squat little boat and were rowed back to the *Bee*, he felt mildly depressed.

Griffin was by no means an expert on the current state of the war; clearly the country was not in the best of financial health, or the government would hardly be suing for peace. But while tax was being avoided, and vast amounts of vital raw materials were regularly being shipped to the enemy, it seemed madness that more was not being done to combat the smuggling menace. Such men as Jones and the members of *Bee*'s crew were doing what they could with the means and manpower provided, but more was needed, and needed fast, if the country was not to entirely collapse: defeated, not by a foreign enemy, but its own internal, and thoroughly rotten, core.

For the smuggling problem to be properly addressed, a large and disciplined force was needed. They should be ruthless and impartial; preferably from out of the area, so that any likelihood of corruption was minimised. Anything less would simply suppress the problem. But the gloom that had descended upon him was in no way the fault of his two companions, so he forced himself to be civil. "Will you stay aboard for a bite to eat, Mr Jones?" he asked.

The riding officer's ready smile returned instantly. "Indeed, sir, that would be most agreeable. And you would be welcome to call me Jackie, as most do."

They were nearing the cutter now. One of the hands stood to receive a line, rocking the boat slightly and causing enough of a diversion for Griffin to avoid making any reply. There might perhaps be more to be learned over a meal, and he was genuinely looking forward to spending further time with both the mate and Jones. But Griffin was still their commanding officer and, even allowing for discipline being more relaxed in the customs service, he felt he had a position to maintain. So perhaps it would be better not to enter into familiarities.

* * *

The following morning the sun stayed with them and Griffin discovered that a cutter's cramped deck could actually be a very pleasant place. Davies had been below since breakfast, and they had dropped the riding officer off at Worthing the previous evening, so he shared the space by the binnacle with no one, other than Forsyth at the tiller. Griffin had discarded his hat and jacket, and was now welcoming the pleasant rays of the surprisingly hot autumn day as he recalled their conversation of the night before.

Jones had told them about Goudhurst, a village not forty miles from Newhaven, which had been in a similar position to Newhaven some years back. There the villagers had rebelled, informing the gang, who had progressed from smuggling to all but ruling their lives and businesses, that enough was enough and they must leave them be. The criminals had responded in typically arrogant fashion, and actually set a date for retaking the place. There was a bloody battle, but the villagers ultimately won.

The Welshman considered Newhaven a potential second Goudhurst, although Griffin did not agree. Not only was there a general acceptance of smuggling, and the Warrens' authority in particular, but he had yet to note any real spirit in the place. Even Davies, whom he was starting to trust increasingly, seemed resigned to allowing a small amount of free trading to go unnoticed, while the staff at Custom House were positively encouraging the practice. And for as long as men were content to help the gang, either through payment, fear or straightforward apathy, they would continue to prosper while Griffin's job became that much harder.

The inevitability of it all was starting to depress him once more, and he began to pace the deck. Having the area pretty much to himself, he found he could do this most effectively by walking across from bulwark to bulwark, rather than the fore and aft pattern that was more usual in such an exercise. *Bee's* broad beam made the distance reasonably satisfying, and he was just getting into his stride when a call came from the masthead.

"Sail ho, sail on the starboard beam!" They were heading east, up the Channel on a southerly breeze, and a good many ships and small vessels had already been sighted. But there was something in the lookout's tone that alerted Griffin, and also caught the attention of all on deck. "Square rigged, and topsails in sight, though she's adding t'gallants, and headin' north, almost straight for us," the man continued.

Davies had also apparently heard, and emerged from the officer's companionway shortly afterwards. He was bareheaded and with a dozy expression on his pink face. Griffin glanced up, diplomatically giving his attention to the masthead while the mate straightened his uniform and brushed a few stray curls of hair back into some semblance of order with his fingers. The sighting must be a good few miles off, but it was still strange for any ship to be adding sail when heading for a lee shore.

"Good day to you, Mr Davies," Griffin said formally when the mate had finished, and most of the evidence of his mid-morning nap was gone. They had actually breakfasted together not three hours before, but Griffin felt that some acknowledgement was necessary. The older man muttered a reply, and went to salute before remembering that his hat had been left below in his cabin.

"We will turn to meet the sighting," Griffin announced briskly. "Port your helm; bring her as close to the wind as she can manage. And set the main."

The cutter, which had been pottering along under fore alone, turned closer to the breeze and, as her huge gaff sail was raised, began to power through the waves, and out towards the open sea.

"She's an Indiaman," the lookout called. "Well-laden, and running afore the wind. You'll be catching her off our starboard bow any time."

Griffin considered moving forward with the glass, but the spray was high, and even under a bright sun he had no desire to get wet.

"Strange behaviour for a merchant, sir," Davies chanced.

Griffin remained silent. Indeed it was; in all his years with the Company every captain he had ever encountered had been cautious to the point of obsession, and would never have made for a shore so, with the wind on his tail. Presumably the merchant had been heading up the Channel to the Downs; it was probably a quick dash for safety at the end of a long trip and was now diverting for some reason. She would be carrying all manner of valuable goods, and there was only one cause that Griffin could think of for her to suddenly crave the doubtful security of a dangerous coast.

"Clear for action, if you please, Mr Davies."

The mate glanced at him for a second before giving the order. Then, within moments, all thoughts of a leisurely sail were wiped from the minds of the crew as they went into what was clearly a practised routine. The galley fire, smouldering gently and due to provide them with their midday meal in less than an hour, was hastily shovelled into buckets and thrown, hissing and steaming, into the water, while the mess tables and benches were taken up and secured. The medicine chest, always locked, and with Griffin carrying the only key, was brought up from the forward hold, and the two small-arms cases heaved out and unbolted. On deck, sand was liberally sprinkled and dampened down, while the spare hammocks, usually stowed amidships next to the sail locker, were broken out and added to those already stuffed into the side nettings to provide additional protection. The guns were run out, with extra charges brought up from the magazine under Griffin's quarters, and stowed in the salt boxes behind each pair of cannon while aloft, metal chains were attached to the yards to re-enforce the lifts.

"Cleared for action, sir," the mate reported. He was still looking at him strangely and Griffin suddenly realised that Davies was not entirely sure if his captain had sensed trouble, or was merely testing the men's readiness. The Indiaman was now in plain sight from the deck; she was still running before the wind, but had altered course slightly to intercept them.

"What do you see beyond the sighting?" Griffin called.

"Clear sea, sir," the lookout replied confidently. It sounded like the same man who had missed the cooper two nights back. Griffin trusted that he had learned from the mistake and would be taking no chances today.

After the excitement of clearing for action the inactivity that followed seemed more apparent, and time passed slowly; the hands started to fidget and mutter amongst themselves and Griffin began to grow uneasy. His order could have been premature; the merchant's captain might have spotted a revenue cutter, and decided to close for a number of reasons. But that did not account for the sudden increase in sail; even now, the Indiaman must be making nigh on five knots, a substantial speed for such a lumbering hull. She had probably travelled from the Far East, with no chance of extensive repair for upwards of a year or more, and be carrying influential passengers into the bargain, so would be unlikely to crack on the speed, even so close to home. Yes, he assured himself, her behaviour was unusual at the very least.

"She's turning to starboard now," the lookout reported. "An' looks to be heaving to. I think there might be a signal, but the flags are flying straight for us."

At that news Griffin began to relax, the merchant's captain had given him the clue he needed, and now the rest could be assumed. "Masthead, are you sure there is nothing beyond?" he bellowed.

"Clear sea, sir – no, wait! There might be something to windward."

Davies pulled a face, but Griffin did not react. If what he suspected had been hidden amidst a large merchant's tophamper, it would have been easy enough to miss, and he was simply pleased to have his suspicions confirmed.

"It were masked by the Indiaman," the lookout declared in a lower tone. "But yes, it's a cutter."

A buzz of excitement spread amongst the crew as the man continued, "She's a deal larger than us, an' with a dandy rig – I can see her jigger now, plain as day."

The extra mast, set as a mizzen, was not uncommon and would hardly mark her out as French, although Griffin was quite certain of the sighting's identity.

"Keep her as she is," he said. "With luck we'll be hidden from her in the same way she was from us."

Now Davies was regarding him with amazement, and Griffin was actively enjoying being more knowledgeable about something; it had been a rare enough occurrence of late. The Indiaman was wallowing in the Channel chop, and *Bee* would be passing close by her prow: an ideal situation for what he had in mind.

"Cutter seems to be turning," the masthead reported. "She's coming on to a broad reach, starboard tack."

So be it, Griffin decided; they had probably been spotted, but now at the very least there would be a sailing competition. The bulk of the Indiaman grew closer with every second, as *Bee* sliced through the waves. Already figures could be made out on the merchant's deck, some waving, others obviously cheering, and there was one man on the forecastle holding up what looked like a signal flag.

"Take her near," Griffin muttered to Forsyth. "All but clip her jib boom if you can."

Bee already seemed as close to the wind as she could bear, but the northerner was an experienced helmsman, and held her on the very edge of the luff. "Aye aye, sir," he replied, his gaze constantly switching between the sails and the merchant, while making minute adjustments to the cutter's head. Then they were passing, and doing so at considerable speed. It was unusual for *Bee*'s performance to be judged by so close an object and, as the Indiaman was all but stationary, the effect was magnified. The small vessel shot by the bowsprit like a greyhound passing a fallen oak, with shouts and waves being exchanged between both crews. Then she was gone, and the only thing ahead was a dark and sinister French privateer. She was in the act of turning further to starboard, and would soon be heading for her own coast and safety.

"She's a big one, and no mistake," Davies murmured, as they were finally able to see their opponent with any degree of clarity. "Upwards of two 'undred tons; maybe more." The mate was right, the enemy's black hull was definitely heavier, but it wasn't just her bulk that was causing the man's concern. "An' she would be well armed, sir," he continued. "Nine pounders at the very least, though the Frogs fire a heavier shot; one to be wary of, I'd say."

Griffin knew that Davies was doing his duty in warning him, and he was right to be concerned. The Frenchman was also bound to have a full complement; after all, her raison d'être was to fight and capture foreign shipping, so she was probably even over-manned to allow for potential prize crews. Conversely, there were few revenue cutters quite so well provided for. Most had ample to serve their sails, but guns were not expected to be used beyond the occasional warning shot. And *Bee* was several hands down.

"I hear you, Mr Davies," Griffin replied gently. "But think we may risk a closer inspection. Colours, if you please!" The last words were all but snapped, and the ensign ran up to the crossjack and broke out.

The enemy continued to turn and soon was heading away, both from the Indiaman and the cheeky little cutter that had the impudence to chase her. It was to be expected; her captain must be either a businessman or responsible to one: there would be little financial gain in sinking a Treasury cruiser and much to be lost. Griffin felt he might follow her for a while, but knew that close action was to be avoided. If he made one slip, one error of judgement, which exposed his craft to the enemy, or took damage that made subsequent flight impossible, everything would change and they may well be sunk or taken.

"I think we may have the edge on her, sir," Davies said cautiously when both vessels had settled to the chase. Griffin said nothing in response, but was well aware how much wishful thinking could be involved in such a judgement.

He picked up the deck glass and studied his opponent carefully whilst collecting his thoughts. Yes, she was certainly big, and not as slow as many of her size. She would also have a hand-picked crew; a privateer, with the promise of prize money and adventure, had her choice of seamen, and currently there were plenty ashore in France to select from. Added to that her frame was bound to be stronger, and provide a far steadier platform for her guns – guns that were bound to be more numerous, and heavier, than any *Bee* carried. And then, Griffin finally admitted, there remained that last piece of evidence in what was turning out to be a very unequal equation. A privateer captain was, by necessity, a professional fighting man, and he could hardly say the same about himself.

Griffin's entire life at sea had been spent in the merchant service and, whatever aspirations he might hold he had limited experience of single-ship actions. Three years ago, in the old *Empress*, he had commanded the Indiaman's armament, and fought off two pirates; sinking one and disabling the other. It had been a noble effort, and one loudly applauded by officers, passengers and his employers alike. But all his efforts had really amounted to was using the blown-out cannonades to their best effect. The captain had been in charge of the ship, although there had been precious little manoeuvring and certainly no fancy tactics; she had merely acted as a floating fortress while he managed the armament in the same way an artillery officer might have that of a fortification. And now here he was, in absolute command of a minor warship, with which he had scant experience, facing a superior enemy who also happened to hold the windward gauge. He had been lucky two nights back; this time more care would be needed. While she was running he was perfectly entitled to chase, but if the enemy should turn he knew it would be wise to do likewise.

"Beggin' your pardon, sir; but you do understand she is a privateer?" It was a different voice, and the words were delivered in such close proximity that Griffin, still deep in contemplation, almost jumped in surprise.

Lamport, the deputed mariner, must have come aft from his usual station and approached unnoticed. Griffin had yet to form a firm opinion of the man; he was somewhat downcast in appearance, with a long face that bore an undeniable likeness to a donkey. In helping to capture the smack the petty officer had performed well enough, although so far he had yet to endear himself to his captain, and using a quasi-confidential manner, as he was now, would hardly aid the process. The question itself was on the verge of acceptability, but Griffin guessed he might be posing it on behalf of the hands, and made both allowances, and his answer as comprehensive as possible.

"Indeed, Mr Lamport, I am fully aware of the situation. She is a touch larger than us, but that need not worry anybody. It is strange to find one so close to our shores, but I would guess the lure of a fat John Company ship was too much for her."

"We have seen a few over the years, sir," Lamport replied. "Navy sends a brig or a frigate in to chase them off on occasion."

"Is that so?" Griffin was genuinely interested.

"Yes, sir. The *Brazen* was wrecked only a year or so back doing that very thing."

"It were on the Ave Rocks, as I remember," Davies commented, joining them and regarding the petty officer guardedly.

"Every man aboard killed, but one," Lamport added, his dark eyes rolling in wonder.

"And has the *Bee* ever engaged a privateer?" Griffin found himself asking.

"Oh no, sir," Lamport replied, as if mildly affronted.

Davies cleared his throat. "I understand Mr Dobson is not in favour of us risking ourselves unnecessarily."

The more Griffin learned about the attitude at Custom House, the less it surprised him. "Well, Mr Dobson is not in command," he replied, instinctively, and in a voice pitched to carry to as many nearby as was possible, "I intend to take appropriate risks, if it means we are doing our duty. And you may tell that to the men, Mr Lamport, should you so wish." As he said the words he realised he was committing himself, but there was little he could do to take them back, even if he wanted to.

"Very good, sir," Lamport replied, saluted formally, and left.

"The lad can have an unfortunate manner on occasion," Davies said in a low tone after a moment, but Griffin's thoughts were already racing ahead. It might well be an unequal fight, but that was no reason why they should run at the first opportunity.

"Mr Blackman, give the word when you think we might reach her," he called, consciously blocking all thoughts of retreat from his mind. The gunner, standing alongside the foremost starboard cannon, looked up in surprise, before turning and knuckling his forehead. Memories of Dobson and the attitude at Customs House had raised the blood in Griffin's veins, and Lamport's question, along with Davies' cautious attitude, was all that was needed. It might be madness, or just plain foolhardy, but he was damned if any Frenchman was going to be let off without a fight.

Chapter Eight

They had crept to within a mile of the privateer now: long range for a six pounder. A good deal of distance would also be lost in yawing to bring the guns to bear. And probably they would do little good if *Bee* did fire off a broadside but, as they were so close to the enemy, it seemed a crime not to at least try.

Griffin took a turn across the deck, dodging the bulk of Davies and two seamen as he did, while enjoying the heightened sensitivity that the danger had awakened inside him. Despite the time spent in pursuit, and even against such over-mounting evidence, Griffin's confidence was growing with every second. Single-ship engagements might not be in his blood, and the *Bee* was indeed a relatively new command, but he still felt equal to the task. The rebellious streak that first led him to travel all those years ago had been unusually active of late, and any thought of simply running for home was becoming increasingly repugnant. Experienced or not, he felt he knew the cutter well enough; besides, the current opportunity was surely the main reason he had abandoned the comfortable life of a merchant in the first place.

"Oh, for a pair of chasers," Davies grumbled, but Griffin was quite content. They were gaining steadily on the cutter, and must bring her to battle before so very long.

"I think I might find her with a lucky one now, sir." The gunner's voice sounded from forward, and returned Griffin to the real world.

"Very good, Mr Blackman, stand by." He looked again at the Frenchman, and noticed she was already manoeuvring.

"Starboard your helm," he called to Forsyth, and the hull dipped as the rudder bit. The enemy cutter completed her turn as *Bee*'s sails were still being trimmed, and the British craft was marginally behind when she eventually settled on a finely diverging course.

"We should reach her comfortably," Davies said, after a minute or so. The mate was right, Griffin decided, but it was an asset shared and, even as he thought, a ragged line of flame rippled along the hull of the privateer. The sound of the cannon fire came almost simultaneously with that of ball striking wood, and a round shot dug deep into *Bee*'s starboard bulwark.

The hit sent up a shower of fine dust that caught the wind and spread untidily about the deck, but caused no injury. When the *Empress* had been struck by a heavy ball the splinters had been far more deadly. Griffin looked up at their tophamper, but the mast and spars remained untouched; in fact several of the shots had fallen short, though not, he suspected, through lack of range. Unless there was something seriously amiss with their pieces, *Bee* should have been easily in the enemy's grasp; he suspected the French gunners had been rushed, or failed to account for their having the windward gauge.

"Shall we not reply, sir?" Davies asked.

Griffin's face suddenly flushed. "Fire!" he shouted. What could he have been thinking of? They had received a broadside and he was calmly ruminating on his opponent's lack of aim, and the nature of splinters. Admittedly he had only been in command a few days, but if he wasn't able to concentrate in such a situation he may as well hand the job over to someone else without delay.

Bee's starboard six pounders spat back at the privateer. No hits were reported but, even as the pieces were being secured, Griffin's mind was properly focused, and he prepared to manoeuvre once more. With sudden insight he realised that this was the ideal moment to turn for home. Despite what he had said to Lamport, no one could blame him for running from a superior enemy; besides, he had even released one solid broadside, taken token damage and may have inflicted some in return. But it was that very broadside that strengthened his resolve; the sound of the cutter's guns being fired in anger had fuelled something primeval inside him, and he could no more have turned away as hauled down the colours.

"Port your helm!"

The cutter shot back into the wind, and was soon close hauled once more, this time with the enemy off the larboard bow, and soon to be coming across their beam. With luck, Griffin might have the range to rake her stern: if not he should at least gain enough distance to be able to turn again, this time with the wind to his advantage.

But the French captain was not content for that to happen. Even as *Bee* drew closer, he was also changing course to the north and, Griffin thought, might be intending to jibe. Only now was the *Bee*'s crew attending to the starboard battery, the majority having been involved with trimming the sails, and he had only the larboard guns to rely on. It was the side that now faced the enemy, but that could soon change, especially if there were more clever tricks to come.

"Keep her as she is," he said, aware of the enquiring look from Forsyth at the helm. Whatever the Frenchman had in mind, he was determined to secure the windward gauge: if just to cut off her retreat should she decide to run.

"She jibes!" someone forward shouted, and Griffin looked up in time to see the enemy cutter swing round and begin to creep back towards *Bee*, on the opposite tack. That extra mast might give her an edge when on a reach, but made her less tidy to manoeuvre.

"A touch to larboard," Griffin ordered, and Forsyth pressed the helm over. It was important that any attempt the enemy might make to rake his own stern was thwarted, although the privateer showed no inclination, and was obediently coming up on Bee's larboard quarter instead. Both vessels were closing again now, and presenting undischarged broadsides, this time with the advantage slightly in favour of the British, and Griffin wondered if he should be the one to fire first. Once more the decision was taken from him, however, as the Frenchman suddenly yawed to larboard, and her side was temporarily shielded by a cloud of white smoke.

"Here it comes!" the same anonymous voice called out, and Griffin was fast to note there was not a trace of fear in it. Then the broadside began to rain down upon them.

It could have been luck or judgement, but this was better laid and struck the British vessel squarely, with all but one of the shots finding a home. The Bee's mainsail was punctured near to the foot, and a ball took out the chimney to the stove with a loud, ringing clang. And there was greater damage to come: two men leapt clear as the sternmost cannon was struck muzzle on, and whipped to one side, while a seaman was hit by a slither of oak that ran up his thigh and left him screaming like a pig in slaughter. The larboard elm-tree pump head was neatly removed, and a ball took out the mounting to one of the forward swivel guns, knocking the barrel free to roll about the crowded deck. But there was no material damage to the cutter, she could manoeuvre and, with the exception of one long gun and a swivel, was still able to fight.

"Fire!" Griffin shouted, his voice cracking with excitement. The privateer had returned to her southerly course, but was well with the range of *Bee*'s main armament. There was a pause, but it was a sensible one. None of the gun captains were rushing to apply their linstocks, instead careful aim was being taken and when *Bee*'s broadside did finally roll out, it was effective.

A ragged cheer rang through the cutter as the Frenchman's stumpy mizzen mast was neatly knocked down, and Griffin saw at least one shot strike her hull just by the main chains. Her jib was also holed in two places and, with the sudden imbalance in her rig and possible inattention at the helm, the privateer flew up into the wind.

Now was the time to press home the advantage, but with *Bee*'s limited crew he could not order her about as well as having the empty guns served. Griffin gauged the wind, and signalled for Forsyth to bring her to larboard. "Spill the wind!" he shouted, and the main and fore were released; the alternative was to luff up, but his present course was more logical and must take them across the bows of the privateer. It would be the ideal firing position, if only they could get the guns loaded in time.

The men were certainly not slow in grasping the situation; even Lamport was manning the flexible rammer on number three cannon, but there was no doubt that they made poor and slow practice. *Bee* was creeping closer to the privateer, while the French crew were taking in their battered jib in an effort to proportion the wind pressure more effectively. Griffin wondered if the enemy had enough men to serve their cannon, and decided for the second time that they probably did. A privateer's role was to fight; there was little point in setting sail without adequate and well-trained men, and with a hull far larger than *Bee*'s there would be sufficient space to accommodate quite a considerable number.

They were creeping steadily down upon the wounded Frenchman now, but only one of the British gun captains was signalling his piece loaded. Two more were just being primed and the rest, including Lamport's, had yet to heave their weapons into the firing position.

"Ready!" The call was more in hope than expectation, but another man raised his hand. The privateer's prow was temptingly close. "Fire!"

Two shots rang out, followed by a third a few seconds later; then, after a considerable pause, one more. A ball hit the Frenchman square on the prow, and Griffin was sure he saw splinters. The enemy's forestay was also struck, and her foresail collapsed in a heap.

But despite the damage, the privateer was still moving and, at that moment, started to luff up, clearly intending to use her momentum to turn straight into the wind, and bring her larboard guns to bear. It was a move Griffin had not anticipated and he watched, horrified, as the row of gaping cannon was slowly turned to face him.

"Bring her to starboard!" It was vital that they did not continue on their present course as there was every possibility that the privateer's broadside was already loaded. Forsyth started to guide the cutter round, but they had lost speed and it took slightly longer to sheet in the slack sails. *Bee* would soon be moving again, but Griffin doubted they would be fast enough to miss a severe drubbing.

The first enemy gun spoke as they were beginning to turn, and was followed almost immediately by the others. Most of the shots fell neatly beyond her counter, but one crashed into the hull, just below and astern of where Griffin was standing. He felt the crunch of broken wood through the soles of his boots, and then a second thump as the spent shot passed through the frail hull.

Davies made for the companionway; the cutter was still accelerating, but such damage must be investigated without delay. To be holed was bad enough, but there were also various flammable stores in the main cabin that could set the ship alight and beneath, in the deepest lazarette, was the powder magazine.

"What do you see there?" Griffin demanded, as he peered down the hatch after the mate. Davies was standing in the doorway to his quarters; the carpenter had got there before them and was already inspecting the damage.

"We seems to have been hulled, sir; shot came in by the breadroom bulkhead, passed right through your cabin, and out just afore the chart room."

Griffin closed his eyes for a moment; it was what he had feared, and they had been unfortunate. *Bee* had an extremely broad beam but towards bow and stern it narrowed dramatically. He looked again and Davies was standing to one side, allowing the carpenter to pass him.

"Could be worse," the latter said, looking up and blinking at the sunlight; in action he was the only man stationed below, and had been on hand as soon as the shot struck. "Made a proper mess of some of your dunnage, sir, an' there's a pair of extra scuttles we could well do without."

"Any structural damage?"

"No." The carpenter was reassuringly positive. "We're in luck; main frame timber's not been touched either side, but a couple of strakes are stove in. I'll do what I can to plug them but would not hold out much hope until we can get her back to harbour."

"How high?"

"Almost on the waterline," the man replied. "For'ard one is slightly lower but neither are botherin' us too much at present. I might be able to get some lead across, or maybe jus' stuff an' batten for now, but it's not an easy place to reach, and I wouldn't hold out for anything quick or permanent."

Bee was currently on the starboard tack and not showing much of a heel. Were they to attempt any form of fast manoeuvring, the cutter would simply fill with water. Griffin heaved himself back up from the hatch and looked to where the Frenchman was steadily being left behind. One pump was out of action, but even with two he would have little choice.

"We shall break off," he said, as Davies rejoined him. "The enemy is larger than us, and probably better manned; I cannot afford for her to get close."

"Aye, sir," the mate replied evenly. Both knew that *Bee's* only advantage lay in her speed and agility, and both had effectively been taken from her. "Do you think yon Frenchie'll give us more trouble?"

"I should not doubt it for a second," Griffin replied dolefully. The privateer had a workable main, and in time would be able to raise another foresail. She was also between them and their shore; the British still held the windward gauge, but that was of little advantage if they were unable to take on too much of a heel. He swallowed; this was just the situation he had feared.

"We shall have to bear up and pass her as soon as we can, with luck they will still be adjusting their rig. Take her to larboard."

The last words were addressed to Forsyth, who duly pressed the tiller over and *Bee* began to alter course. Her sails were released as the wind took her further on the beam, and Griffin was certain he could hear water slopping in through the shot hole below. Then, as the turn continued, she righted herself and, with the privateer now more than a cable off their larboard bow, settled with the wind coming over her counter. Topsail and topgallant were raised, and she took speed with minimal heel, but they still had to pass within range of the Frenchman's guns.

"How is the larboard battery?" Griffin asked.

"Two guns primed and ready," Davies replied. "The others will be yet a-while." Setting the additional square sails had taken manpower, and only now were the recently fired guns being swabbed and reloaded and then not especially quickly. "We shall just have to see how busy our friend has been."

The range was long, and increasing steadily, but it would not take much to damage *Bee*'s rig and bring her to a halt. She would then be at the enemy's mercy, and Griffin cursed himself for the impetuous fool that he had been. They waited as the cutter bore down on the Frenchman, which was now broadside on and almost abeam. The last gun was just being hauled in as Griffin raised his hand and was about to give the order to fire when, yet again, the French anticipated him.

All could see the roll of flashes, and several ducked down below the cutter's bulwarks. It was long range and Griffin drew brief comfort from the fact that the French gunners would not be able to reach *Bee*'s masts, and must aim at her hull. As he did so he realised with a shock that he was actually glad he, and his men, would be the target. In the event several shots fell short, two slammed into the side nettings, sending a bunch of tightly packed hammocks bouncing merrily about the deck, while another whined higher, passing through the gap between Griffin and Davies and mercifully missing them both.

"Fire!" Griffin ordered, as soon as the men had recovered. The broadside rolled out in a neat enough ripple, and they watched as the shots rained down upon the privateer. The mate shook his head sadly; no hits could be detected, although it was long range for six-pound shot.

"Never mind, Mr Davies." Riding out that last broadside had been enough for Griffin; he had not hoped for more. "I think we left our mark."

Bee was now running at a truly credible speed, one that the Frenchman would be hard to match, and the coast of Britain was edging closer with every second.

"Aye, sir," Davies reflected. "And we didn't put up a bad show, really; not for a little 'un."

Chapter Nine

"You can't kill a man just because of the uniform he wears," Sophie stated defiantly. Her brother and father appeared uncomfortable; both knew that the Warren family had done exactly that to Griffin's predecessor. But then the circumstances had been entirely different and the Horsebridge gang were ultimately responsible. Commander Griffin was a separate matter entirely, and one, it seemed, they must remedy by themselves.

"We have no wish to kill anyone," Matthew said, his voice low, even though it was late, and the darkened parlour otherwise empty. "But he has shown himself to be a nuisance, and must be kept in check."

"And Stanton Warren told you to do so," Sophie added, glaring at the two men who meant more to her than anyone else in the world. "You make me sick, both of you."

Her father's gaze fell in shame. "It wasn't Stanton, it were his son."

"Oh, so now you're taking orders from children?"

"The Warrens supply everything we need," the old man explained. "Without them there would be no inn, no business, and no home."

"Not so," she all but spat in reply. "They just supply it cheaper."

"But price is price, Soph," the old man appealed. "We can't be judged more expensive than Hodges at The Bridge or Matthews at The Buckle."

"Well if you all went legitimate there wouldn't be a problem. Besides, Matt here can provide." Sophie's look had lost nothing of its intensity. "He has barely been trading six months yet already brings in more than can be sold elsewhere."

"You don't understand; it is hardly so simple."

"Oh, I find it simple enough," she snapped. "Sure it is simple to see that you are both too afraid to stand up to a bunch of London priggers what needs you more than you need them."

Her father raised a hand in supplication and she stopped, although her eyes still blazed in the evening light. "I'm not saying he should be killed," he said. "But if there is any more interference it could be the worse for us." He seemed to consider this for a second or two, then continued: "should we do nothing and the Warrens take over, they will show no mercy to your friend. Or us, if it came to it."

"He is not my friend." Her face flushed. "I hardly know the cove."

Her father smiled knowingly. "Be that so or not, we wish him no harm. But, for his own safety, he must be kept away from here. He knows nothing of the town, or the places where he should not venture, and naught of how we live. In short, he cannot judge what is right, and what is acceptable."

"Aye," Matthew agreed. "And such a man is a danger at any level; but when he wears the uniform of the revenue service, it is the worst we could wish for."

* * *

Bee crept over the bar with barely inches to spare, but even so it was late, and the men, many of whom had been occupied with pumping, were tired. Davies turned away from supervising her moorings; his face half hidden in stark shadows from the overhead lanthorn.

"Will you be stayin' aboard, sir?" he asked.

So much had been required of Griffin over the last few hours that it was not a question he had anticipated. The

Frenchman made no effort to chase *Bee*, or the Indiaman, come to that; last seen she was beating south to lick her wounds. But there remained the task of nursing the leaking cutter safely back to harbour before, for the second night in three, sending a boat in with wounded aboard. Whilst waiting for the tide, the carpenter had started work in the stern, and much of Griffin's cabin was already dismantled. All his personal possessions and a good quantity of stores lay spread about the chart room, so he supposed he would have to bunk with the men, if he didn't wish to evict one of his officers from their quarters.

"No, I have a room in the town," he said. "I will return at first light."

Davies' look grew anxious. "Do you think that wise, sir? With the general feeling, I mean."

Griffin was tired, troubled and not a little confused; so much so that he felt a wave of defiance rise in him, and it was with an effort that he did not snap back at the mate. "I shall be fine, thank you, Mr Davies," he said; then, feeling the need to mollify his statement somewhat, added, "but your concern is appreciated."

There was little left to do, he supposed. The hands had been fed while waiting for high water, and Davies was sound enough to see an alert anchor watch set; he could head off for The Star whenever he liked, and perhaps get a bit of rest.

He collected his hat, which had been lying on the skylight since the end of the action, and thoughtfully buckled on his sword, before pulling his jacket about him, and setting off for the newly positioned gangway, muttering a goodnight to Davies as he went.

The air seemed to get colder as he walked and there was a trace of fog, which made his isolation feel more complete as he settled to the journey. What those at Custom House would make of the afternoon's activities was yet to be seen. There could be no doubt that Griffin had done his duty in tackling the privateer: the country was at war, and enemy vessels must be engaged wherever feasible. Reports abounded of revenue craft fighting long, drawn-out battles with French raiders and those who proved triumphant were praised and rewarded. But his minor action could hardly be regarded as a victory; *Bee* was damaged, and would require extensive repairs, whereas the French vessel, although larger, and dissuaded from taking a valuable Indiaman, was probably not severely hurt and might be back on patrol within a few days. If he tried, the collector would be able to find a dozen reasons for censure, and by now was likely to be under pressure from the Horsebridge mob. They would want him out of the way; Griffin expected nothing less. Dobson had all the power he needed to do it quite legally, and may have been given the opportunity that very afternoon.

The steady rhythm of his walk encouraged deep thinking, and Griffin's mind travelled back to his second interview with Dobson before moving on, inevitably, to the scene at The Star that preceded it. He had not seen the girl since she had been shocked by his uniform, but still her presence haunted him far more than was reasonable in the circumstances. And, despite the fool he had undoubtedly made of himself, he found that thoughts of her were immeasurably preferable to anyone at Custom House.

Griffin judged himself to be reasonably experienced with women. There had been several affairs in his life, ranging from an engagement to the daughter of a factor in Bombay who finally succumbed to a warmer offer, to a series of shorter encounters aboard ship or in dusky harbour-side hotel rooms. Some of the latter had ended with a financial contribution from him that had come as a surprise, and rather shocked his naïve nature, but none compared with his current feelings for the girl.

She was at once fascinating, and slightly frightening. At the moment it was clear he was not in favour, and yet there remained an attraction that was far too strong to ignore, and he was quick to acknowledge that a major reason for returning to the inn was the chance of seeing her again.

His thoughts kept him company that far, and he was approaching his lodgings, and anticipating having to wake the boy for a second time, when he noticed lights in the front parlour. Through the partially boarded window he caught sight of two men, and yes, she was there as well; they were sitting at a table and seemed deep in conversation. Feeling a sudden warmth that had no place on such a night, he made for the door, and rapped loudly.

* * *

"I hope I am not inconveniencing you," Griffin said, his confidence waning at the strange look that she treated him to. He supposed anyone would be surprised to see a guest quite so late, but that hardly accounted for such a reaction; it was as if she had seen a ghost.

"No, not at all, sir; do step in." She stood to one side and he passed, delighting in their brief intimacy.

"My father and brother are in the parlour," she said, and there might have been a hint of mischief in her voice. "Would you care to join them for some bishop?"

Griffin said that he would, although it was a toss-up as to which was the greater attraction: mulled wine or the girl's company; the prospect of meeting with the two men was hardly any incentive at all. He allowed her to pass him this time, and was reasonably certain she did so closer than was absolutely necessary, then followed through to the dim room where the others sat by a glowing fire. The younger man stood up suddenly on seeing him and, for a moment, nothing was said. Griffin looked more closely at his face and gave a short laugh.

"Well, that is a coincidence," he said. "Though I suppose we cannot expect anything but, in a place so small." The lad looked across to his father for reassurance before taking the extended hand cautiously. "We met not the day afore yesterday," Griffin continued, addressing the older man. "Your son here led me in a right royal chase, though it were down to him that we finally bagged a smuggler."

Both men were now decidedly ill at ease, although Griffin felt suddenly reckless, and was thoroughly enjoying the situation. And so, he suspected, was the girl.

"Matt, ain't that a fine thing?" she exclaimed. "And so good to hear you have been helping his Majesty."

The young man looked angrily back and forth then, realising he was being teased, smiled sheepishly. Griffin laughed again, to show there were no bad feelings.

"I had little idea, Matthew." The landlord spoke for the first time. "Was you involved with the capture of that Warren smack?" His tone was cautious: some might say frightened.

The lad went to explain, but Griffin was ahead of him. "Not involved in any way, Mr Ward." He sensed there was some importance here, even before he had fully reasoned it out. "Though, had I not diverted to search his vessel, I should have failed to make the capture."

"But your boat was rummaged, Matt?" the older man persisted and once more Griffin cut in.

"I merely stopped and asked questions," he assured them. "He had done nothing wrong, and was most obliging."

The lie settled the atmosphere somewhat, and a chair was found for Griffin.

"And have you taken any more villains today?" the girl asked wickedly, as she passed across a steaming tankard. Griffin shook his head.

"No, today I have been speaking with Frenchmen," he said, accepting the pot with a wink. He noticed the two men were watching him closely, and wondered if he had been too forward, before realising they were far more interested in his conversation than any designs he might have on the girl. "Large yawl, well-armed, and fast," – he felt that little could be lost in embellishing the story.

"Dark hull and a patched mainsail?" the landlord asked.

"Indeed, you know her?"

"That would be the *Amelia*," Matthew Ward told him. "We sees her quite a bit round these shores, though she is never much of a nuisance."

Griffin raised an eyebrow. "Is that the case?"

"We're fishin'," the lad blustered. "No Navy wages war on us."

Griffin was prepared to accept the statement at face value, even if the entire world knew just why such leniency was extended.

"Did you fight her?" the girl asked, and Griffin was forced to confess that he had. Both men looked up with surprise and something approaching respect.

"That's a heavy match for your little cruiser," the landlord murmured.

"Well, I can't claim complete victory, though she were sent back to France with her tail betwixt her legs."

There was a moment of silence, then the younger man asked, "And is the *Bee* damaged?"

Griffin was in the midst of drinking his wine and took a moment to think before answering. "A mild impairment, nothing more. She should be a'sea again in no time."

"Still, good to be fighting the French," the girl prompted.

"Aye," Griffin agreed, wiping his mouth with the back of his hand. "They make a far better enemy than my own kind..."

The silence returned and this time held an extra edge. Griffin's eyes swept all three faces, but none would return his stare. Then he spoke.

"It is my duty to fight for my country." His words came slowly, and he pronounced each with care; he wanted no misunderstanding. "If that involves the occasional milling with Dutch or French, then so be it. I also have to check against smuggling. It is every bit as important, especially as we are fighting a war." He held their attention, although neither man would meet his eye.

"And it is a war that will be lost if we continue to allow gold, wool and other vitals to be exported, while undermining our Treasury by trading with those who would see us defeated."

Still the glances remained elsewhere.

"I might be nought but an unlicked cub, but have learned enough to understand what goes on hereabouts. It has been made clear to me that this town, and most of the area about, is controlled by some disreputable men who are far more my enemy than the occasional smack carrying a tub or two of contraband." He was looking directly at Matthew now, and the lad blushed as he finally returned the gaze. Past conversations with Davies and Jones came back to Griffin as he continued. "Should I catch your vessel with ankers filled, I will take and charge you, be sure of that. But I do not wish to concentrate my efforts on small game; I am after bigger prey: far more evil folk that do greater harm to your town and country than I think you know."

"You're wrong," the girl spoke, despite her father's sudden warning hand. "And no, I will not stay silent." She turned to Griffin: her face was red, and for a moment he wondered if she were about to burst into tears. "We understand better than you give us credit."

It was just as he suspected, and Griffin tried not to show his relief.

"And we do not approve, no matter what you might think or have been told." Her voice was thick with emotion, and she seemed to be directing every word at Griffin, and he alone.

"Soph, stay silent, girl," her brother urged, but no one was taking any notice of him.

"If you are serious, the gang must be faced." Griffin's voice also became more intense. "Unless you do, they will be impossible to counter."

"It is not so simple," she replied. "Many hereabouts are bothered by their actions, but we cannot be sure who is to be trusted. Most of the members we know, and some can be guessed at, but a good few ordinary folk are forced to have dealings with the Warrens, and even those that do not might seek favour by turning informer." There were reluctant acknowledgements from the other two.

"Well I am prepared to act against them," Griffin said after a moment. "But can do little without support."

"Then you have it," the girl spoke quite loudly. "You have it from us all," she continued, glaring hard at the two men by her, daring either of them to contradict, and finally receiving nods from both.

"That is good to hear," Griffin said, his tone reverting to normal.

"And though we may not be able to spot all the informers, some, who are in the pay of the Warrens, are certainly known."

"For sure?"

"Yes." She was positive. "Little can go on in a place like this without such things becoming common knowledge. I dare say we can tell you most of those who regularly work for the Horsebridge gang, and will make a list if you wish."

Her brother and father began to object, but Griffin shook his head.

"Merely naming names will be of scant use and may only serve to incriminate you. But give me evidence, or at least support from others, and I will act. In such an instance any wrong that you have done could not be ignored, although your assistance would be taken into consideration."

"Might we be punished?" she asked, biting her lip.

"Possibly not," Griffin said earnestly. "Much can be allowed. There are examples a plenty of King's Evidence being used to prosecute in such situations, and I would do my utmost to see that your help was acknowledged, though I could not give my word that you would all go scot-free."

"You're playing a dangerous game, girl," her father cautioned.

"And what have you been doing these last few years?" she went back at him, before turning to her brother. "Or you, Matt, if it comes to it. At least, with Commander Griffin here, we are taking a risk that might improve matters."

Both men were shamed into silence, and the girl continued.

"Yes, we will work with you, and may the Warrens be defeated, but first there are other arrangements to be made. You cannot stay here; there is too much danger for all if you do."

Griffin pursed his lips as he considered for a moment. Her words made sense; assuming it were possible to work alongside the Wards, they would have to continue with their current dealings, and that would be all but impossible with him, an officer of the revenue, living in the same house. "What do you suggest?"

"We can find a place." The landlord spoke this time. "Somewhere safe, there are those I have known a fair while and can rely on. And what the girl says is right, though I do not approve of her manner of saying it; far too much like her mother," he added, giving a grudging smile.

Griffin knew it strange to be speaking as frankly with people he had no reason to trust and had only just met, but there was something in the girl's manner – in the very atmosphere of the room, if it came to it – that convinced him of their sincerity.

"I am glad," he said. "But we will have to meet occasionally, if we are to combat this menace."

"I may speak with you," the girl said quickly, and Griffin felt his heart skip a beat. "It is not uncommon for me to be abroad; more so than Father, at least; and Matt might not wish to spend too much time at the cruiser," she added lightly.

All appeared to be in agreement, and Griffin drank down his wine in one before slamming the pot down on the table.

"Well so be it. And if I am to risk one more night under your roof, I should be abed," he told them. "Thank you all for this drink, and conversation, I hope we will talk more in the future."

He left the room conscious of the murmurings behind him. They would have much to discuss, he supposed, but Griffin had only thought on his mind. Sophie: what a truly excellent name that was.

* * *

He was up before dawn and reached *Bee* in the first of the daylight. She was sitting oddly, her bows down, and counter strangely raised; stores must have been moved to alter the trim and make accessing the damage easier. Coal smoke rolled greasily from her foreshortened flue, and as he grew closer he noticed the smell of bacon in the air. A party of seamen were already at work on a rough platform rigged about the stern, and the cutter itself had the air of purposeful activity that immediately made him feel guilty. Griffin peered over the wharf, and could see the carpenter lying on his back, looking up at the fractured strakes.

"Good morning, sir." It was Davies' voice, and Griffin looked round to see the mate clumping down the gangplank to join him. "We made an early start," he said, indicating a row of lanthorns that were hanging from the cutter's counter and harbour wall.

"So I see, Mr Davies," he replied, a little shamefaced. It was clear that much had been achieved while he had been doing little more than eating his breakfast. "Highly commendable."

The carpenter was easing himself upright, and muttering to the man assisting him.

"What do you find, Chips?" Davies shouted down.

The man looked up and seemed surprised to see the cutter's captain and second-in-command on the harbour side.

"Well, it could be worse, gentlemen," he said, scraping the slime from his hands. "There's two strakes gone on either side, and by rights they need replacing in the complete length."

144

Griffin winced; *Bee* was clinker built, and such a repair was bound to entail the dry dock, and an extensive refit.

"But I think I might be able to scarph them well enough, even though she's clench, and pretty tight in that area."

That was better news. "How long will it take?" Davies asked.

The carpenter pulled a face. "No knowing, and I'm not saying it will even be possible. But if I may retain Wooderson here to assist, I reckons a day an' a night should see us back on the water. It won't be a full job, mind; she'll be tender for a few days, and never as sound as she should be."

"Never mind, Mr Jeffreys," Griffin interrupted him. "If you can get it done in twenty-four hours, it is far more than I could ever have expected. Is there anything you require?"

The carpenter seemed to consider this for a moment, then shook his head. "I've lumber enough for now, sir, and help." He glanced at his companion, whom Griffin recognised as the older man who had spoken up the previous morning. "We will be able to do much. I could use young Harry and the spirit stove to boil up some glue later."

"I'll send him down straight after he's eaten," the mate replied. "And you'd better stop an' get some scran yourself."

There was the sound of tearing wood; Jeffreys had gone back to examining the damage, and was ripping the splintered timber away with his bare hands.

"Bit of bacon in some soft tack will suit me fine, thanking you, Mr Davies," he shouted back. "I'd like to get started, if that is straight with you."

"Would you care for some breakfast, sir?" Davies asked Griffin, as they walked towards the gangplank. "Men have been up for close on two hours, so I reckoned it right to give them a decent feed. They'll probably not eat again until dusk."

The memory of his recent meal, taken in comfort and with Sophie attending, came back to haunt Griffin.

"No, I shall be fine, thank you, Mr Davies," he said. "And please make sure the hands have all they require. Send for more provisions if there be need, and I trust they will allow me to sup them royally tonight?"

The mate beamed. "I'm sure that will be greatly appreciated, sir," he said.

Thinking about his breakfast had reminded Griffin of another matter, and it was with an effort that he kept his mind on the job in hand. "What else do you plan for the day?"

"We must attend to the galley chimney once she is cold, and there are other areas where shot has struck. They can be smoothed down for the present, but I should like to get a couple of coats of paint on them for safety. Then there's sail to be patched and the bo'sun wants to replace the larboard preventer stay."

"I'd say you had your work cut out. If I am not needed I have another matter with which to attend, then shall pay my dues at Custom House before looking in on the wounded."

"Very good, sir," Davies replied, just as the steward called the hands to breakfast.

Griffin turned away and started back towards the town. It was good to have a second-in-command as solid as Davies, and the news was far better than he could have expected. With luck, in less than two days, *Bee* would be serviceable again. More than that, he now had an optimistic report to present to Dobson, should the interview turn bad. But before then there was something far more intriguing to attend to. The paper Sophie had slipped him was still in his pocket. On it was written an address; she had murmured something about it being a safer place for him, and Griffin was keen to discover more.

He paid his toll and crossed at the drawbridge before turning onto the path that led to the Tide Mills. The industrial buildings looked far larger than they had from the sea. Most were three-storeys high, with peg roofs that must take a good deal of punishment so close to the shore. As he drew nearer he could hear the sound of the mill race, with regular creaks from the turning wheels, and the buzz of grinding stones deep inside the buildings. There were carts travelling back and forth, while two barges, laden with sacks, were waiting to be unloaded by a small wharf. He stood and watched; the whole place seemed fired with the activity of an ant heap, and all the energy to run the mechanism was provided by nothing more than the tide. Much had been made of Mr Watt and his diabolical steam engines, but Griffin decided that this was a far more effective use of water.

By and by he found the house; it was just the other side of a bridge that spanned the mill stream, and looked out over a bleak coast. It was one in an irregular terrace, and had paint peeling from the window frames, and glass that might not have been cleaned in years. But there was a light burning within, and Griffin sensed it would not be too early for him to call.

He rapped at the front door, and heard the sound of someone bustling about inside. Then there was a small crash, followed by gentle swearing, and eventually the door opened to reveal a tall, rather elegant figure. He was clad in silk pyjamas, a heavily embroidered dressing gown, and a small round cotton hat was perched upon his bald head. The man, who could not have been younger than sixty, considered Griffin's uniform with obvious interest.

"Good morning, I am looking for a Mr Willett," Griffin said, feeling slightly uneasy. It was still rather early, and the apparition before him was not what he had been expecting.

"Then you have been successful," the man replied, with a pleasant expression. "Would you care for a glass of wine?"

* * *

The room that Willett showed him took up much of the first floor of the small building and was serviceable enough. Griffin explained that he needed it principally as a base for his luggage together with some personal and official items that could not be stored in the cutter, in addition to the occasional night's rest. Most of the time, he proposed to be aboard *Bee* and preferably at sea. Of course for a number of reasons he would rather have kept his quarters at The Star but, as the Wards had intimated, he might well be in danger, and he supposed a change would not inconvenience him so very much.

"That would seem to be fine, Mr Willett, but it troubles me where you may be sleeping."

The man gave Griffin the benefit of his surprisingly white teeth. "Why I have a bed below, and will be of little concern to you."

Willett was starting back down the stairs. Griffin followed, and indeed noticed a small portable bunk set almost next to the stove in the single downstairs room. Apart from that there were three small cupboards, and two kitchen tables: one supported a tin bowl and another had a couple of rickety chairs drawn up to it. The walls held no pictures or ornamentation of any kind, but instead were lined with row upon row of books that seemed to stagger on a series of erratically placed shelves. Most rested on bricks, lumps of wood or, in one case, an upturned bucket. Griffin had no idea as to the number, but they were far more than he had ever seen outside of a library. It was obvious that the old gentleman had few other possessions, and lived extremely simply.

"And the rent, sir?" he asked, when Willett had shown him to a table and set a large and previously refused rummer of red wine in front of him.

The man looked up from refilling his own glass. "Shall we say a guinea a month?"

Griffin raised his eyes; his own wages amounted to slightly less than four, and this was hardly salubrious accommodation. But besides rent, his living expenses were remarkably light, and he had been particularly lucky with seizer money already.

"That would be all found," Willett added, hopefully. "As much as you wish to eat," he paused, before adding with emphasis, "and drink."

"Very well then." For all the man's eccentricities, Griffin could not help but like him and the feeling was clearly shared. Willett immediately tried to encourage more wine into Griffin's already full glass, leaving a considerable quantity to spill and form a puddle on the dusty table top.

"I have some things to move from The Star," Griffin said, taking a careful sip of the wine.

"All shall be taken care of," Willett assured him, with the air of a stage magician. "I shall send a boy down this very morning. I know the Wards well, and have done so for years."

"Indeed?"

"Oh yes, long before the mother took ill. Young Matt is grown up and fishing now, so I hear, and that Sophie has turned into a rare beauty. Why, I can remember when she were but a child, and would play naked in the street." Willett reflected. "'Tis a pity the habit waned."

Griffin cleared his throat. "So you have lived here a while?" he asked.

149

"The town? All my life. My niece married young Billy Catt who owns the mill; they let me stay here, as long as I look after the place." Griffin glanced about; it was clear that Willett was not keeping to his side of the bargain. "Afore that I was riding officer for nigh on ten years, and a tide waiter previously."

"You worked in the revenue service?" Griffin asked; it was yet another in a long series of revelations.

"Ah, that was some while ago," Willett confessed. "I have moved on apace since then."

"And what do you do now?"

"Is it not obvious?" he replied, before draining his glass in one huge swallow. "I read," he belched quietly, "and I drink."

Chapter Ten

Griffin was back at the harbour by four. After meeting with Willett, he had gone to call on the collector. Dobson had been strangely unavailable and Dwyer, his deputy and comptroller for the sector, had seen him in his own office, which was only slightly less grand than his senior's. The man had been business-like to the point of brisk. It was clear that Griffin's actions in tackling a privateer were not approved of; they might be at war with France, but the job of actually engaging the enemy fell to the Royal Navy. Griffin's duty was as an enforcement officer, with taxation, or its avoidance, his only foe. However much he might choose to risk his command attacking French coopers and perhaps the occasional enemy merchant, he was not expected to engage other fighting ships.

It was twaddle, of course, Griffin knew that, and nothing Dwyer said was going to make him change his mind, or affect future actions in any way. As far as he was concerned a revenue cutter sailed under the authority of the King, and it was every serving officer's duty to fight his sovereign's enemies, should the occasion present. Griffin suspected the comptroller's attitude could partly be blamed on the problem he had already caused by seizing one of the Warrens' boats. The family, or their representatives, would have had ample time to speak with him, or Dobson, by now and Griffin guessed that relations with Custom House would be decidedly less cordial in future.

He also realised that his position in the town itself was becoming more perilous. The parish surgery sat to the western side, where the streets were generally busier and included several groups of well-dressed young men apparently walking about without purpose. On two occasions he had been forced to step into the roadway when confronted by them, and one openly tried to trip him as he passed. Another spat in the dirt, and there had been shouted insults and even the banging of a tin pan from behind a fence as he walked up the High Street. But, undeterred, he made the trip and met with those of *Bee*'s crew who were injured.

It had been a slightly awkward visit, primarily because he only knew the men's names, and had just the briefest idea of their responsibilities. They were healing well however and one, who had been hurt when boarding the smack, was allowed to leave under his care. Having a wounded man with him, Griffin begged the use of the surgeon's carriage back to the cutter, and suspected he might have avoided a good deal of unpleasantness in doing so.

But the scene at the harbour was enough to gladden any heart. Davies, the carpenter and all of *Bee*'s crew had done remarkably well. The larboard strakes were already neatly patched, with the starboard needing only final fitting and fixing. Griffin's cabin was a mess, of course, but a party was already starting to apply thick, marine paint to the new wood. Above deck several fresh items of standing rigging were in place, in addition to the preventer stay, and the cutter had even gained a new larboard pump head. This differed slightly from the standard pattern and as neither he, or anyone at Custom House, had authorised a replacement, Griffin could only assume it had been liberated from elsewhere, and decided not to pursue the matter further. The entire job had been carried out by five hands who had no experience or qualifications for such a task, other than being skilled seamen. The damaged swivel gun mounting had been repaired, the larboard six-pounder was back in place on a rebuilt carriage, and they had a brand new flue, a fine copper affair that shone extremely proud, although it did bear close resemblance to a drain pipe.

Griffin finished his inspection on the prow and spotted the mate standing by the binnacle. It was the ideal time and occasion, and he called along the crowded deck: "Mr Davies, you have achieved much in a short time, I am mightily impressed."

The mate beamed at him and touched his hat. "Thankee, sir; the lads really set to with a purpose."

"So I see, so I see." Griffin walked slowly sternwards, smiling as he passed the men, patting some on the arm or shoulder as they gave small mutterings of self-deprecation. The faces were all familiar now, and even most of the names came to him as they grinned back. "You have all done really splendidly – I could not have asked for more."

He reached the mate and, catching the older man's eye, continued in a voice far louder than was necessary for normal conversation: "Now I seem to remember a small promise I made earlier, Mr Davies."

"Indeed, sir." The mate was just as experienced, and replied in an equally carrying tone: "You were to sup with the people, I believe; shall I pipe 'hands to dinner'?"

"Oh, I think we can do better than a bite of cold biscuit and cheese. Have they eaten at all today?"

"Not since the morning, sir." Davies replied. Griffin had also gone without food, although he guessed that his breakfast had been better, or certainly a good deal more enjoyable, than any the men had eaten.

"Then we will send to The Star," he said. He intended taking the entire crew to the inn, but thought better of it. The bad feeling noticed in the town earlier was still very much on his mind; tired and hungry, the seamen might not be quite so able to ignore an occasional slight as he had been. Besides, there would be over thirty of them, and as they were bound to drink, something a little more contained was required. "Here, where's Harry?"

The cutter's lad appeared as if by magic. Griffin dug into his pocket and pulled out a guinea. "Make for Mr Ward, lad. Tell him to send provisions for forty. Cold meat, cheese, bread – whatever he thinks that need not be cooked; an apple pie or two, or some duff should he have any, and a barrel of his best Stingo. Give him this, and tell him I will settle later if it be more."

The boy caught the money and ran off without a pause. Griffin knew that speed and agility would see him past any unpleasantness, even if his age did not.

Half an hour later a cart arrived, with Harry sitting importantly next to the driver who, Griffin noticed with a slight intake of breath, was Sophie. He reached up to her cautiously while more confident hands began to unload the provisions.

"I had not expected you to come as well," he said, as he helped her down. Then, realising that it was not the most gallant of statements, hurried to make amends. "But it is good to see you: good indeed."

Her face relaxed into a slightly teasing smile, and Griffin thought was made even more lovely.

"Oh, I have to make sure the plates and such are properly cared for," she told him.

"Then you must stay and be certain," he said, as she set foot on the ground.

It was a warm evening. Mess tables set on casks were already in position and the food was quickly stacked upon them while a fire, lit from the damaged timbers the carpenter had removed, began to crack and splutter into life and soon was giving a cheerful glow to the scene. The convivial atmosphere usual when a group exert themselves to a common purpose carried them through until strong ale took over, and in no time the men were eating, drinking, laughing and showing signs that they would soon be ready for song. Griffin sat at the far end of one table next to Sophie, with Davies on his left and Lamport to her right. He looked along the line of faces and was satisfied. Even though he had been their commander for no more than a few days it was clear that a team was being forged. Davies was silent for a rare moment, and Griffin turned to say something of this to him when he saw Jones, the riding officer, approach.

"Mr Jones; a welcome visitor indeed," Griffin called, rising slightly in his seat. "You must join us, do." The man looked momentarily awkward but when Lamport shuffled along the bench, and a fresh plate and mug were found and filled, he soon entered into the spirit of the evening.

"There is something I have to tell you, sir," the Welshman said, when they had all eaten well, and were starting to grow listless.

"Then you must," Griffin replied, beaming genially. "Would you speak with me alone?"

Jones' eyes flashed briefly across to Sophie. "That might be a wise move, Commander."

"I should attend to our plates," Sophie said, and rose from the table. "You will excuse me, I am sure?"

Griffin was silently grateful for her understanding, and she made off to the second table, where the men greeted her with good humoured, if robust, comments that were expertly countered. Jones leaned down to be nearer to the cutter's officers, and spoke in a low tone.

"There is to be a run in three days' time," he said, watching their eyes intently. "I cannot tell you how I know, but it is of the finest source, and not one I am inclined to mistrust. Warren's lot are organising, and there are to be at least three vessels and nigh on eighty ashore attending to the landing."

For the second time that evening Griffin felt his pulse increase. "Where's it to be?" he whispered.

"Brighthelmstone, or at least a beach close to."

"But that's out of our sector, Jackie," Davies said, his disappointment evident.

"Officially, maybe. Though it need not mean we cannot get involved."

"We could come that way by chance, you mean?" Lamport suggested.

"Or follow one of the Warrens in; that would be hot pursuit," Davies added, brightening slightly.

"There are no end of ways," Jones agreed. "If you are willing." The man's eyes flashed across to the head of the table.

"I am keen to act," Griffin said quickly. "But wonder if not the Shoreham office should also be involved. The Warrens will have three boats, you say; we could combine, with *Bee* working alongside the *Hound*."

"It is a possibility," Jones conceded. "Though I think enough can be raised ourselves, and we are only talking of smacks no bigger than the one you took the other night."

"So small a force?" Griffin questioned.

"It need not be large," Davies murmured. "Even a forty-ton lugger can carry enough to keep many men busy unloading, and may even be towing more booty behind." Griffin nodded; there was still much he had to learn. The mate was speaking again. "But we could still make it a joint operation. Why are you playing so cagey, Jackie?"

"I do not wish to compromise the situation, see?" Jones' voice had suddenly grown harsh and defensive. "Informers are everywhere; there are certainly some hereabouts that I would not trust, and a good few more elsewhere." He drew back and considered Griffin. "You spoke of wanting to crush the Warrens, sir; well, this is an opportunity. But it will be lost if we spread the word too wide."

Griffin took the point. "What of the land forces; who will you approach?"

"Colonel Douglas at Lewes," Jones replied instantly. "I can go to him direct; it might not be the correct protocol, but he is a regular officer, and will understand."

"Should it not be the militia?" Lamport asked.

Jones shook his head. "I would not wish to involve them, nor anyone at Custom House for the same reason."

Both the food and not a little beer were starting to take effect on his senses, but Griffin was still aware that this was a chance not to be missed. He glanced across to where Davies and Lamport were considering Jones' proposal. Lamport was clearly concerned; his expression, rarely cheerful, was currently pinched in thought, making him appear even more mule-like than ever but in Davies, Griffin saw a revelation. The older man was also inclined to caution, and definitely lacked spontaneity, yet here he was, face bright and eyes distant in contemplation.

"A hit like that could certainly fix their wagon," the mate said, to no one in particular. "It would be a major loss, especially if we took their boats as well. And it might teach them Warrens we are not to be meddled with."

"To my mind we have already made an impression," Jones agreed. "Such a run would normally be handled in our territory; there are a number of suitable beaches, and yet they choose to move somewhere less convenient. Why is that, do you think?"

Davies nodded heartily, and even Lamport seemed to agree.

"Well, if such is the case we must enforce the belief," Griffin found himself saying. "Strike while we have the initiative, and be sure they are kept on the run. Mr Jones, you have done exceptionally well. If you will organise matters from the shore, I shall commit to meeting you off Brighthelmstone at an agreed time."

"You will not mention this to Dwyer or Dobson?" the riding officer asked.

"I shall say nothing," Griffin confirmed, picking up on Jones' thoughts instantly. "Indeed, I agree; the fewer who know the better. Mr Davies, when would we be set to leave once more?"

The mate, whose thoughts were still clearly elsewhere, brought his mind back to the question. "Why, on tomorrow's tide, if you wish it. The paint may still be tender, but will serve until the next refit, and we are customarily provisioned for several weeks. Water is low, of course, but that can be rectified in the morning."

"Then let us be at sea by tomorrow night," Griffin said.

Jones and the mate looked their approval, and even Lamport's expression could be called cheerful.

"Shall I inform the men, sir?" he asked.

"No, I think we will let that come as a surprise," Griffin replied. "In fact, I think all should be kept very quiet for now, they can learn of our plans once we are free of the shore and there is no question of more discovering them. Until then, this must be kept very firmly amongst ourselves."

There was a moment of seriousness, then Davies began to chuckle, and soon all four were laughing heartily. Griffin looked up and caught sight of Sophie; she was standing by the far end of the second table: their eyes met, and she smiled also.

* * *

The Tide Mills contained a number of smaller buildings besides the modern stone industrial structures. There were offices, and a wagon shed, stables, a smithy and even a massive glass house that stood next to an allotment area as the owner, William Catt, had a passion for growing vegetables and fruit trees. There was also a row of fine cottages for favoured workers that stood with their own communal wash house. Beyond them, and rather too close to the sea for comfort, were the less salubrious houses. Willett and his new lodger had one and, quite by chance, Joe Lamport lived next door to them with his small family.

He had moved there four years ago when he and Emma were married, and for most of the time they had shared the small dark terraced home with his mother-in-law. It was cold in winter, hot in summer and damp all the year through. Wind and salt water crept through both window and door frames, and the roof was in need of constant attention. When their first child, a boy named Joseph, who suffered from colic, appeared the modest living accommodation was suddenly unbearably cramped. Both the women had worked in the mills but, almost simultaneously, Emma's mother became ill, and the baby too dependent. It was only through a good deal of persuasion from the other workers, and an undertaking that they would return as soon as practical, that William Catt allowed them to keep their accommodation. Then, not more than a month ago, the old woman died and two days later Emma discovered herself to be pregnant.

That morning Lamport hurried out, drawing his thin, worn coat about him in a vain attempt to block out the searching wind. He had stayed late at the cruiser the night before, and was leaving without breakfast; there being nothing beyond the heel of a four-day-old loaf in the larder. But at least he had eaten well the previous evening, and should benefit from a further meal as soon as he boarded the *Bee*. They were likely to be at sea for some while, so he would also be fed for the foreseeable future. It was a prospect that could not be shared with his wife and child, and added guilt to the long list of his negative feelings.

He loved Emma; nothing would change that. Even when her youthful looks faded so quickly and she began to pile on weight, even then there was no one else for him, neither would there ever be. But at times he felt he did not want her to be there constantly, not so close, not every day. He hated the tiny house that always managed to be both stuffy and cold. The incessant screaming of the child wore him down, and in the back of his mind he knew that the next would be along shortly and could only add to the misery. But most of all he hated the responsibility of a family, and the fact that he was bound to his job, the area and what seemed destined to be wretched living accommodation for the rest of his life.

He was far too young to be tied down. It was a big world and he wanted to see more; travel further than the confines of a revenue cutter's sector, and see sights other than the bleak cliffs of Beachy Head, or the shoreline at Cuckmere Haven. There was much a young man like him could achieve, and yet he seemed locked on an all too predictable course. It was a necessary one to provide for his present obligations, but still it bored and depressed him in equal measure.

That morning he hurried along the cinder path that led to the harbour, giving scant regard to workers from Newhaven passing in the opposite direction. The mill ran for ten hours in every twelve, the starting time constantly changing with the tide, and they were late: Lamport knew from the noise of grinding wheels that could be heard even at such a distance. Each was likely to be fined by the ever watchful Mr Catt, but Lamport could feel little sympathy for them; he had his own troubles.

The current one was finding a place to live. They had the house until the end of the month, but then must move on. In normal circumstances that would cause no great difficulty; Lamport drew a regular wage as deputed mariner, and his position was as safe as any in a country beaten down by almost ten years of constant war. There was also the tidy sum that should eventually be coming to them from the haul made a few evenings back, but their immediate situation was still dire. His mother-in-law's medical expenses had been high, and Emma could not find anyone willing to take on the care of young Joseph so she could also work. Consequently they owed small amounts to the three stores in town and a great deal more to Franklin, the money lender. The old man's heart was of solid stone and, working directly for the Warrens as he did, he had a sure-fire way of seeing that debts were repaid on time.

The next few days might bring better tidings; were they to seize a goodly amount, his credit would undoubtedly increase. But government money took an age to be paid and however much was owed to him would not solve the present difficulty. For that he needed coin, and it must be immediate; preferably in his hand before they sailed.

Lamport had hoped to run into Matt Ward on his way to the harbour. His friend's hide was set in the beach to the east of the Tide Mills; it was a dank and slippery cellar that the two of them had dug out during a string of summer evenings three years ago. Matt used it to store contraband and it was not unusual to find him returning from his hoard first thing. The two had not met up since *Bee* stopped his boat a few days back, and Lamport was vaguely worried that the incident might have caused ill feeling. But, as the mass of hurrying workers gradually faded, he was soon alone on the path, apart from the three men in long coats that had been following for some while. By and by they caught him up and, as the harbour finally came into sight, Lamport was not in the least surprised when one drew alongside.

"Cold morning for a sailor," he commented. Lamport gave a weak smile; he thought he knew the men, or at least could guess where they were from.

"Ask me, this one could do with a new piece of cloth," another said, rubbing Lamport's shoddy coat between his gloved fingers.

"No, it ain't the want of rig that ails him," the third added, with the slow voice of authority. "Our friend has greater troubles beyond keeping warm." By mutual but unspoken agreement they all stopped walking, and Lamport looked cautiously from one to another.

"Name Lamport?" the first asked. Joe said it was and blinked; it was devilishly cold, and it must be the wind that was making his eyes water.

"Work on the cruiser, do you?"

"That's right."

The third man's expression relaxed, although the look lacked any warmth or comfort. "Then we'd like a word with you," he said.

* * *

Griffin awoke the next morning with impossibly bright daylight streaming through the bare windows. He groaned, and covered his eyes with the back of his hand. There was no need to look at his watch; even without the light he knew he had slept long past his normal rising time. Slowly the memories of the previous evening came back to him, and he was comforted by the fact that he would not be alone in his present condition.

He had no idea of the source of the brandy that made an appearance towards the end of the evening, but already knew enough about the revenue service not to enquire. He had said goodnight to Sophie shortly before, which he supposed had precipitated his drinking to some extent. They had walked together as far as the drawbridge and, with the patient horse being led at an incredibly slow pace, were able to talk in private. So much was said in such a little time; he told of his life, ambitions and most of his fears, while she more than matched him in secrets, revelations and foolish childhood stories. More than that, when they reached the end of their journey and really could not stand in the cold autumn night any longer, she offered up her lips to be kissed and in the darkness Griffin had been only too pleased to oblige.

On returning to the cutter he felt a muddle of mixed and contrasting emotions; she was clearly his for the taking, and yet there was so much to stop them being together. Consequently, the glass of Nantes brandy that Davies handed him seemed very welcome; it offered an instant release from all concerns, and was downed in one to the obvious approval of the rest of the crew.

The evening then continued for far too long. The approbation of his men was important to him, but it was one thing to feel comradeship and optimism with brandy in his stomach, quite another to have to face the real world with a sober head that throbbed with every heartbeat the following day. Griffin rolled out of bed and achieved a vaguely upright position, while rubbing his eyes and moaning softly. There was water enough for a wash, which did much to restore some degree of normality, although he still eyed the razor warily, before collecting the strop, and brightening its edge. His skin was slightly bloated and the cold blade cut through the stubble, making a faint rasping sound, but it was the last shave he could expect on solid ground for several days, and he resolved to make the best of it.

As the soap was slowly scraped from his chin, he felt his spirits rise with the thought of what those days could bring. The only man outside the cutter's crew who had any inkling as to their movements was Jones, and he would be contacting the dragoons at Lewes that morning. Apparently one of the Warren sons was expected to be present at the landing, so there was every chance that Wednesday night would see a member of the family in custody.

Little more would be required, Griffin decided, while carefully bringing the blade down over the peak of his chin. Once the Warrens were shown they could not behave as if they owned the place – that every man, however powerful or well-connected, was subject to the laws of the land – the gang would be beaten. They might strike back, maybe try to re-assert themselves, but the point would have been made. All it needed was a bit of effort; goad what were intrinsically good men into taking action, and the evil would not survive.

But Griffin was not blind to the responsibility he had taken on. All had been relatively content to submit to the status quo, accepting that the Warren family were too large and powerful for them to fight. Now that he had come along with his fresh broom tactics and a couple of bold moves, a latent enthusiasm had been awakened. That was fine, as long as he were successful; should Jones' plan go awry, or some mistake occur that allowed the Warrens to escape, possibly at the cost of a member of his own force, he would be answerable, if not legally, then at least to himself. As it was Davies, Jones and Lamport were backing him, whereas he had repaid them by drinking too much brandy and wakening with a hangover.

And he carried a similar obligation to every one of his men. *Bee*'s repairs had been carried out in record time: something that Griffin suspected was due in part to his arrival. They all could see a chance to actually make a difference, and maybe correct something that had been allowed to go bad for too long. Griffin stared back at his reflection in the mirror and could not be impressed. The hollowed eyes and pale complexion made him appear several years older, and yet he lacked the experience of even the rawest member of the cutter's crew. He could only hope for a measure of luck that would make him worthy of their trust.

On the good side, neither Dobson or Dwyer, nor anyone else was aware of *Bee*'s present condition. When she docked, the night before last, the damage had appeared far more serious, and none of them would be expecting her to be repaired so quickly. High tide was at one, so there should be sufficient water to see her over the bar by about eleven and thirty. They would take *Bee* out, ostensibly for a shake-down cruise after the repairs, and stay at sea for a good few days. Acting independently of the shore, Griffin could then fully explore the area and, if they happened to drop by a certain Brighthelmstone beach on Wednesday morning's high, and chanced to fall in with one or two Warren boats, they might discover a measure of action.

He wiped his face and mopped at a small spot of blood next to his ear, before throwing the towel down and stuffing two spare shirts, together with the last of his clean laundry, into a ditty bag. A glance about the room and he was ready to go, but a chill ran down his back, and made him pause.

Whatever his feelings the night before and even today with the prospect of what lay ahead, his move to the revenue service suddenly felt to be a mistake. Perhaps he was not really cut out for such a life. Maybe, in reality, he belonged in a safe, solid merchantman, where the greatest danger lay in offending a passenger or catching the pox. This time last year he had known security and held a respected position, now he was living in a house with a drunkard for a landlord, while doing a job that attracted little regard and actually placed him in very real fear for his life. The current plan could go horribly wrong; men might well die because a bored and probably spoilt merchant mate had decided on a change of career, and fancied he may have a flair for revenue work.

But then there was Sophie, he reminded himself, and her existence alone made sense of much of the madness. Besides, he was committed to the path at least for the time being and, however hard his head might be hurting, the well known rebellious streak was still present.

He knew that whatever mess he might have placed himself in would be seen through to its conclusion, and acknowledged the fact that a part of him was actually beginning to relish the prospect. His sword hung on a nail by the door; he collected it, noting how the decoration was starting to tarnish, and buckled the belt about his waist. Then he slipped the jacket across his shoulders and slowly headed down the stairs to where Willett would doubtless be pouring himself breakfast.

Chapter Eleven

"Steady... Steady..." Davies' voice was low and could barely be heard above the scream of the wind rushing through the cutter's lines and the hammer of heavy raindrops on her deck. The night was dark, and made doubly so by the solid bank of cloud that blocked out all starlight, and seemed to wrap about them like a sodden blanket. *Bee* crept forward on the still-rising tide, until slowly the headland gave a slight lee, reducing the sound of the tempest to a mere whine. But the rain fell down relentlessly and, to those aboard, it felt as if it always would. They were crowded along the starboard bulwark, straining to see into the dark inlet, and each was equally wet and miserable.

"No bottom." A hand was forward with a sounding rod that would strike less than a fathom below their keel. It was a faster and easier method of measuring the depth considering the conditions, although lacked some of the information given by a properly cast lead.

"There's movement ashore, sir," Davies said, pointing a gloveless hand; yes, several darker masses on the beach could be defined. It was a veritable crowd, in fact, Griffin decided, as the flash of an ill-kept dark lantern revealed at least one group. Soon he fancied he could hear the snorts and grunts of truculent horses, even against that of the rolling surf, but there was no sign of shipping; neither had there been as they approached. "There's a chance that the landing's already occurred, and they're clearing after it," the mate continued.

"Hell of a night," Griffin grunted. The water was streaming down his sou'wester and had found its way past his oilskins in at least three different locations.

"Aye," Davies agreed. "They couldn't have asked for better."

Forsyth was being supported by Conway at the tiller, due to the strength of the storm. Of them all, they seemed to be the only ones not staring at the shore or out to sea. "Starboard your helm," Griffin ordered, and the men pressed the bar across, their eyes never leaving the luff of the sails.

Griffin felt they were relatively safe to stay as they were but, without a vessel that could be engaged, the *Bee* was more or less redundant. The cutter's deep keel prevented her coming much closer, and the tide would be starting to fall soon. If Jones had done his job properly, a sufficient force of dragoons should be amassed and be preparing to strike at any moment. Griffin might send in a landing party to assist, but the twenty or so he could raise would be difficult to set down in any safety and may even be taken for smugglers by the military. The cutter rolled in the heaving waves while every available eye peered through the storm. With luck more boats may be expected, and she must remain on station: a ketch or a smack might be intercepted coming in, and then it would be down to the *Bee* to deal with them. For that to be the case they must also stay as invisible as they could; a signal from the shore would be seen miles out into the Channel and might spoil everything. But it was miserable work, and bound to last a good while longer.

They had been at sea for three days, and were inspecting this particular beach for the second time. It was one of the advantages of an extended cruise; Griffin could go pretty much where he pleased and when, without worrying that his future movements were being revealed to anyone on shore. There was just the knowledge that Jones had shared a few nights back, and none of the ordinary seamen was aware of that; besides, *Bee* had sailed the next morning, so the only thing to fear, beyond the current storm, was chance.

For each of the preceding days their time had been spent almost out of sight of land, and they should have been all but invisible to any watching eyes. During that period six small fishing craft were boarded, but nothing found of any concern apart from two half-ankers of brandy that were in a pandle boat heading back for its home port of Seaford. Griffin was disinclined to believe the fishermen's story about the booty having been dragged from the bottom by chance; it was a common enough method of getting small crops of contraband to shore, after all. The man was well-known to Davies and some of the crew, however and, as no major crime had been committed, he allowed the boat to proceed. Full details had been taken, but Griffin guessed the captain would not be charged. And if he was, his defence, that he had every intention of reporting the matter as soon as he was able, may well see him clear of a fine. Griffin was equally cynical about his own men; the booty was currently in his cabin, where he guessed it would have the best chance of remaining safe until *Bee* next saw harbour.

The cutter was keeping position in the dark, moonless night but the tide was now definitely on the turn, and would soon be taking her out to sea. The wind had backed slightly in the last half hour, and only needed to do so a couple more points to create a lee shore. It was still pitch black and, despite the cold, the wet and the inherent danger that grew almost by the minute, no one on board spoke, or even moved, unless it was absolutely necessary.

The time at sea had also been used in exercise. Throughout his career in the East India Company, Griffin had nurtured an interest in ship's guns that had come very close to obsession. Even the cannonades, short-barrelled monstrosities that the Company used to arm their larger ships, were maintained and exercised to the highest level as soon as he was given their charge. So keen was his fascination that a later captain had seen fit to censure him; apparently his excessive drills were disconcerting some of the more sensitive passengers. But now he was in command and, even though *Bee*'s broadside weight was little more than one shot from a large John Company piece, Griffin was determined to see that his fire-power was effective.

The cutter carried less powder and shot than a Royal Naval vessel, so live firing was limited, but every morning several hours had been spent with practice broadsides. Gun crews were changed periodically, with each man given the chance to try a different station, until all knew the entire operation of their particular gun. Then Griffin himself took charge of judging each for their capabilities, and reassigned the crews, so that now he felt he had the optimum mix of gun captains and servers. Consequently their broadside rate had all but halved and, on the two occasions he had allowed the guns to actually be fired, the crew's new-found pride in their craft showed through.

"We'll have to stand off soon," Davies said, his voice ringing out above the storm. A shout from further forward announced that the sounding rod had struck bottom, and Griffin ordered them round. The boom swept past silently overhead, and *Bee* began to edge slowly out to sea as the heavily reefed sails were sheeted home. She soon settled onto a southerly course, and her bows began to break through the oncoming waves. Griffin looked up to the masthead and resisted the temptation to call. The night was dark and as dirty as they came, but Nairn would keep just as good a watch without any chiding from him.

That was another thing that had improved in their short cruise; the work with the gun crews had shown benefits that had nothing to do with their weaponry. Griffin had started to properly learn his crew; already he could identify all of the men, both by face and name, and was beginning to understand their particular skills, as well as the subtleties of certain personalities. Gadd, Griffin decided, was not quite the miserable old soul he pretended to be. On several occasions over the last few days he had been surprisingly supportive, so much so that Griffin was even wondering if a small degree of promotion might improve matters further. And there was Wooderson, the older man whose innate wisdom was dulled somewhat by a propensity to spout biblical text. He had been made carpenter's mate after assisting Jeffreys with the repairs and was responding well, accepting the promotion with a degree of pride that even Griffin had not expected. For a reason way beyond his commander's atheistic mind, Wooderson found being recognised as a carpenter immensely pleasing, even if the old man's scriptural referencing had, if anything, increased.

"Deck there!" The call from the lookout merged with the noise of the storm, although to those below it cut through like the crack of gunfire. "There's a ship in sight, almost dead ahead."

"Harry, get yourself to the masthead and relieve Nairn," Griffin snapped, and the ship's boy sprang up as if propelled with a pin. In no time he was skimming up the starboard shrouds like one born aloft, while Nairn dropped down to the deck via a backstay.

"Less than a mile off," the lookout confessed. He was below average height, and stood sure-footed on the heaving deck as he reported to Griffin and Davies. "A smack, I'd say, though could not be certain. She's showin' no lights, sir, an' it is perishing dark out there." Nairn's voice was a mixture of concern and bravado. No blame could be attached to him for allowing an unlit vessel so close, however; the night was truly foul, and the element of doubt as to what he had actually seen was completely understandable.

"What course?" Griffin asked.

"Headin' north," Nairn replied, a little more certainly. "We're neither of us making much way, but even so..."

Even so, the two vessels would be closing quickly enough. A smack was something that the *Bee* should be able to deal with. It might only be a fisherman that had allowed the masthead lamp to go out, but even if it were filled to the teeth with armed smugglers, Griffin felt they could meet with it. If she did turn out to be a runner, the vessel may be intending to land, anchor just off and be unloaded; or she could simply be sewing a crop: releasing a trail of spirit tubs strung together with rope and sunk, to be recovered at a later low tide. That being the case she may be empty by the time they met, making any nefarious activity that much more difficult to prove. But Griffin's defiant nature was making itself known once more, and he was determined to investigate further.

"Give me a bearing," he said, his voice taking on an extra edge now that it appeared likely they were in the presence of an enemy.

"She were fine off the starboard bow," Nairn replied. "I'd say we'll meet her in a matter of minutes."

"Very good, return to your post, but keep young Harry with you. If there is anything important to report, send him down; do you understand?" The wind was building steadily and Griffin wanted no misheard reports wrecking anything he might try to do.

Nairn knuckled his forehead, before making off into the darkness. Griffin turned to Davies. "Guns are ready and primed?"

The older man nodded; they had taken all the necessary precautions before heading for the coast. "Pass the word along; we are closing with an enemy vessel, probably to starboard, but I cannot be certain. I expect to turn before we meet and present the larboard battery; larboard: make sure they understand that. Then hoist ensign and pennant."

No flag would be visible on such a night, but the government decreed that they were to be flown whenever a revenue cutter was in chase, or likely to engage an enemy, and official procedure must be adhered to whatever the weather.

Davies moved away without a word. Griffin waited for the message to be relayed and registered, then called for the cutter to turn to starboard and heave to. Even in such foul conditions the hands moved well, hauling in the main and fore until they were holding their position as much as was possible. They were far enough away from the shore to be safe and *Bee* was lying broadside on to a seaward enemy, making certain that she would not pass. The rain and wind were all but ignored and everyone grew tense as the waiting continued.

And it was then that it happened. A light erupted from the direction of the beach, the brightness almost painful in contrast to the black to which they had become accustomed. It was a rocket, and must be the signal for the dragoons to attack, but it would also have the effect of silhouetting the tiny *Bee*, making her obvious to any oncoming vessel.

"Stand by your guns, men!" Griffin shouted, his voice cracking. The light was not sufficient to reveal anything further out to sea, but all on board *Bee* knew themselves to be extremely visible, and felt oddly exposed in the cold night.

A yell came from the shore, and Griffin turned to see several eerie blue lights being tossed into what appeared to be a large crowd of men and equipment. That would be from the dragoons, he told himself. They must be marking out their enemy before running them down, but the extra illumination was not welcomed by any aboard the cutter.

"Another sail!"

It was the voice of Harry, the ship's boy and Griffin tore himself away from the fascination of the shore.

"Where away?" he called.

There was a pause; clearly the lad was having second thoughts, and Nairn stayed quiet. Either he could not make the sighting, or was even less certain.

"Over there!" Harry eventually shouted, to little benefit. "Windward," he went on to explain. "And it's big."

Griffin fumed, then the more mature voice of Nairn took over.

"Vessel in sight off our larboard bow," he said, after a brief discussion. "Brig, I would say, and coming down with the wind. Looks to me like it's heading for us."

"Bring her to the wind," Griffin shouted, and men began to move about him. In his mind's eye he could see the chart, and knew they had enough sea room to stand off to the east. But the enemy, a far more powerful enemy by the sounds of it, was already under way and would be moving quickly. Soon they might well be caught against them, the wind and the falling tide.

"Take her eastwards, and set the tops'l." Perhaps it would have been better to have spent more time on sail drill, Griffin pondered as the hull turned and picked up speed, even though the crew was proficient in their seamanship. Men made for the shrouds and soon he felt the deck beneath him shudder as the canvas cracked and streamed overhead. She finally came onto the starboard tack and, with the fresh sail set, the small craft began to power through the waves at a fair pace. But they were still close to the shore, and the tide was starting to fall fast.

"What do you see there?" he called up.

"She's coming up on our starboard counter, though may be turning east. And she's a big bugger," Nairn told him.

"Penny to a pound it'll belong to the Warrens," Davies said. Griffin looked to him, but his face was hidden in the dark. "They have three, all over two-hundred tons," the mate continued.

"Yes." Griffin remembered being told of them before. As he recalled, each were well-armed, with guns more numerous than *Bee*'s and half as powerful again.

"I'd say this was planned," Davies went on, relentlessly. "That smack was just a lure, maybe the whole landing was, come to that."

There was still disturbance visible on shore, but Griffin could not tell quite what was about; neither did he care over much: he had his own concerns. Certainly a battle was in progress, and more lights had been added, apparently to mark *Bee* even more distinctly. Then a bright orange flash came from seaward, showing briefly just off their beam and followed by the ripping sound of round shot passing overhead. The dull boom of a cannon came shortly after, and probably less than a cable off.

That would be a testing shot, Griffin supposed. It had passed them just astern, but would be sufficient to allow the opposing gunners to correct their aim. Without doubt they were near enough, and large enough, to do the business. Davies was swearing uselessly, as Griffin tried to clear his head. The darkness in that direction was quite impenetrable; he could only guess at the current position of the enemy, but *Bee* was moving properly now and almost certainly a good deal faster than them. The cutter may still be silhouetted by light from the shore, but in no time would be as invisible to the smugglers as they were to her.

He was proven right a few seconds later. With a tight ripple of flashes that must have come from at least ten guns, the black night was split by the combined blaze of a broadside. Both Griffin and Davies found themselves ducking instinctively, but it was soon clear that the enemy had indeed lost sight of her, and not allowed for *Bee's* increase in speed, as the shots flew a good twenty feet beyond her taffrail.

"Take her to starboard!" Griffin called. Speed was currently their only advantage; he had to add unpredictability and, if possible, even an element of fear.

The hull heeled as *Bee* was brought more firmly across the wind, and her pace increased.

"Starboard battery, prepare!" The men were still trimming the sails for the new course, and there was confusion in the darkness. Someone tripped and yelled, and a flash of light showed briefly as a battle lantern fell from its perch between two cannon, but shortly afterwards the first gun captain was signalling his piece ready.

"There she is, off the starboard bow!" The cry came from further forward and was anonymous, but all followed the direction and the dark prow of a two-hundred ton brig came briefly into view less than a cable off, and bearing down on them.

"Another three points to starboard – bring her round!" Griffin shouted. The cutter heeled further and her square sail began to flap, untended, but *Bee* was now heading to cross the bow of the enemy. They may pass ahead, collide, or let the prey slip by, but Griffin knew he must take the chance, and close as fast as he could.

"On my word!" He had moved from the binnacle, and stood almost next to the sternmost cannon, while peering desperately out into the night. There was just the faintest outline of the brig still on her original course, and Griffin knew, instinctively, that they were ideally placed.

"Steady..." The last thing he wanted was for a gun to go off early; it would both weaken his broadside, and advertise their presence. The enemy was almost upon them now; it was going to be close. Griffin knew he could not afford a collision; a smuggling craft was likely to be well manned, and *Bee* would be taken in an instant.

"Ease off," he muttered to the helmsmen, and the cutter fell back slightly. Then, with a rush that made the whole thing almost feel unexpected, *Bee* came up on the bowsprit of the brig. The other vessel was still a good forty feet off, and Griffin was banking on his next action slowing her considerably.

"Fire!"

One gun erupted on his command, but the others took longer. During their exercises Griffin had made it clear he held scant regard for Royal Navy discipline; far better a ragged broadside and each captain making certain of their target, than crisp and rapid fire where marksmanship accounted for nothing. Light from their own guns blinded those on deck, but still they could see some result from the effort: a fire had been started.

Flames were soon racing upwards and, even drenched as it would be greedily consumed the canvas of the brig's fore topsail. The blaze cast an eerie tint to the scene: there was further commotion as her jib collapsed across the forecastle, and the topgallant yard could be seen to sway drunkenly. Then, with a series of cracks and a tearing that was audible on board the cutter, the enemy's fore topmast sagged, just above its base, and fell to one side in a muddle of canvas, lines and spars.

* * *

Griffin brought himself back from the spectacle with an effort. About him men were cheering, but *Bee* was by no means out of the mire. Another enemy, possibly larger and certainly more prepared, may well be out there in the darkness. Even if she were unable to spot them, the recent broadside would give some indication of their position, and the brig, though disabled, was still capable of landing a devastating broadside if they gave her the chance.

"Starboard the helm," he snapped. "Take her east." The important thing was to move, and do so as quickly as possible: speed was certainly their major asset and if it could be used to get them home and under the protection of the shore batteries, then so much the better. The cutter swung round until she had the wind almost on her quarter and was fairly pounding through the waves. He could maintain this course only for a while, then they would have to head south to avoid the headland and give a measure of sea room before finally making directly for Newhaven.

The thought of allowing smugglers to chase him home was repugnant, but better that than being sunk, or taken, and they had delivered a fair measure of damage to a much larger enemy. The cutter was still darkened, although Griffin had recovered most of his night sight and, when Davies approached, could almost make out his face as the mate spoke.

"Reckon we was hooked good an' proper there, sir," he said, as quietly as the weather would allow.

"Maybe so," Griffin agreed. "But we've made a reasonable fist of it so far. I don't think they expected us to fight back quite as we did."

Davies' teeth flashed in the night. "No, sir; I reckons you're right there. If it was a Warren craft, and I'm sure it were, they wouldn't be used to having someone stand up to them."

Griffin said nothing, but he was warmed by the words.

"Heading back to harbour?" the mate asked.

"I think we must." Having to make a reply helped to rationalise his thoughts. "We might have got off lucky, but I wouldn't wish to take such a chance again."

"Very good, sir." Davies replied.

The brig was still visible astern, and a small fire was burning from within her forecastle; men were obviously attempting to sort the damage, and lights from their lanterns could be seen.

"The coast creeps south round these parts." Davies spoke cautiously, but Griffin accepted the hint in good heart.

"Bring her to starboard once more," he said. "Take in the tops'l and head south."

With the tide falling and the natural curve of the coastline against him, he must remain conscious of the dwindling depth. Knowing where one enemy was gave him a bearing, but Griffin still had the strange inkling that there might be others. From what he knew of the Warrens they would have wished to make sure of the revenue cutter's destruction, and as he stared out into the filthy night he wondered if another really was lurking out there.

The cutter slowed as she turned, and the sails were adjusted, then continued at a more moderate pace. A flash of lightening from the south suddenly lit the area, making all on board jump, and robbing them of much of their night vision.

"Sail in sight!" Griffin's nerves, already stretched to breaking, almost snapped at Nairn's call. "Just off our larboard beam: a small cutter or a smack, and running under a main and fore."

"Heading?" Griffin questioned, as a deep rumble of thunder rolled out of the darkness.

"East, nor-east," Nairn replied, when the sound had finally died. "Set for Newhaven or Shoreham if you asks me, but I only caught a glimpse and cannot make her now."

"Doesn't sound like a Warren," Davies shouted and Griffin felt his body relax. No, the mate was right; far more likely to be a fisherman caught in the storm, or even another smuggler. In either case, the vessel was of no direct threat to them.

The lightening seemed to have killed the tempest; Griffin noticed that the wind was easing and the rain had ceased to fall in quite such volume, but still any degree of distance vision was all but impossible. He glanced back at the shore. Brighthelmstone beach had merged into the gloom of night; only a dim glow showed where a bonfire, or something similar, was burning and might mark the place. He wondered how Jones and the dragoons had fared. Was the whole event a ruse, set up simply to trap him and possibly the land forces? Or had a run truly been intended, and the brig merely brought in to sink the tiny cutter that had been causing such problems of late? Looking at the light he gauged there was enough sea room for them to make the turn for Newhaven now, and had just ordered the cutter back to the east when a second bolt of lightning came to interrupt his thoughts.

"Another sail." It was Nairn's voice again. "Off to starboard, but bearing for the coast."

Now that was far more worrying; on such a night, any vessel that chose to head directly for shore would be doing so for a reason.

"She's cutter rigged, and a proper thumper, more'n an 'undred and fifty tons," the lookout continued. Once more the thunder came, interrupting his words, but Griffin thought he knew the rest even before Nairn repeated: "I'd say it were another Warren!"

Something was moving above, and soon young Harry could be seen slipping down a backstay. Griffin and Davies waited while he gained the deck then, staggering, made for them.

"Mr Nairn sent me," he said, knuckling his forehead. "Says to say a cutter is off our starboard bow, and heading north; he didn't see it for more than a second." His eyes grew large and conspiratorial. "I missed it completely, but Mr Nairn says he's certain, sir."

It was good Nairn had caught the sighting, and had the confidence to report it, unconfirmed. Griffin guessed it would be a second vessel stationed to block their escape, in case they avoided the first. He thought fast; they could either continue on their present course and head all out for home, or turn away to windward, and take *Bee* close hauled and further from the land, hoping to skirt round the new threat. There was no light on shore now, so both would have about the same view of the other and down to luck that Nairn had been looking in that direction when the lightning struck. But had the Warrens been as fortunate? Did they know where the *Bee* was, or had they just seen the gunfire from earlier on and be guessing?

"Mr Nairn is sure of the enemy's position?" he demanded.

"Yes, sir. He was certain. She'll still be ahead." The lad had a quick brain, and was taking the change of course into consideration. "Be about a cable an' a half, sir; maybe slightly more. If we keeps on this heading we'll pass her," he said seriously.

"Very good," Griffin said, keeping his voice purposefully gruff and resisting the temptation to pat the youngster on the head. "Return to the masthead and tell Mr Nairn he was right to send you down."

The boy knuckled his forehead again, and set off for the weather shrouds as Griffin turned to Davies.

"I see no point in trying to evade," he said. "We have speed in our favour."

"Indeed, sir," the mate replied. "An' if we move, we may even make it back over the bar this tide."

Griffin gave a short laugh; the prospect of their home port seemed very attractive, as long as the enemy that lay between and could sink them with a single broadside was ignored.

"I'd like a sharp lookout for'ard, Mr Davies," he said. "And hands to the starboard guns, if you please."

The rain had begun again in earnest, and the men, by now all thoroughly soaked, were crouching behind the shelter of the bulwarks as *Bee* surged on through the heavy weather. Within thirty seconds, the fishing smack came into view from deck and was reported. Griffin moved across and leaned over the side rail, squinting slightly as he peered into the gloom. Yes, there she was, right enough, and they would pass her comfortably. There was something familiar about the rig, and he was just deciding what, when a series of shouts rang out and called him back.

The mystery cutter had emerged from out of a particularly dense patch of squall, and was in the midst of turning to starboard, less than half a cable in front of the fishing boat. She was large, a good two-hundred tons, and her broad hull rolled deep into the tumbling waves as she manoeuvred.

"Port your helm!" Griffin roared. The enemy had clearly intended to pounce on them from out of the storm, and was just a little premature. With luck the *Bee* would be able to pass her to seaward. Then the night was split by the fire of a dozen guns, as the cutter unleashed her broadside.

"She's firing on the fisherman!" the mate bellowed in surprise. Griffin returned to the rail but they were still turning and he could see nothing. He ran back and tried to look past the foresail: Davies was right, the smugglers must have mistaken the smack for *Bee*; they were many tons apart, while the rig was of a totally different size and proportion. But on such a filthy night it was not an impossible scenario. *Bee* completed her turn and was heading south with both the enemy cutter and the fisherman to larboard. The smack's rig had been badly hit: she was totally dismasted, while *Bee* was now creeping up on the cutter, and would soon be in the perfect position for a rake.

"Larboard guns, ready!" Davies shouted this time, and the gunners moved across to the opposite battery, just as the revenue cutter presented her broadside to the enemy's vulnerable stern; they were less than fifty feet from her: it was ideal.

"Fire!" Griffin yelled, and the guns spoke with credible speed, the shots raining down almost as one on the sitting target. As they watched, the stern appeared to crumble and the cutter itself fell off the wind and almost staggered under such an unforeseen assault. Her boom swung with the wind, and she was soon in irons.

"I'd chance they weren't expecting that!" Davies chuckled with glee. From the smugglers' point of view the attack must surely have come from nowhere, so intent were they on firing on what they had taken to be the revenue cutter. The men were already starting to serve the cannon, but Griffin interrupted their efforts and ordered them to secure their pieces. If what he had in mind worked, they would not be needing the larboard battery again that night. And if he was wrong, if he failed, it would hardly matter anyway.

"Take her to larboard?" Davies asked, but Griffin shook his head.

"No, keep her as she is – I want us as close to the wind as we will stand and then some." His eyes seemed unusually alight as he turned to the men at the tiller. "Tell me, lads; can you box the compass?" Forsyth and Conway understood immediately, and the cutter continued to turn.

The start was not entirely smooth, as many were still engaged with the guns, but soon *Bee* was heading away from both the enemy and the dismasted smack.

"Prepare to tack!" Davies shouted, as they came into the wind, but all by now were aware of the captain's intentions, and the cutter moved swiftly through the dead area. Then her boom swung across as the wind found them on the opposite tack, and *Bee* continued to turn.

"Ready starboard battery!"

It could hardly have been tighter; *Bee* returned almost exactly to her previous position, with the damaged smack off her larboard bow and the enemy cutter, apparently out of control, to starboard.

"With luck they won't have a full broadside," Davies shouted, his eyes alight, but Griffin ignored him.

"I want a line passed to the smack," he said. "There may not be anyone alive to take it, but if there is, we're going to tow them out of danger."

The mate responded instantly; even without the threat of a hostile enemy, the smack would be wrecked on the shore in time. Two lengths of three-inch cable were flaked ready by timberheads set at either side of *Bee*'s stern for just such a situation, and Davies himself collected the free end of the lighter heaving line. "Second time in under a week," he reflected, but no one was listening as the cutter bore down on both vessels.

Bee would pass the fisherman seconds before her guns bore on the smuggler, and Griffin watched intently as she closed. Then everything seemed to happen at once. Two figures stood amongst the wreckage in the smack and one waved, clearly guessing Griffin's intention. Davies, who had been spinning the weighted end of the line threw it, almost absent-mindedly, and there was a brief cheer when it was caught and the hawser pulled in and made fast. But the slack had hardly been taken up when the first gun captain was signalling the enemy cutter in range.

"Fire!" Griffin roared, and their broadside bit into the smuggler's hull. A moment's pause, and there came three shots from the larger vessel, although none hit. Then *Bee* was apparently tugged backwards in the water as the weight of the smack came upon the tow. The timberhead groaned, and there was an ominous creak from somewhere deep in the revenue cutter's vitals, but soon the smashed hull of the smack was under control and being hauled through the rolling waves at a speed far in excess of any ever managed under her own sail.

Davies looked at his captain and a deep chuckle erupted from his throat. "Masterful, sir: masterful!" They had all but passed their wounded enemy and Griffin thought he could see figures on her deck. Then another gun went off, presumably firing at the fisherman, or maybe just in frustration. Despite having the smack in tow, *Bee* was making a good six knots and it would take a while for the larger cutter to even get under way. "If we starboard our helm a point," the mate continued, "we can still clear Burrow Cliff but be under the lee of the shore batteries."

Griffin looked to larboard but could see only the occasional light ashore, and had no real idea of exactly where they were.

"You don't mind me saying, sir – only I knows these waters pretty well."

Griffin grinned in the dark of the night. "No, Mr Davies, I mind not a bit."

Chapter Twelve

When *Bee* was finally moored and the smack had been dealt with, Griffin had no mind to return to his lodgings. The strain of three days at sea, followed by the evening's exertions, had taken its toll; he collapsed into his cot, and was still sound asleep when Davies, accompanied by Harry, who carried a tray of bread, bacon and hot tea, entered his day cabin.

"Breakfast, sir," the mate called. Griffin emerged from his tiny sleeping quarters, rubbing his eyes. "Set it down on the table, lad," Davies told the boy and made as if to leave. But Griffin knew the mate well enough to guess that he would have been up since first light, and felt guilty about sleeping late himself.

"Why don't you stay and join me?" He asked, before yawning deeply.

"If that would be agreeable," Davies replied, brightening a little, before adding: "not you," to Harry.

Griffin had pulled on a clean shirt and trousers and sat back on one of the cabin's upholstered lockers while Davies poured two large mugs of black tea, which he proceeded to sweeten to a mild syrup with sugar. The cabin still bore the smell of marine glue and paint, but the scent of freshly fried bacon was stronger and far more attractive.

"You should have wakened me before." Griffin grunted.

"There was no need," Davies told him as he collected a piece of the cut bread and folded it about a chunk of meat. "Been down to the yard to check on the capture, an' Dwyer sent a message that he would be calling later, but I didn't feel there were cause to be disturbing you."

Griffin was grateful. By the time *Bee* had scraped over the bar with the last of the falling tide, he had felt completely done in. There were busy periods during his time with the East India Company, but few competed with those experienced in the revenue service to date. One of the fishermen had been wounded and taken to the parish surgery; another was missing, most probably dead: knocked overboard by the broadside. But the third, and the captain of the smack, appeared perfectly alive and well, and it had come as little surprise to discover him to be Sophie's brother.

Quite what Matthew Ward had been doing out on such a night had yet to be confirmed, although in Griffin's mind there was little doubt. The storm had been strong since the previous afternoon. No fisherman would have chosen to be at sea in such weather, although the conditions were perfect for a landing. He might not have been involved with the Horsebridge gang's venture further down the coast, but probably had other interests to pursue. Consequently it was slightly ironic that Ward should have fallen foul of the Warren vessel, and doubly so that they confused his boat with a revenue cutter.

The smack was currently in the legal dock where in due course she would be searched. Should any contraband be discovered, he would be charged. Griffin had little control over that, nor the outcome, which might even cost the lad his life, although doubtless there was one person who would blame him.

The fact that Ward had already been rescued from probable death might count for something in Sophie's eyes, although Griffin's last thought before he fell into a deep sleep had been to wonder if she was responsible for alerting the Warrens in the first place.

"I reckon someone peached on us," Davies said, unconsciously mirroring his captain's thinking, through a mouthful of breakfast. He paused, took a gulp of tea and breathed out in satisfaction, then continued.

"They were waiting for *Bee* to appear; there's no other reason for two heavy Warren craft to be a'sea: neither could have been unloaded in such weather, even if they was beached." He belched expertly, before adding: "No, they was on the hunt: and with us as their quarry."

Griffin accepted the comment without visible reaction, although there was a cold hard feeling deep inside him. "They wouldn't have been there by chance?" he asked hopefully, but Davies shook his head.

"Unlikely; a run like that would have been a series of small craft; there'd have been no need for such a force; far too expensive, both in men and materials. No, it was the barkie they were after, and they damn near got her." His eye caught Griffin's and he gave a nod. "If it weren't for you, they probably would have. All the lads appreciate what you did, and we reckon it were worth a late caulk."

Griffin felt his face redden; it was a noble speech, especially when delivered by one such as Davies, but undeserved all the same. Admittedly he had brought the cutter back undamaged, and dealt out a few costly broadsides to the Warrens in return, but that didn't excuse the fact that Griffin had placed them in danger in the first place. If Davies discovered it was his captain who had effectively given the game away, he might hold a very different view. It was one thing to risk his command and crew in pursuance of revenue business, quite another to consort with someone who would reveal their plans to the enemy.

He was reasonably certain that nothing had been said on their walk back, but Sophie could easily have overheard the discussion with Jones. She had been standing only a few feet away, after all. Were it to have been any other civilian Griffin would have delayed talking with Jones until they could do so in private. But because it was Sophie, because he had a liking for her, and she had made a brief and unsupported promise to help, he had allowed her to stay. And with her related to two known smugglers... really, what could he have been thinking of?

To know exactly where *Bee* would be at a certain time was valuable information in itself, and that was ignoring any trap the Warrens might be intending to spring. Sophie would have been well rewarded, or at least owed a favour or two. In the cold light of morning he could also see that, if the cutter had been caught, or should he or any of his men have been taken, even killed, it would have made life so much easier for her brother and father. Jones was too strong a man to have let the information out, and the dragoon commander must, by his very nature, be sound. Both were professionals, after all, and either would suffer personally if the plan were revealed. He found himself wishing there was some other likely candidate; that he had told all to Dobson, or Dwyer, or even the drunken Willett. But no, Sophie was not just the only one who could have spoken to the Horsebridge gang: she also had the most to gain from doing so.

The more he thought about it, the bigger fool he felt. He had trusted her for the simple reason that they had enjoyed a couple of intimate conversations, he particularly liked the look of her face, and some absurd inner feeling told him that he could. Worse; simply because he was such a purblind fool, he had assumed her to be likewise, and expected a grown woman to have forgotten any loyalty and affection for her own family, in favour of a man she had only just met.

"Are you feeling quite well, sir?" Davies asked, clearly concerned, and Griffin pulled himself up. He must indeed have gone quiet, and his hand was all but crushing an untouched lump of breakfast that would now be cold.

"Yes, splendid; thank you." Griffin took a bite from the bread and began to chew, although his mouth was inordinately dry and he would far rather have spat the food out. "Just thinking of what we must to do today," he continued, after he was finally able to swallow.

"Ask me, we have to meet up with Jackie Jones," the mate continued, helping himself to more bacon. "It's likely the land force made arrests; I'd like to find out who."

Griffin's mood lifted slightly. "Yes, there could be a Warren or two taken," he said. Strange, he had never met any of the family and yet, for a number of reasons, they were currently the most hated people in his life.

"I'd be doubting that," Davies said. "I still thinks we were the reason for last night's little jaunt. My guess it will be a bunch of bought men, working for the gang. And it may not even have been a proper run."

"Surely they would not have gone to so much trouble?"

"Oh, I've known it before. You might not see it but, to the Warrens and their like, there is only one war, and that is against the Treasury. Forget Frenchmen, we are their true enemy: once they have dealt with us there is little to stop them doing exactly what they will. Why, you yourself could be a rich man if you let the Horsebridge gang take you into their employ. Once the land guard and the revenue cruiser is working for them there is nothing left to worry about, except maybe the occasional inquisitive Navy ship."

"But we are at war; the French are all but ready to invade, and the country is close to bankrupt: surely they must see that?"

The mate shook his head. "They don't see nothing beyond their purses, and would go to any amount of trouble to shut us down. Less than a year ago they were trying to discredit your predecessor, Commander Carter. Sent a pair of luggers in to the Cuckmere on a moonless night and we gave chase. Even in the dark we could tell they were filled to the gunwales; it looked like a prime seizure. We brought them both to book, right enough, and saw them into harbour: then what did we find?"

Griffin waited.

"All the tubs were filled with spring water, and the crates held nothing more than ships' stores and exempt goods. Made us look like right chubs, I can say. Then the Warrens takes us to court and sues for wrongful retention. The Treasury was forced to pay out handsomely and we had to escort their boats back out of the harbour."

"That is ridiculous; could no one see there was ample cause for suspicion?"

"Oh yes, the Commander made quite a scene, as I recall; not that it did him any good. The magistrates were hardly inclined to listen, and who could blame them when they were as keen as anyone to see the service under Warren control."

Griffin shuffled uncomfortably on the locker. This was certainly proving to be a task far harder than he had imagined. He glanced up at Davies, and a sudden impulse made him ask: "And have you ever considered working for the Warrens?"

"Considered it?" The mate snorted in surprise. "You mean turn a blind eye, like Admiral Nelson did in the spring?"

"Exactly."

Davies laughed. "Oh, certainly; we all has, at one time or another. An' to be truthful, I'm not against letting the occasional small trader through now; not for money, but if I knows them and their situation. With the Warrens it's a different story, though. You might convince yourself that a single run can go unnoticed and ain't going to cause anyone no problem, then discover they got you as firmly as if you were permanently on their pay roll. I'm all for a quiet life, but there has to be a limit."

"And Matthew Ward was below that limit?" Griffin asked.

"When he was running the occasional tub and a bit of illicit baccy there weren't no real harm," Davies replied. "If he'd stuck to that he would have done fine; we could have ignored him, and he wouldn't hold it over no one's head." He glanced at his captain cautiously. "But it don't do to give them Warrens an inch of leeway, or you'll be in their grip for eternity."

"I'll confess I came here with a different understanding." Griffin spoke slowly. "Illicit importing is what we are here to stop, and giving even the smallest trader a free run means we are failing in our duty. To my mind you did young Ward no favours by being lenient; it was only a question of time before he got greedy. We captured him last night, but that was pure chance. Had we not, there is no telling where it would have ended; next thing you know he'd have been recruiting more, and buying a second boat. And afore long, we'd have another gang on our hands."

"So you'd be against it, then; turning a blind eye, I mean?" Davies' own eyes were twinkling.

Griffin gave a short laugh. "I said I thought we should always uphold the law, and still do, though admit my views have changed a touch of late. In certain cases there may be the need for discretion. A blind eye is all very well, if used selectively: perhaps as a stiff warning, and one that is followed up with action should it be ignored. But that must be as far as it goes. We cannot do our duty with both eyes shut."

Davies considered this and was about to reply when sound of a landsman clumping unsteadily down the steps to the chart room alerted them both. They were silent, as the murmur of a man's voice could be heard, then there was a sharp tap on the deal frame. Griffin was about to call for whoever it was to enter when the door opened, and both he and the mate were surprised to see Dwyer outside the cabin.

"Ah, Commander, and Mr Davies; I see you are still at your breakfast: forgive me," he said, easing himself in through the door and peering superciliously down at the two officers. "Though I would have thought an early visit to Custom House would have been more appropriate in the circumstances."

"I had no appointment," Griffin said, the defiance strong in his voice. "I will doubtless call on the collector in due course but first, yes you are correct, I am taking my breakfast – as you undoubtedly already have. If not you would be welcome to share ours, though you may see, we have little room."

"I was up in good time, sir," The comptroller snarled, drawing himself up and allowing his head to brush the overhead beam.

"And were you at work half the night?" Davies asked.

"It is indeed that work that I wish to speak with you about," Dwyer continued, otherwise ignoring the mate. "It seems your actions have upset several, including some important members of the community."

"If you mean the Warrens, then yes, I fired on two of their vessels and seized another belonging to a smuggler. Such action is the nature of my craft, sir; indeed it is why all of us are employed."

"You seem to fire rather too readily, Commander," the man spat back. "Mr Dobson has spoken of it to you before, I believe."

"We was under attack," Davies said belligerently. "What would you have us do?"

"I would have you behave like responsible officers of the revenue." Dwyer glared down on them, but each were equal to his stare and, even in the act of setting his breakfast down and standing, Davies seemed to be carrying out a rare act of aggression.

"I don't know what you are trying to do," Griffin said, taking the mate's lead and bringing himself as upright as he could in the low cabin. "But if you think you can board my command and speak to me in this manner, you are very much mistaken."

"Sir, it may not remain your command for much longer." Dwyer curled his lip slightly. "Mr Dobson is about to make his regular return to the Board, and is talking of calling an enquiry into your actions: unless you change your ways, that is."

"I have no fear of any investigation you may wish to mount, Mr Dwyer. And, by changing my ways, are you advising me to follow your example?" The previous conversation had already woken Griffin's rebellious nature, and it was perhaps unfortunate that the comptroller was presenting such a suitable target for its force. "Should I be in the pay of the free traders, or is that an advantage only certain people may enjoy?"

The civilian began to bluster, but Griffin was well into his stride. "You speak of me not doing my duty; I trust that you have sufficient evidence to back such assertions. I have my journals, and can call on certain people to support what they contain. And do you think I did not attain my present position without sound connections in some quarter?" He watched as each of his shots struck home. There was no reason why Dwyer should know that his uncle was now dead, and nothing in the man's weasel face said that he did. "I am certainly not afeared of an enquiry; indeed, should either you or Mr Dobson continue in your current manner, I will be only too pleased to call one myself." Griffin knew that he may be overstepping the mark, but sensed Davies' support, and gave his anger full vent. "Do not presume to intimidate me, sir. I had thought it already plain that I will not be bullied."

Dwyer's gaze flashed about the tiny cabin, as if looking for reassurance in the wooden panels and plain furnishings. "You shall hear more of this, I promise. In the meanwhile, I trust you will present yourself to the collector at the earliest opportunity – and properly dressed." His glance took in Griffin's crumpled shirt and trousers judging them as if they were little more than sackcloth. "And I will expect you to have a suitable explanation for the booty I see in your own quarters."

With that he scuffed his boot against the two half-ankers seized a few days earlier, before turning and storming, as effectively as he could, out of the tiny doorway.

* * *

"Couldn't raise the dragoons as I intended, see." Jones told Griffin as they walked away from Custom House. The morning was cold and the road still damp, even though the rain had finally stopped. There was a change in the wind as well; it had continued to back during the night and was now blowing from the east. They had been to speak with Dobson, although little had been added to what Dwyer said earlier. Jones was very much the hero of the hour, but Griffin's popularity seemed decidedly on the wane. The collector at Shoreham was posting an official protest to the Board of Customs, both about the withholding of information, and *Bee* being active in his sector, and it seemed likely he would be listened to. While that was being considered, Griffin had also been handed an official letter advising him that future unnecessary endangerment of the lives of his men, or the fabric of his command, would result in his immediate dismissal. He was angry, but also concerned; it took little imagination to see how Dobson might present the previous evening's events in a report. Griffin could be shown to have been reckless, even incompetent, and with a positive queue of young naval officers vying for his position, this time next week might easily see him on the beach. But Jones was still speaking, and it was with effort that he tried to concentrate on his words.

"Colonel Douglas was not unwilling to help, but there was a shipment they had to escort on the same day. Looking back I'd be willing to bet the Warrens might even have got word of it, which was why they chose last night for the landing."

"The yeomanry did well enough, however," Griffin commented absent-mindedly.

"Oh yes, it were fine, as far as it went," Jones agreed. "Though you can't expect much from a bunch of farm hands on cart-horses. We might have done better with the military behind us, but it would still be a fair bet there wasn't a Warren on land within a mile of Brighthelmstone."

"So who did you arrest?"

Jones shrugged. "Thirty-eight assorted wastrels and labourers. They'll be up at the assizes at the end of the month. Most will get off with a fine, as they are needed back on the land. A few might be held for a judge, but only if we can discover who was supposed to be in charge. Oh, and then there's your man Ward; he is an exception, of course."

Griffin flushed. Why should Jones refer to Sophie's brother as 'his man'? Was their relationship less of a secret than he had thought? Then he reminded himself that, as the cutter had been involved in Ward's capture, it was natural for Jones to speak so. Besides, even if the entire world knew about him and Sophie, it meant little now.

"He will be tried separately, I assume?"

"Oh yes." Jones was positive. "No denying what he was up to, nor that he was in charge. They might send him to Lewes, or London. If he is especially unlucky, he may well end up swinging at Newgate, then hanging in chains on Bishopstone Common."

Jones' words sent a chill down Griffin's back. This was not what he had intended from the night's work. He cleared his throat.

"And what of the Warrens?" he asked.

"Nothing seen or heard of them," Jones replied. "None have been anywhere near Newhaven, far as I can tell. Mind, I'm not sayin' they weren't afloat; old man Warren is 'specially fond of his war ships, even though he could never be called a seaman himself. All of them cost a small fortune to buy and maintain, so it's rare they sail without at least one of the family on board. If you'd have made a capture last night, we might be telling a very different story."

"Both were considerably larger than the *Bee*," Griffin replied coldly. "I think we did well by simply damaging them." He felt that if he didn't say something in his defence, no one else would.

"Oh no," Jones hastened to reassure him. "I'm not suggesting you could have, just that things might be easier now if you had, that's all." He gave Griffin a brief sidelong glance, then continued. "But wherever they are, they're sitting pretty and, just because they ain't around themselves, that doesn't mean their work is not being done by others."

Griffin supposed he was right. The family might have lost a bit the previous evening, but that would have been expected if they had been trying to lure him into the area. Perhaps the *Bee* had not been destroyed as they intended, but if he was to be dismissed as her commander, the job was all but completed anyway.

"So what do you intend now?" Jones asked. They had left the town far behind and were close to the road that led to the Tide Mills, where Griffin still had a room.

"Get back to sea as soon as possible," he replied gloomily. "At least then I have some control, and there may not be the opportunity in a few days from now."

Jones looked up suddenly and stopped. "There's strange," he said in wonder. "What in goodness is going on over yonder?"

* * *

Sophie saw the smoke at roughly the same time. A thick greasy column that wafted over the town with the wind. She paused for a second, before breaking into a run, her dress flying wildly as she hurried down the path to the mills, dodging the occasional passer-by who had paused to watch, or was making a slower progress towards the scene.

The far row of cottages was properly ablaze, and probably had been for some while. A line of men with buckets were throwing ditch water from last night's storm through a broken downstairs window of the central house, but it was clear that it, as well as those to either side, was a loss.

"Is there anyone inside?" she asked, breathless, as the heat from the fire brought her to a halt. One of the men was the blacksmith from the mills; Sophie knew him as a regular in The Star. He broke away, handing his empty bucket to another bystander.

"Cannot say for sure," he told her. "Old Mr Willett lives there, and he ain't about."

Sophie closed her eyes for a second; she had actually forgotten about the elderly man. "But there's someone else," she insisted. "A customs officer: he took a room here just the other day."

The blacksmith went to laugh out loud and would have, were it not for the concern on the girl's face. "Well, if he's in that lot he'll no longer be a trouble," he said, obviously controlling his pleasure.

She glanced about in desperation, but almost immediately turned back. "Well, aren't you even going to try?" she demanded.

This time he did smile, although the expression was without humour. "There wouldn't be the point, duck," he said, his voice now a little more gentle. "Fire's spread too thick, there won't be a stairway. And look, it's already up to the roof."

Her gaze travelled upwards, just in time to see the entire structure collapse onto the house in a mass of burning timbers and cracking peg tiles. The flames leapt higher as fresh air found them, and the couple instinctively took a step backwards with the increased heat.

"It'll do no good standing watching," the man told her. "I'm used to a bit of warm, but it won't make you any the prettier. There's the Lamport girl over by the bridge. Hers is the house next door, and there's little we can do to save it; chance is she could do with a friendly word."

Sophie followed the man's pointed finger and saw Emma standing next to the mill pond holding young Joseph in her arms. The two had been friends for most of their lives, attending the same dame school as Matthew and Joe. A group of men were starting to rig a pump next to the mill pond; Sophie moved across and gently guided the girl to one side.

"Come on, Ems; they'll be the better for us not getting in the way," she told her. The girl appeared to be in a trance, but allowed herself to be guided to the rail fence opposite where Sophie helped her sit on the top bar. She also went to take the baby, who was enjoying a rare moment of sleep, but Emma had him locked firmly in her grip, and Sophie relented.

"Was Joe in the house?" she asked quietly, rubbing her friend's back.

Emma shook her head. "No, no he didn't come back last night." Her voice was weak and frail. "I was afeared for him, particularly when I hears the cruiser had come in." She gave a half-smile. "Now it looks as if he were safer at sea."

"Well, if he wasn't in the house, and the cutter's back in harbour, you have nothing to worry about," Sophie said in her firmest voice. "He's probably in the boat; don't take on so."

Emma flashed a look in Sophie's direction. "Don't take on so? My home's a burning, and I'm not supposed to be concerned?"

Sophie fiddled with the tie of her dress. "Well, it was hardly a very nice house, Ems," she flustered. "I mean, you made it wonderful, but it wasn't yours. Old man Catt charged a small fortune for living there, an' it were never that warm."

"It's warm enough now," Emma replied, and rested against her friend's shoulder.

"Come and live with us at The Star," Sophie said gently, wrapping an arm about her. "There's plenty of room for all, an' you can help out in the parlour, if it makes you feel any better. Not for permanent; just till you gets another place."

The pump was in use now, and clouds of steam began to erupt from the lower levels of the buildings, while further sparks flew up from the roof. Some of the mill workers had finished their shift and were standing in groups watching, fascinated, and even William Catt was there, speaking to one of the foremen, and pointing at the cottages with his cane.

Then Sophie saw Griffin running up to the cottages with Jones, the riding officer, puffing behind. Her body grew tense, alerting her friend.

"That's the commander," Emma told her. "Do you know him?"

"He was staying at the inn," Sophie said, in a tone as flat as she could manage.

"Was he indeed?" Emma gave a wicked smile. "An' you never said."

"I don't tell you about all our guests," Sophie retorted. "Come on, let's see if he knows where Joe is about."

They stood up and walked towards Griffin, who was talking to one of the men. He glanced round on seeing them approach, then registered Sophie's presence with a rapidly changing expression.

"Mr Willett is dead," he told her, as if in wonder. "And they think it was meant."

Sophie shook her head. "Meant?"

"Fellow here says the fire was started in two places," Griffin replied. He stared at the girl with confused emotions. There could be no doubt that she had betrayed him, but still he retained an implicit trust in her, and was suddenly desperate for some form of reassurance. And he was also conscious of an undeniable feeling of guilt; for all he knew she was totally oblivious to her brother's fate and, more importantly, his involvement in it.

"Have you seen my Joe?" Emma's question burst into his thoughts. "Only he didn't come back last night, and I'm concerned for him."

Griffin had to contain a sigh; they all seemed to have someone to worry about at present. "Joe Lamport?" he asked. "No. Last I saw he was in the cutter, but that was a few hours back. You could go and look if you wish."

The girl thanked him, but stayed where she was, and Griffin found himself looking deep into Sophie's eyes. Somehow, to be in her presence – to see her face, hear her voice, scent her very fragrance – it was impossible to believe she could really have betrayed him.

"Your brother was taken last night," he said softly, despite himself.

"Taken?" She was clearly unaware. "By who?"

His gaze fell away. This was far harder than he had thought; he shouldn't have started it.

"By me, I fear," he confessed.

Her face froze, but she was silent.

"It's the bloody Warrens," he said at last. "I should never have come."

"It always seems to be the bloody Warrens these days," she replied.

* * *

Lamport had been detailed to join two of the Custom House tide waiters who were rummaging Matt Ward's boat, and it was the last straw, as far as he was concerned. The smack had been severely mauled, and would cost a pretty penny to put right, although any damage was probably the least of its owner's worries. At that moment Matt was in a cell awaiting trial and would probably be blaming everything on whoever it was who tipped off the Horsebridge gang, while Lamport was having to deepen his crime further by gathering evidence for his friend's eventual destruction.

Actually there had been little need to search; it was more a question of unloading the cargo. He and the others had taken two score of half-ankers from the smack. Each was filled with a variety of over-proof spirit that would finally make up to several hundred gallons of liqueur. There was also a large quantity of tobacco and snuff, several bolts of lace fabric and a pipe of port wine. It was a phenomenal load, and far more than Matt would have usually traded. Either he had obtained a special order, or was trying to up his game. But with such a quantity there would be no chance of the lad getting off with a fine and a stiff word from the magistrates.

When Lamport was finished, and Davies declared him free to check on Emma and the baby, he had set off with every intention of doing just that, but the whole business had sent his fragile mind on the well-trodden track to depression. On the road from the legal quay his dark side took control and, rather than turning right, onto the cinder path that led home, he carried on to the drawbridge that crossed the harbour further up.

The tollkeeper knew him of old and seldom charged long-term residents, but Lamport stamped across without acknowledging either the man, or his favour. Once on the other side of the river he continued, still with no set purpose in mind, but in exactly the opposite direction to the cluttered little cottage where he lived. The cliff road came into view before long, and he began to climb. He felt his heart start to pound as he mounted the stone steps until, before he was even properly aware, he was walking on the short, dense grass of Castle Hill.

He passed the shore battery where the smell of cooking food went totally unnoticed, and only paused when he reached the edge of the cliff itself. Staring down at the *Bee*, moored far below him he could see Fuller, the lad Harry and what might be Calver standing in a group at her taffrail. Wooderson came to join them, and even though they were a good way off, Lamport could tell they were laughing. Excepting the boy, he had served with them all for many years, and yet never felt quite so easy or confident as to indulge in light conversation or enjoy a joke as they clearly were.

He rarely relaxed in any form of social company. Most of the time it was as if it were a part he had to play; only with Emma, and occasionally Matt did he ever truly feel comfortable and allow the real Joe Lamport to be revealed. Consequently he found his shipmates' effortless social grace a positive insult to his current mood. He glanced about. The nearby gun emplacement swept an arc that just about covered the inner harbour. Had he had been able, there was nothing he would have liked more than to have flattened the group with a broadside from the heavy cannon. Smashed them all to pulp, and sent the hated cutter to the bottom along with all the rules and petty regulations that were currently cramping his life. He continued to stare, but did nothing; there was nothing that could be done: he was totally ineffectual, as he always had been. Once more they had beaten him, and he was growing tired of always being the loser.

He drew a breath, then settled down on the cliff top, pulling his knees up to his chin and hugging his legs as he looked away and out towards the grey waters of the Channel. Thinking of his wife, and the circumstances at home, unleashed further thoughts, although not all of them were depressing.

When the Warren men gave him that guinea, he had taken it straight back to the house. As long as old Mrs Newman had not insisted on Emma paying back what she already owed, it would buy them food for at least a month. But that was the one and only image which might be called positive; he had many others, and some were far more sinister.

Taking the money had put him very much in the pocket of the Horsebridge gang and it was quite conceivable that it would be the last coin he would ever see from them. There would be little need for payment from now on, not when they could simply threaten to reveal his past actions to Dobson or Dwyer. Either would revel in a chance to raise their status with the Board of Customs who, once they were informed, would have no hesitation in dismissing him from the service. With luck he might avoid gaol, but must still provide for his family, and Lamport was singularly lacking in any skills save those of a seaman.

He could try for the merchant service; wages were high and men in demand at present, but there was no protection from the press such as he enjoyed in the revenue. Years could be spent away from England, only to find himself plucked from a home-bound ship and sent to spend an immeasurable time serving his Majesty in a man of war. He thought on for a moment, imagining the life, and slowly his attitude began to change, as Lamport's moods so often did.

Actually the Royal Navy was not such a bad idea; ordinary seamen could grow rich on prize money and an intelligent person like himself might well advance: it was not unknown for lower deck hands to emerge as officers, and even take command. Overhead a shaft of sunlight broke through the cloud, highlighting the change in his temperament. Yes, he would enjoy being a captain, and Emma would like it too. He could see her as a fine lady, ordering servants about, while he drank port with his fellows or hunted to hounds. The thought of joining voluntarily suddenly became unusually appealing, and he felt the urge to laugh out loud. He might then choose his berth, and where he would serve, and up to ten guineas could be claimed as bounty by one as experienced as he was. Go away for a year or two, and come back rich and maybe an officer. That surely sounded grand in his mind, and his spirits rose further. Emma would be provided for; he could see to it that she drew his pay monthly, and there would be a soft and comfy wife waiting for him whenever he returned.

But even as he sat there thinking about what might be his new life, something caught his attention, and he glanced to the right. A small vessel was labouring against the wind, her sails oddly set as she continued towards the shore. The professional side of his brain took control now, and he watched her tack, a slow and awkward manoeuvre that brought her far closer to the cliffs than was advisable. Eventually she was round, however, and set on the larboard tack, and he continued to follow her idly as she clawed her way off and into safer water. She was a brig, he decided, and seemed to have taken damage: her fore topmast had apparently been replaced by a far lighter spar, making the entire rig ungainly and gauche.

Then he looked again, and more carefully. Slowly his brain interpreted the signals, and his blood began to pound. He could alert the battery, only a few yards to his right, but the vessel was heading away from the shore, and by the time he had made himself known, and understood, she would probably be out of range. No, there was only one course he could take, and that was to get back to the cutter. He paused, looked again, and was positive. Then, turning back for the path, he started off at a brisk walk that soon turned into a run.

Chapter Thirteen

Griffin left Jones at the scene of the fire. The adjoining houses currently untouched by the blaze had been stripped of their furniture, and several tubs of spirit and other items that were directly of the riding officer's concern were brought to light. He supposed he could have stayed to help, but the smoke had attracted quite a crowd, and Jones was well supported by two other revenue officers, as well as several clerical staff from Custom House. It was only a matter of time before Dobson or Dwyer made their appearance, and Griffin had no wish to speak to either of them. Consequently he avoided the cinder path to the harbour, and walked instead along the shingle at the very top of the beach. The tide was making, but he was far enough from the breaking waves to remain dry while allowing their regular pounding to clear his nose of the clinging stench of the fire. He had lost everything not in the cutter, although that was hardly a major concern. Possessions could be replaced, people were something entirely different. However much he might tell himself that Willett's death could be laid squarely at the door of the Warrens, he knew in his heart that he was ultimately responsible, and found the slow walk cleansing.

When he reached the harbour the world came back to meet him. The wind, still holding in the east but now blowing stronger, carried the smell of smoke, and he supposed the hands that gathered round *Bee* would be gossiping about the fire, as much as their adventures of the previous night. After towing Ward's smack in, the cutter was moored on the eastern wharf. Davies was not there, but the men greeted Griffin cheerfully. They knew nothing of his discussion with Dobson; neither could they guess that the chances of him remaining their commander for very much longer were slight. All each of them understood was that he had proved himself worthy, in their eyes at least, and as they bantered easily he felt a sense of comradeship rarely known before.

The sound of Lamport's calls interrupted their conversation, and Griffin glanced across the harbour with some annoyance. The man was standing on the opposite wharf, and seemed unduly agitated as he waved, and pointed out to sea while shouting something that was lost against the prevailing wind.

"Gloomy Joe's after a ride," Gadd said; then realising his captain was close, clapped his hand theatrically across his mouth as the others grinned and chided him.

"Clear away the quarter boat – the galley," Griffin ordered. The cutter was at rest and there was little else for anyone to do, although he was inclined to agree with the muttered questions that centred around why the miserable bastard couldn't walk up to the drawbridge like a regular human being.

Two men rowed across and it was not a quick passage. The tide was coming in, and three luggers that had been waiting in the roadstead were riding it. When the squat little boat finally did reach Lamport he all but jumped in before it was even made fast. There was a moment of discussion before they started back and when they did, the pace was a good deal quicker than on the outward journey. Griffin watched with interest; whatever had affected the petty officer was clearly contagious. Then, as the galley was still half a cable off, and had just appeared from behind a coal barge, Lamport stood up and bellowed. The words came clearly, despite the wind, and suddenly Griffin's mind was washed free of all other concerns.

"Where is Mr Davies?" he shouted to Harry, who was standing next to him by the bulwark.

"He's gone down to the dockyard stores with the boatswain, sir. They were to see about some fresh three-inch cable," the lad told him.

"Go fetch him," Griffin commanded. "And run – the rest of you, stations for leaving harbour!"

"Tide's still making, sir," Wooderson said, almost apologetically, as the lad skipped down from the cutter and started to sprint along the wharf.

"We have to be off," Griffin told him, "just as soon as we have the depth. See to it, will you!"

* * *

"Come on, girl, you're doing no good standing here," Sophie told her. "Let's get you back to The Star; there's space enough for the time being. You can find somewhere else later."

"What about Joe?" Emma whined. "He won't know where I am."

"There are folk hereabouts who saw you fit an' healthy," Sophie replied, collecting two bags and a coat that were all the Lamports' possessions rescued from the fire. "He'll soon put two and two together, and find you with us."

Emma pulled her shawl tighter about the baby, then glanced back at the burning wreck that had been their house. "Seems so strange," she reflected. "One moment you have a home, the next it's gone."

"Well at least you're not gone with it, like poor old Mr Willett," Sophie told her soberly, and started off on the cinder track. A short, stout man with a double chin and armed with a cane stepped out from the crowd as they were passing, and Emma stopped.

"I'd like a word with you, young lady," he said. Sophie turned back, and realised it was William Catt, owner of the Tide Mills and Emma's landlord. "There's seven weeks' back-rent you're owing, and little sign of payment, I'm guessing."

Emma lowered her head and began to mutter something in reply, but Sophie took control. Reaching back she grabbed the girl by the arm, and pulled her away. Then, glancing over to the fire that had now spread to the entire line of houses, she shouted, "So why don't you evict her, then?"

* * *

Davies could be seen coming towards them. His face was red and he was alternating between running and walking quickly, with the boatswain puffing behind and young Harry scampering between the two like a dog with errant sheep.

"The Warrens' brig has been sighted off Castle Hill," Griffin all but shouted at him as he staggered up the gangplank.

"I know, I know," the older man gasped, wiping his brow with the back of his hand. "Have Taylor and Cartwright returned? I gave them liberty to see their families, though they should be back by high water."

Griffin shook his head. "We can't wait for them, and I'm not sending anyone else off. We must leave; there is no time to waste!"

Davies looked about the harbour. "It'll be low over the bar, sir," he said, his breath still coming in deep draughts. "I'd give it another half hour, at least, maybe more."

"Can you get us out now?" Griffin demanded, and the older man paused.

"I suppose there is a chance," he replied.

* * *

Ten minutes later *Bee* was under way, heading out towards the roadstead under foresail alone. The easterly wind was constant, and she could have travelled very much faster, but all aboard knew that, for the moment at least, the cutter's speed was not an important factor.

"Take her to larboard," Davies said, as he stood with Griffin by the binnacle. A hand was at the bow with a sounding rod, but the mate had yet to call for the depth. There was no set channel to navigate, the bar was solid and even, only varying by a matter of inches across its length. But the older man knew the area well, and for the moment was content to conn the cutter by eye and instinct alone.

Griffin was trying hard not to fidget. His blood had been up since receiving news that the enemy was nearby, and he felt he would burst unless some form of physical exercise were found. This might be no more than a fool's errand; a vessel that was too large for them in the storm last night would be no easier in the bold light of day. And even if they were to take her, she would probably carry little evidence of smuggling. But Griffin knew in his heart that it was a battle he must fight. The Warrens were a wily bunch, although even they would find it hard to explain the damage *Bee* had already inflicted, and why they had happened to be off a certain beach on a moonless night when smuggling was in progress. They may have the more powerful vessel, and probably would account for him and his tiny cutter, but still he felt justified in doing all he could to stop them.

He glanced round the crowded deck; the tension steadily growing inside was like steam in a heated boiler, and almost as difficult to contain.

212

"Why not take a look from the masthead, sir?" Davies asked, eyeing him as warily as a father might a much loved but troubled son. "You'll get a better view of the bar from that height, and may even be able to spot the Warrens."

Griffin made for the larboard shrouds. Soon he was climbing up at a credible speed, while Davies, along with Forsyth at the helm, breathed a shared sigh of relief.

"Keep her steady," the mate muttered. "Give me a depth, there!"

Bee crept forward, the wind regularly spilling from the single sail to check her pace. It was one of the problems of the cutter's hull; the bow rode relatively high, drawing little more than a heavy rowing boat, but from there it deepened steadily until over two fathoms of water was needed to clear her stern. Fuller, at the sounding rod, had called eleven feet, but the waves were running high, and there must be a broad margin for error. At best Davies knew there was probably less than a foot below her keel, and worst she would touch the bottom in the next thirty seconds.

If they chanced to ground it would be no great problem; the bed was shingle and at the speed they were travelling, no great damage should be caused. But the cutter may well be trapped, and have to remain until the tide came to lift her off, and there was always the chance of the wind rising further. They would be left, prone on the bar with the foresail released, as a sudden gust might lay her over: a humiliating and frustrating experience while with every breath the Warren brig was clawing further away.

Slowly *Bee* eased forward, her hull pitching gently in the waves. She was making progress, and for one glorious moment Davies thought they were going to pass safely over. Then, with a slight bump that was really more of a caress, she stuck.

"All for'ard!" Griffin's shout came from the masthead, although no one moved for a moment. "For'ard, I say," he repeated, and Davies suddenly understood. Grabbing Harry and Colclough, who were standing nearby, he began to run down the deck, shouting for the others to follow. Only Forsyth remained steadfast at the tiller as the entire crew began to crowd together at the prow. The cutter began to sway again almost immediately. They were free, but it was obvious to all that there was little chance of any further forward progress for a while.

"Keep her as she is!" Griffin yelled. "Let the wind take her west, then we'll try again."

Davies pursed his lips and exchanged a glance with Wooderson; both knew the harbour bed well, and had never found any great difference in its depth. The cutter rocked from the vagaries of both wind and current, and Forsyth struggled to keep her head straight as they were pressed crab-wise across the bay.

"A sounding, if you please," Griffin called down from the masthead.

There was a pause while Fuller swung himself over the side and reached down, almost to the water's surface.

"Just off ten, sir," came the reply, the sounding rod being marked off in feet rather than fathoms.

"Very good, remain where you are, but bring the foresail to the wind once more."

Davies nodded, the sail was sheeted in, and *Bee* began to creep forward again. Everyone held their breath; by all accounts they should not have the depth, although the added weight forward would make a difference and they were quite possibly past the point where they had grounded before. Nothing was certain in such a situation, however, or any accurate judgement possible, and the tension continued. Then, as it slowly began to dawn on them that they must be clear, the men began to chatter and laugh like a bunch of schoolboys. Griffin clambered down the shrouds, and landed on the deck to an ironic cheer.

"Make sail, if you please, and steer east, as close as she will bear," he ordered. "Harry, join Nairn at the masthead; both of you keep your eyes peeled for the brig."

Davies was nettled, not so much by Griffin's apparently superior seamanship, but more from the crew's favourable reaction. "I was aware of no channel," he said, when they had regained their accustomed position by the binnacle.

"Neither was there one," Griffin replied cheerfully. "I felt easing slightly to the west might see us across, however. And it seemed to have worked." He paused and winked at the older man adding, almost as an afterthought, "it was either that, or the weight of you lot sitting atop the catsheads; in truth I shall never crave a lean crew again."

* * *

Sophie swept into the parlour and smiled her apologies at Jenny, who looked after the lunchtime trade and should have left over half an hour ago. The girl was bound to have commitments of her own but Sophie had been extremely busy and, as she hurriedly tied an apron about her waist, could feel little sympathy for other people's troubles.

Emma and young Joseph were finally installed in an upstairs room. Sophie's father had complained of course, but that was to be expected. More to the point, if the baby behaved to form, there would be further objections from guests unable to sleep through the constant crying. And Matt was in custody in Lewes Gaol; they had been less than helpful at Custom House, but from what she understood he was to be held for trial and would be lucky to escape the noose. Just what part Griffin had played in his capture she could not be certain; the collector's clerk said *Bee* was responsible for capturing the smack and yet, when she spoke with Bert Taylor, one of the cutter's crew, he was emphatic that the commander had probably saved her brother's life. All would doubtless be settled in time, but now she had other and far more immediate problems with which to concern herself.

She checked the room; it was still reasonably crowded, even at this late hour. Three small groups of local workers sat finishing their drinks in quiet conversation while, in the far corner, six better dressed men were making rather more noise. Their table was littered with empty glasses, as well as two broken pipes and the remains of an abandoned game of dominoes; Sophie guessed they had limited their refreshment to drink and tobacco. Such a group could prove troublesome, even during a quiet lunchtime; Jenny seemed to have given them a wide berth, and she would also.

Sophie's arrival apparently encouraged the other guests to leave, and soon there was only the noisy crowd in the corner. She knew their like well, even though it was a relatively new addition to the Newhaven community. They were the kind with no trade or obvious means of support, yet kept a horse and flaunted all the newest London fashions and gewgaws. Arrogant and superior, they would treat any working man or woman like dirt, while carrying themselves with all the swagger of judges or politicians and, in her mind at least, were every bit as despicable. At present they were playing; each taking a turn at adding to a pile of empty glasses upon the table amidst childlike giggles, nudges and immature comments. They had reached the height of five by balancing one upon the other, and Sophie was about to intervene when the sight of the last one, a rummer heavier than the rest, made her stop. She watched, fascinated, as it was lowered into position by a pock-faced lad a few years younger than her, who was smirking at his own skill. The glass was released, and even stayed for a moment, before the tower began to topple. There was a roar of laughter and derision from the table's occupants as the glasses tumbled down, with some then rolling to the floor where they smashed into countless pieces.

Sophie hurried across, collecting a broom as she went. The group greeted her arrival loudly, but she was in no mood for the usual niceties of inn work and ignored them. The broken glass had spread widely, but was soon brought into one tidy pile by a few swift strokes. Then, taking the hearth brush and shovel from the fireplace, she turned her back on them and bent to sweep up the debris. An unexpected draught came from behind, followed by a chorus of lewd laughter. She stood up as she realised what had happened and, turning, snatched the hem of her dress away from the man who had been holding it up. Sophie glared at the group with true hatred; they leered back with rosy red faces made plump by drink. One she recognised as the young Warren's companion from a few days back, and several of the others also seemed familiar. She winced as a slap caught her square on the rump, and there was more laughter from the table as another rejoined his friends after a trip to the privy.

She felt her own colour rise, and her hands began to shake. "Get out of here!" she said, waving the hearth brush as her anger finally broke. "Get out, and take your loutish manners with you!"

The group were quiet for a moment and then one, a slightly older member who wore a supercilious smile and gentleman's clothing, raised his hand.

"My friends meant no harm, miss; we are merely celebrating a recent piece of good fortune. Now send along another run of bottles, and we'll say no more about it."

The others looked at her with different levels of expectation; some, she could tell, were contemplating far more than simply wine.

"We ain't servin' anyone else today," she said coldly; there were seven of them and one of her, and yet she felt strangely equal to the odds. "I knows who you are, and you're nothing but scum; I only hope your mothers don't know the way you behave."

Something in either her words or tone struck home, and the atmosphere was suddenly void of all humour. The older man preened himself slightly, then regarded the girl with a mixture of proprietorship and disdain.

"I would advise you to moderate your tone; you are clearly unaware of whom you are addressing."

Sophie shrugged. "I could hardly care less. Now will you leave this place, or do I have to call my father?"

At this the laughter did return, albeit more restrained. But the older man was not amused and looked her square in the eye.

"To what ends, my dear? Have us arrested and up before the local magistrates?" This time he did laugh, and the others obediently followed. Sophie guessed that if he were not a judge himself, he had the power of one.

"If need be!" she spat back. "And if they won't listen, I shall take it higher." She glared round at the group, contempt written bold upon her face. "This was a decent town 'til the likes of you were seen, and it will be so again when you are gone."

The men were now more bewildered than amused, and whispered comments as they looked from Sophie to one another.

"Go on," she continued. "I want you out of here!" She raised the hearth brush and banged it loudly against the shovel, creating a shower of dust over the nearest man. He stood up in sudden anger, and made to grab at her. She stepped back, but continued to bang the shovel; a loud and penetrating sound that hurt the ears and raised the tension in the room.

Now all were standing, and Sophie had to retreat further. She backed away until the ledge of a table stopped her, then bent back in an effort to put as much space between them as she could. But they were coming for her and, though she continued to beat the shovel mightily, all knew that this would not end well. One snatched at her wrist, and another took hold on the cloth of her dress, and she was just starting to struggle when a slightly different sound was heard.

It was further banging, but this time far louder. She turned, and saw Jenny, the lunchtime maid. She held a large saucepan in one hand that she was striking with the side of a cook's spoon. And there was Emma, seeming smaller without the child in her arms, but carrying instead an iron frying pan. As Sophie watched the girl smacked it with a rolling pin, causing the entire room to reverberate with the sound. The men seemed disconcerted by the din, and looked to each other in confusion.

"Come on, get yourselves out of here," Sophie shouted, retrieving the initiative. One man took a step back; she filled the space and began hitting the shovel again. The two girls came to either side of her and together they advanced, driving the men from the room.

Outside, they seemed to regroup. The hallway had a higher ceiling that absorbed the sound somewhat but the girls were not stopping and continued to make for them. One, the man who had accompanied the Warren son, went to speak, but it was impossible amid such a cacophony. Another, the older one, was clearly angry, and waved his hands at the girls, but again there was little in the way of threat, protest or complaint that could be heard against such a racket. The noise attracted others into the hall and several small groups gathered to watch as the women steadily herded the men towards the door. Jackson, the butcher who supplied The Star, jeered at a recognised face.

"That's Smokie Samuels," he shouted, pointing at one who blushed under the sudden attention. "Wants ten shillings a week for me to keep my windows – when I couldn't pay last week he took my Sunday britches, but he's not so bold when it comes to dealing with a bunch of women, eh?"

Other shouts followed, and Sophie became even more certain she was dealing with members of the Horsebridge gang. But it would have been impossible for her to back down now, even if she had wanted to, and the women continued to advance.

They were soon joined by others, who massed behind them as they slowly drove the men towards the door and followed when they were outside. There the constant barrage of sound continued while still more guests and tradesmen gathered, and others from the street joined in. Some knew what was about, a few might have been no more than inquisitive, but in no time the following crowd was vast, and seven scared men began to run.

Hoots and catcalls were screamed at them from their pursuers, but none seemed in any mood to respond. The gang members met with several more of their like half-way down the street, although there was no question of turning back on the mob that seemed keen to swallow them. A stone was thrown from the back, and passed over the women's heads, before landing square on the waist-coated man's head. He reached up, apparently in surprise, as blood began to flow, but there was little chance of examining the wound further. Seeing the blood enraged the others, however; one drew a small hand-gun and aimed it roughly at the mob and there was a pop as it exploded.

The women stopped, momentarily at a loss; no one appeared to have been hurt, but this was all now far beyond their control. The gunshot proved to be the final note for the rest of the crowd; nothing more was necessary to enrage them to an absolute frenzy, and they pushed past and fell amongst the gang members in a stampede of boots and fists.

Sophie dragged herself free and clung to Emma and Jenny for support. It was a mob brawl, and frightening in its intensity, although, as they watched, there was also something undeniably cleansing in the violence. To one side the waist-coated man was being tossed up into the air, while Jackson, the butcher, had knocked the one he had addressed as Samuels to the ground, and was now roughly relieving him of his britches.

"Looks like we've started something," Emma said, holding her friend close for support. Sophie could only agree.

* * *

The wind was still in the east, the general direction the brig would need to head to reach Rye, and that was an advantage, as far as Griffin was concerned. With a fore and aft rig, *Bee* could sail several points closer than a square rigger, and as the chase was also damaged there would be very little chance of her losing them. However, when the Warrens were caught, when they had to close against that deadly battery of nine pounders, was when the odds would really start to stack up. *Bee* may be fast and manoeuvrable, but they had already discovered just how fragile her frame was. One shot from a privateer had hulled her at long range; today she would be facing a far heavier broadside and probably fired a good deal closer. It would take seamanship, skill and a lot of determination: Griffin felt he was really only able to supply the latter.

"Deck there, I have a sail, fine off the starboard bow."

There was silence as the masthead lookout considered for a moment. "It's a brig, or a snow. Square rigged, least ways, and beating east for all she's worth – wait, she's tacking." Another pause, and Griffin felt the urge to fidget, then: "Yes, she's about and on the larboard tack now, I can see her more clearly, and her rig. It's a jury fore, just like Joe says. She's the one we met last night."

Murmurs of discussion greeted the news but Griffin said nothing. So, they had her. Now all he needed to do was claw to windward and they could engage. The brig's home port was still some miles off: there should be plenty of time, but did he really want to close with an enemy so powerful?

"Any other sail in sight?" he bellowed.

"Two luggers an' a smack," Nairn called back. "Fishers, I'd say; nothing more."

No Navy ships, nor anything else of any weight; it had been a long shot, but he supposed everything was down to him alone. Slowly his mind ran through the available options. He could speed on and attempt to reach Rye before the brig. With luck they would raise the revenue officers there and arrange a suitable reception. With his statement, and if one of the Warrens was on board, a charge could be brought. But he would be relying on a good deal of cooperation from Rye Custom House and, for the Horsebridge gang to be allowed a berth in the first place indicated a degree of acceptance by the locals. Something might be achieved, but Griffin had already learnt enough about the corrupt ways of government officials not to hold out much hope. No, if they were to stop her, he must engage, and there was only *Bee*'s eggshell hull to hand.

He glanced up at the sails: both the main and fore were board tight, and the cutter's stem was creating a good deal of spray. He supposed he might add the jib, but recent experience had taught him it would only force the bow down, and probably for no increase in speed. They were cleared for action, and every man was at his station, so there was nothing for him to do except wait for the moment when the brig came into range. The time gave him a chance to think, and they were not pleasant thoughts.

This would be his last chance, he could see that now. He had already burnt his bridges as far as Sophie was concerned; the few worldly goods he possessed beyond those in the cabin below had been destroyed, and his only friend in England, outside of those whom he commanded, was dead. And it was all because of him, and the actions he had taken: there could be no dispute in that. Soon, even if nothing else disastrous occurred, he would be officially dismissed, and forced to try for a warrant post in the Navy; that or go back, cap in hand, to his old employers. And meanwhile the Horsebridge gang, the force he had opposed, was quietly prospering, having hardly been affected by any of his actions. To take their brig would put matters straight, as far as he was concerned at least, but one important question remained. Should he really be risking his command, and the lives of all aboard her on what had become almost a personal battle?

The men were about him now, and seemed eager enough to be going into action against a Warren craft. He remembered the doubtful bunch he had encountered no more than a week ago; all seamen in the main, but seemingly lacking the initiative or enthusiasm to properly carry out their duties. They must have become worn down by months, probably years, of Dobson's mismanagement. Even his predecessor's attempts would have hardly improved matters; Carter had tried to make a stand and failed in the most final and public way possible. That would have convinced all that opposing the Horsebridge gang was a fool's game. He supposed he had done well to reignite something of their ire but, were they to be disappointed yet again, there would be little prospect in toppling the Warrens' reign for many years to come.

No, he decided. That could not happen, and they must close with the brig. Men may be injured, and probably some even killed, and they could easily lose the *Bee*, but she would go down fighting, and at the very least it would be an example worth building on for whoever was sent to follow.

"We have her from the deck, sir." Davies broke into his thoughts at exactly the right moment, giving Griffin no more time to consider or recant his decision. Yes, there she was; a blurred image on the starboard horizon. "Shall we steer for them?"

Griffin shook his head. It may well be that they had been spotted, and the brig was making out to sea, but he thought not. The Warren craft had survived what must have been a foul night. Extinguishing the fire and setting that jury rig during the storm could not have been quick or pleasant tasks, and then they would have had to claw back against a fierce and contrary wind; it was unlikely that any on board had slept at all and, with their home port almost in sight, he doubted they would deviate when rest and safety lay so close. The wind was still against them, and the brig was having to beat into it; far more likely that she was on the southerly leg of a tack. "Keep her as she is, if you please," he said. There could be no doubting that the image was gaining clarity by the minute; if he kept *Bee* as close to the wind as she was, they would continue to gain, and must ultimately catch her. Then the fun would truly begin.

The cutter's broadside was inferior, both in weight and number, and her hull far more vulnerable than a well-set-up brig, but the *Bee* would have speed on her side. Speed and manoeuvrability, as well as the not inconsiderable advantage of a body of men who Griffin knew were totally behind him. Ultimately, though, it would be down to his skill as their captain; it was a position he had held for just a few days, yet he must command them as if he had done so for all his life. Anything less would be a betrayal.

Chapter Fourteen

The crowd poured into the inn, full of cheers and bravado. Sophie and the other women followed them through to the front parlour as her father appeared, and soon all four were filling tankards and pocketing money like it was the very best of Saturday nights. The faces were bright with smiles; a welcome contrast from the gloom that had crept up so subtly of late and, as Sophie passed about the tables, she also felt unaccountably happy.

Her brother was in gaol, and likely to be tried for his life, while the man who had placed him there was the only person outside of her family she felt she could trust. But none of that altered the fact that the Warrens had been taught a lesson, and one they would remember for a while to come.

More beer was being called for, and she hurried across to the same corner table that members of the Horsebridge gang had occupied less than half an hour ago. She captured the empty tankards expertly in both hands, and went to make for the servery when an unexpected face was seen at the door.

She was not the only one to spot it, and the general clatter of conversation and self-congratulation dwindled as Jones, the riding officer, strode boldly into the room.

"There's no need to take on so," he said, apparently surprised at the silence he had caused. "You knows well enough who I am, and what I do, but that's not why I'm here."

"Then why are you, Jackie?" Jackson, the butcher, asked. "We've already got rid of one lot of ragtag this afternoon; it wouldn't take much to drum out another."

"An' is that what you think you've done?" Jones glanced at the filled tables all around him. "You think the Warrens are going to take account of a bit of horseplay an' a few sore noses?"

The silence was complete now, and made more sinister by the contrast to what had been before. "Oh, I'm not saying you haven't done well," he continued. "Excellent work, lads, and I'm truly proud of you. But it'll take more than that, if you want to see the Warrens out of Newhaven for good."

"So what do you suggest?" Abrahams, the wheelwright asked. "'Cause if it's another Goudhurst, you can forget it."

There was a chorus of support from the others, and Jones had to hold up his hand for quiet.

"What I'm saying is simple enough: you should finish what you started. The Warrens have been allowed far too much slack in this town. There is no one to blame other than yourselves, and it is up to you to put them straight. It won't be easy, and will certainly involve a few changes – it just depends on whether you have the pluck to carry them out, see?"

"Go on," one of them prompted, although it was clear from the sullen expressions that the room was not in favour.

"Well, first we have to start with the main problem, and right now it's looking at me. You're greedy; every one of you. All moan and gripe about the Warrens, yet each of you trades with them in one way or another." Jones' voice rose above the crescendo of protests. "Oh, you think I'm wrong, do ye? So shall I name a few? Michael Newman, you've been spotted working as a tubsman, carrying liquor for them on several occasions, and you, William Winton, tell me you don't keep an ash bat behind your door for the nights you're a working on a landing." The murmuring died down and several tried to avoid the riding officer's eye.

"Most of you is guilty of some small crime, be it running goods, buying or selling them. And even those who don't exactly break the law... supplying feed or shelter, or some other service: you're still cooperating. And just because the revenue don't choose to go for the small fry, and would rather set their bait for true sharks, you look upon us with contempt. Well, where has it got you?" He glared round, now truly angry. "Is this how you wants to live, in fear for your lives and those of your loved ones?"

"We've little choice." Jackson spoke again, his voice now low and sullen. "There are more of them than us."

"And they got money," another added with a little more defiance.

"Well of course they got money," Jones replied. "Much of it came from you in the first place; don't those with shops pay a regular sum, just to keep your roofs? An' as for the number, I didn't notice too many just now, out there on the street. Old Man Edwards hasn't been so shook up since his honeymoon, and that Samuels will probably still be feeling the cold come summer."

The laughter returned for a moment, and a pair of moleskin britches were thrown across the room to shouts of joy. Jones waited until the noise died down, then began again.

"So that's what you have to do, realise you can be a body, and behave like it. You, Jackson, next time they tries to sell you a sheep, tell them you don't need one; and you, Wainwright, if they want bread, or cake, claim you haven't got any, or offer them stale at twice the price. Show they're not going to get anything from you, and they'll soon move on."

"That's fine, and when they burn us down, we'll be that much the better off."

"They ain't going to burn you down," he said with rare certainty. "Today was just a warning, and you'll note did not affect their income in any way. The Warrens need the town far more than you realise. And if you are looking for support, there may be some available. I was speaking to Colonel Douglas of the dragoons not three hours ago; he's hardly pleased about what happened at the Tide Mills, and is quite prepared to act, if someone will only give him the evidence to work with."

"Little he can do at Lewes." Jackson again. "By the time he's got his men in the saddle, the Horsebridge lot has melted away like fat on hot coals."

Jones regarded the butcher warily. "Well, let's see about that, shall we? But for now we have to put a stop to what's been going on; that is, if you are prepared to do it."

They watched as he pulled a sheaf of paper from inside his jacket.

"I want to know everything – every last detail; who you've been selling to, and buying from, and exactly what the Warrens have been demanding. Anything they have borrowed, or stolen has to be listed, along with whatever threats or intimidation they used against you."

The men seemed mildly appalled, staring at one another in disbelief and shaking their heads, but Jones was not finished.

"And it isn't going to stop at the Warrens," he continued.

They waited.

"Many of you accept that Custom House is well in the grip of the Horsebridge gang, and some know more than others. Now I'm quite happy to stand up against my superiors, but could do with a little help. A number of you have got off mighty light with fines and the like on more'n one occasion."

His eyes fell on two men sitting at the nearest table; both looked straight ahead, but said nothing.

"I want a written statement from anyone with dealings with those in authority, saying what you paid to see you straight and who you paid it to." A rumble of discontent started, but subsided as Jones spoke again. "No one will come to any harm by what they do, I can assure you of that." The silence returned. "You know me, and that I have always been fair."

"You're asking us to fight the Warrens," Abrahams said softly. "More, you're asking us to fight the revenue men, and they can see any of us hang as easy as sneezing."

"I'm not asking you to fight anyone," Jones replied without blinking. "All I want is the information; with a bit of luck someone else will do the fighting."

* * *

"Now there's a mess, if ever I saw one." Wooderson stared at the brig from his position at number two cannon. They had advanced steadily on her for most of the afternoon and now, as the light was starting to fade, she was less than a mile off their starboard bow, and the cutter was still gaining.

"I seen worse jury rigs," Gadd muttered. "But they was on ships that were sinking."

"Silence there!" Both men jumped as Lamport's voice rang out, cracking slightly as he shouted. He passed them by, and continued his inspection of the guns. The two seamen exchanged looks.

"Old Gloomy Joe's been a bit touchy of late," Gadd said quietly.

"Probably nothing more than needing a caulk. 'Wherewith his spirit was troubled, and his sleep brake from him': Daniel two, verse one," Wooderson said, after considering for a moment. With a superior enemy to windward, none of the men were feeling exactly relaxed, but Gadd was right, for several days the deputed mariner had been unusually brittle.

"I hears his wife has another chit on the way," Calver added.

"That so?" Gadd raised his eyebrows. "Never known it wear you out quite that much."

* * *

Griffin was also tense. For all the time *Bee* had been closing on the brig he had been conscious of his heart beating nineteen to the dozen and, now that the enemy was almost within his grasp, he was sure it would shortly burst. It was his first single-ship action to have offered any degree of preparation; the previous instances being rushed upon him in such a way that planning had been impossible. But this was quite straightforward; two vessels upon an effectively empty sea. A simple game of chess, one where there was all the time in the world to consider the next move. Both players had individual strengths and weaknesses, or different pieces missing, and it was up to each to make the best with what was left.

He tried to consider tactics; the enemy's hull was strong, but would be slower and not as manoeuvrable. Her fire-power was also greater and she probably carried more men. In opposition he had a light, lithe and extremely fast vessel that could turn tight, and sail far closer to the wind, but would not take much in the way of punishment. He told himself this would be little more than a text-book problem for the average fighting captain but, with limited experience in command, and almost none as a deputy, Griffin would have to rely on instinct and luck if any of them were to see the following day.

While gauging the wind and staring once more at that hated brig, he found he was gripping his fists tight. She was making heavy weather of it; her jury rig had only allowed the setting of a jib: the main reason she was still out battling against a contrary wind, and not already sitting safe in harbour. He must use her lack of weatherly progress to his advantage, and there was only one way he could envisage doing so.

"We'll keep her as she is, Mr Davies," he said. "I want to pass and gain the wind."

"Very good, sir," the mate confirmed. They were a fair distance off, so it was hardly a chancy move. A fortunate broadside from the enemy, fired on the roll and well laid, might see one or two shots reaching them, but it was too far for any damage to their rig, and the rounds would be all but spent by the time they arrived. Besides, he was assuming the brig was mounting long nines, or equivalent guns with extended barrels. It was more likely for a vessel that might also be used for trading to carry something shorter, which would be less accurate at extreme range. And how would the enemy react to seeing *Bee* take up position to windward? What was an aggressive stance for a small craft could jog the opposing captain into acting rashly. But then he was probably more experienced than Griffin, and might not be as susceptible to such emotions. He may even know of a simple ruse for the situation, one that would totally devastate the cutter while killing or capturing her crew. Griffin swallowed; this was certainly not going to be easy.

The brig was now on the starboard tack, and *Bee* was keeping her distance as she crept up on her. As soon as they had passed he might bring the cutter nearer to the breeze, and properly claim the windward gauge. It would block the enemy from gaining her harbour, although he was uncomfortably aware that this was where any form of strategy effectively ended. He had no fixed plan in mind, or any real idea how he might use the cutter's speed to the best advantage. The sky was darkening more quickly now, but there was no sign of last night's storm returning, and the wind was holding steady. Throughout the chase he had hoped to meet with reinforcements. Another revenue cutter or, better still, a passing Navy vessel would sweeten the odds in his favour, but no, this seemed destined to be a single-ship action, and all the responsibility was to remain with him.

"Looks like they're holding their fire," Davies said, and Griffin supposed he was right; the brig was now hard on their beam, with her broadside guns bearing on the tiny craft. He went to reply when there came the first of several flashes, followed by a cloud of smoke that was soon whipped away by the strong breeze. They waited, while the sound of the barrage rolled out to meet them, and a series of splashes, none closer than half a cable short, rose up in the sea. The mate gave a wry look. "Might have been a touch hasty, there," he said, and Griffin could only agree as he felt a little of the tension ebb away.

He had learned a lot from that broadside. It had been delivered in near-perfect conditions, with guns that would have been loaded carefully, without the pressure of battle. The firing had not been instantaneous, neither was it a controlled ripple, in fact the whole procedure could be described as sloppy in the extreme. But the main point, and the one that reassured Griffin the most, was that they had fired at all. It looked like his earlier hypothesis was right on the head; whoever ordered the broadside should have been aware of their range, and known there was little chance of actually hitting the cutter. He was either inexperienced or angry that such a little craft, one that had already dealt them considerable damage, should have the temerity to forereach on them, and both conditions were as agreeable to Griffin. He brought his hands up out of his pockets and stretched. Yes, he was now feeling decidedly better about the whole affair.

"I think we might bear in a point," he said, and Forsyth duly brought the tiller back. Knowing the range of the brig's guns was a distinct advantage and, as there was plenty of room in hand, he may as well be in the best position for when they finally took the windward gauge.

* * *

The cutter was a little closer now, and edging nearer; five minutes had passed since that first broadside, so they might assume the brig's guns to be loaded once more, but *Bee* was at the very extent of the previous shots, and almost out of the enemy's arc of fire. As soon as she was well ahead he would act, Griffin decided. Come closer to the breeze and gather some sea room, then turn back. With luck, and what would be almost a following wind, he could run down on the enemy, before jibing tight across her bows, delivering his broadside into her already damaged prow, and beating back and out of danger. It was just the sort of move he was looking for; one that, even if no serious damage were caused, could be repeated and would sap the spirit from his opposite number. Even as he thought, he could feel his confidence rise. In fact, so deep was he absorbed in the idea that, when the second enemy broadside was fired, he almost missed it.

This one was far more professional; the guns went off almost as one, were better laid and, more to the point, seemed to have gathered a good deal of range. The sound of passing round shot took them all by surprise; they had hardly closed a hundred yards, and yet the cutter's mainsail was holed a good way up, and a backstay parted with a ringing twang. Davies roared for the boatswain's crew to see to the shroud, but Griffin's mind was on other things.

His face had grown red, and once more both hands were balled up into fists and thrust deep into his pockets. He had been fooled, duped, by what was probably the oldest trick in the book. The brig's captain must have planned that first broadside extremely carefully: ordered it low, loose and badly aimed, just so that someone as stupid as Griffin would be taken in. And he had swallowed the bait perfectly – hook, line and sinker. Assuming that only an idiot would fire his guns at anything other than full range, Griffin had ordered his little cutter right inside the enemy's reach, while concocting elaborate plans that would probably have little, if any, chance of success.

"Larboard two points." He spoke as if it were just another order, and was in no way an admission of failure, but inside Griffin knew he had already sustained one major defeat. *Bee* had hardly been damaged, which was fortunate, but the other captain may have many such tricks up his sleeve, and a new boy's luck could not last forever.

* * *

The parlour at The Star had taken on some of the aspects of a schoolroom. Tables still held beer-drinking customers but at each sat one with pen and ink, who was soberly making notes as the others took turns to speak. Sophie had already covered three pages, and was starting on a fourth. Across the room she could see Emma, baby firmly tucked in the crook of her left arm, similarly employed, while Jones along with Jackson, who had a fair hand for a butcher, were at other tables. Her father was also fully literate but would take no part in the writing, although he and the girl Jenny were working hard enough delivering drink whenever it was called for. By the time they finished the afternoon was all but spent, and light from the fire cast a friendly glow about the place that strengthened the feeling of cleansing that each enjoyed. The men stood up and chatted softly, while the writers sat back and flexed their fingers. On every table there was a sizeable pile of notes that would implicate many. A single one might have been open to dispute in a court of law, but together they formed a sizeable body of evidence which would be far harder to refute.

Jones went from table to table collecting. No one had left, the room was still filled with people, but the exuberance and celebration of a few hours ago was nowhere to be seen. Each was fully aware of the risk they had taken. Any one of them could expect retribution of the darkest kind, if their part were revealed. But they had strength in numbers, and trusted that this was a certain way to permanently rid them of the menace that had tainted their lives for far too long.

"You going to be careful with that," Jackson warned Jones, as he thrust the wad into his satchel. "Word gets out to the Horsebridge lot, and there'll be the devil to pay."

"This ain't going anywhere near the Warrens," the riding officer told him firmly. "There's my own journals to add, and I want to interview the officers of the cutter, but first it will be taken straight to Douglas in Lewes."

"An' when's he going to act?" David Powell, the shoemaker, asked.

"I have no idea," Jones conceded. "But can be certain he will."

The men were heading for the door now, each feeling unwilling to leave alone. Emma had gone some while back and was upstairs feeding the baby and soon the room was empty, apart from Sophie, her father and the riding officer.

"With luck I should reach Lewes before dark," he said, not meeting the stare of either of the others.

"Before you go, we need to ask you something."

Jones half-closed his eyes, guessing what was to come.

"It's Matt," Sophie continued. "Do you know what will happen to him?"

"I do not," the riding officer confessed. "By rights, the whole matter is totally out of my hands and you should be speaking to Dobson or someone at Custom House."

Sophie went to protest – the last few hours had shown the futility of such a move – but Jones stopped her. "I do have an idea, though, and one which might conceivably save him, but it is only that." He raised his hand again. "I will follow it up as soon as this little lot is delivered."

The landlord grunted and Sophie muttered her thanks as Jones headed for the door. The important thing at that moment was to get the package to Colonel Douglas: afterwards he could try and help the Ward boy. What he had said was quite correct, there was a chance that the lad might avoid the noose, but a lot had to happen before then and most of it was still very much in the balance.

* * *

Bee had now properly gained the windward gauge, and was actually pulling away from the brig, which had tacked, and was making heavier weather off her starboard counter. Griffin knew he must act soon, but was still at a loss for an actual plan.

"Would you have us take in some sail, sir?" Davies asked. Griffin shook his head; speed was still their main advantage, but how best to use it, and when?

"No, keep her as she is, but be ready to ease the sheets." It was probably a hackneyed manoeuvre, but better than none at all. "Starboard battery prepare." He turned to Forsyth at the tiller. "Port your helm."

The cutter began to wallow as she presented her beam to both wind and enemy. Griffin had forgotten to allow for the movement.

"Haul in a little," he said, partially countermanding his previous order, and *Bee* started to take up speed again as the hull stabilised. The brig was at long-range for their six pounders, but it was worth the effort, if only to show the Warrens they were prepared to take them on. "Fire as you will." The last was less of an order, and more the granting of permission; a dramatic roar from him might easily excite a nervous gun captain, and waste shot.

But the men were more than equal to the situation, and each took careful aim as *Bee* moved across the brig's oncoming bows. All, by the binnacle, were watching the enemy for some sign of movement. Her foremast was disabled, but it was still unlikely that she would simply stay as she was and allow the impudent little cutter to take pot shots at her.

And so it proved; even before the first of the revenue guns spoke, the brig fired off two shots from her bow chasers. Both were wild, one falling way off to starboard and the other raising water midway between the two vessels. Then the enemy began to turn to larboard, and was attempting to bring her own, far larger, broadside to bear as the cutter's reply rained down about her. Griffin cleared his throat; it was long range, and none of their shots would have worried any aboard the enemy, but now that he had actually returned fire, the well-remembered feelings came back and he felt more equal to the task.

"Starboard your helm," he yelled. Then: "sheet her in!" and the cutter immediately took up more speed. The brig continued to turn, and then there came the first flash of her starboard broadside.

The shots landed close, but not dangerously so. The cutter's impudence in firing at all must have annoyed whoever it was in charge of their guns, and they had wasted the chance of dealing them serious damage. Griffin felt a wave of relief break over him; the rash action proved his opponent was not so clever as all that: maybe they would have a chance after all.

"Very good," he said, when the last splash had settled. "Reverse the helm; take her to starboard."

Now the inspiration was truly starting to flow, as *Bee* bore down on the brig's stern. There had been no calculation; a mixture of guess work and intuition was responsible for the order but, as the cutter accelerated in front of the brig's temporarily impotent larboard battery and closed on her vulnerable counter, Griffin felt his confidence increase further. The one doubt in his mind was whether their own starboard battery would be re-loaded in time, but that was something only the future could reveal.

The enemy captain had noted his manoeuvre, and was trying to claw back into the wind, but the brig was clumsy, and the speed of the cutter proved more than enough to keep her safe. Griffin glanced down to where his gun crews were hurriedly serving their pieces. This was where the previous days of exercise should pay off; three had clearly loaded, and were hauling back into the firing position, with the others not so very far behind. His gaze switched to the brig, now appreciably closer, and her vulnerable stern just off their starboard bow. He held his breath, not believing his luck: it was almost the perfect angle.

The fastest of the crews were priming their guns as the cutter sliced through the dark waters. Griffin could not tell if the enemy was continuing to turn, but knew *Bee* was going to skim her quarter, and should be able to deliver a deadly load, without receiving a shot in reply.

"On my word, men!" They were still at the last stages of serving the guns, and soon would be laying the pieces before firing. Griffin strode to the starboard side, watching as the ideal moment approached and praying they would be ready when it did. The positioning was ideal; they just needed to have a full broadside prepared. An inner feeling warned him that it was perhaps a little too perfect, but there was nothing he could do now: they were committed.

Figures could be seen on the deck of the brig, and soon they might recognise faces, but there was no time for any thought other than releasing that broadside at the most effective moment. One gun captain had his hand raised, and there was another, but they would be passing in a matter of seconds. The crack of a musket ball startled them as it embedded itself into the bulwark, to be followed by several others, but no one on the small craft gave them any thought. Griffin raised his hand: it was so nearly time.

"Fire!" Everything seemed to happen at once: the brig's stern was almost close enough to touch, and yet at the speed *Bee* was travelling, would soon be gone. The guns went off in a ragged clatter, causing maximum damage.

"Starboard your helm, bring her round!"

A nearby seaman swore softly as the gunners looked back at their work. The brig's stern windows were a mess of fractured crown glass, and half the taffrail had been knocked in. But the rudder appeared to be intact and, even as they watched, it kicked to larboard.

"She's turning back!" Davies shouted in surprise.

"Starboard battery reload!" Griffin snapped. He had no fixed idea what to do next, but it was foolish in the extreme to waste time staring when there were empty guns to be served. Certainly he had not expected the enemy to take up the fight quite so willingly. It meant drawing her away from her destination, but the captain was clearly willing to trade that for a chance of hitting back at his tormentor.

The brig was moving slowly, but soon she would have the wind on her quarter and must accelerate. With every degree the broadside arc moved dramatically: Griffin knew he must avoid *Bee* encroaching into that danger area, whilst staying close to allow for another pass.

"Keep the helm to starboard," he shouted, even as the thought occurred.

Bee wore round and swept up like the beautiful creature she was, and shortly began to take the wind on her larboard side. The brig was still turning, and Griffin wondered how long she would continue to do so. Should he turn also, or claw away to windward? It was like fighting with a dense, slightly clumsy, pugilist, but one that still could pack a solid punch when called upon to do so.

"Stand by to tack; ready larboard battery!" If he could only repeat the previous exercise they might cause yet more damage, but Griffin doubted that the enemy would be quite so obliging and was shortly proved correct.

The cutter swept through the eye of the wind in record time, while the brig continued to turn. Soon she would be wearing, the invisible sweep of her broadside slowly creeping towards the area where *Bee* would have to travel. It was purely a question of time; if the cutter were fast enough they would close on her stern and deliver another deadly load. They might even be gone before she could react, leaving the enemy that much closer to defeat; but that trick had already worked once: the Warrens were no fools, and

Griffin was dubious about trying it for a second time. What looked far more likely, both in odds, and from the evidence before him, was that the brig would be in the perfect position to receive the cutter when they did arrive.

"Belay larboard battery, we shall be taking her to starboard." His order was unexpected and started a dozen different conversations. Griffin stepped forward and addressed the men in a clear voice. "I intend to feint an attack on their stern, but turn in front and address their bows instead; does everyone understand?"

That they did was as obvious as their apparent approval of his plan, but that hardly helped him with the final problem. The first turn would have to be made at the very last moment: to be early, and signal his intention, would simply give the game away. They would have no time to set square sails, but must run under main and fore alone, and make a high speed pass through the brig's larboard broadside arc. With luck the manoeuvre would be both unexpected, and fast enough to avoid too great a damage. Then the cutter must check her speed, before veering across the enemy's bows, and discharging her own guns. It was by no means an impossible manoeuvre, but not one they had practised under Griffin's command. Even if they avoided the brig's broadside, they would have to move quickly. If there was any confusion – should Griffin time it badly, or *Bee* be crippled – they could fall foul of the enemy's bowsprit, or be left vulnerable and have to face the brig's guns at devastatingly close range.

Bee was bearing down with her customary speed. Never, in all his days at sea, had Griffin experienced a craft so fast, or manoeuvrable; he simply wished there had been more time to get to know her better. The enemy was starting to wear and seemed confident that the cutter would be aiming for her stern once more. Griffin considered the angle: it was conceivable that they could even have pulled it off: a bolder commander than himself might think it worth dodging a broadside head on for the opportunity of delivering what could well be the fatal blow. With luck such a possibility would make what he was about to attempt even more of a surprise.

"Larboard a point." He spat out the order, cross that they were a little too far off the enemy to make the manoeuvre smooth, and hoping his correction would not be noticed or interpreted. The cutter responded, but it was still a little out of line: no matter, they were getting perilously close to the brig's broadside now, and had to move.

"Wear ship," he said, unconsciously using the command he had grown up with. "Take her to larboard."

Forsyth pressed the tiller across, and the boat baulked slightly.

"Ready starboard battery!" But the men needed no urging, even as *Bee* came around, and the boom swung overhead, some were heading back for their guns. This was the dangerous time: *Bee* was sweeping through the broadside arc, and might expect a devastating barrage at any time. Griffin waited, wondering for a moment if he were the only one aboard the cutter sensible to the danger. The gun captains were squinting down their barrels, and waiting patiently for the enemy's prow to come into view, while the rest of the servers were ready at the sheets. He stared fixedly at the brig, gauging the moment as finely as he could. Then, at his shout, the tiller was pulled back, and *Bee* turned her head to cross the enemy's bows.

"Larboard a point." Griffin repeated. He wanted to be close, but not too close; the brig was making progress, and at the speed *Bee* was going, it would be easier for the gunners if they had slightly more room.

The gun crews had all returned to their pieces now, and there was nothing left for anyone to do other than watch the proceedings. The brig was clearly trying to turn, and avoid the inevitable, but her hull was not as lithe and *Bee* would be upon them in less than sixty seconds. Once more, by a mixture of judgement and luck, Griffin had placed his command in a good position, and it was down to the individual skill of each gun captain to make their shots tell. He found himself beaming at Davies, who grinned back, as if they were any two lads abroad on a jaunt. For a long moment he had forgotten the problems of the last few hours, so absorbed had he become in the duel. Besides, it was hard to think of anything else when *Bee* was thrashing through the waves at her customary exuberant pace, and it was at that moment that Griffin realised just how much he loved the cutter.

And it was a genuine love; one that he had never before thought possible. Of course, he had known others express such affection for their particular ship; the seaman's term 'barkie' was common enough, and seldom used for any vessel who had not actually won their hearts. But with the spray from her bow reaching him as he stood far back by the binnacle, Griffin knew for certain that *Bee* was special and would have given anything to remain her captain for the rest of his life.

He longed to explore her ways: learn the good and the bad, and grow old in her company. For one who usually considered himself the most rational of souls, it was certainly a revelation but, even as he acknowledged the fact, he also knew that it was not to be. They were currently closing on a vastly superior enemy and, while he enjoyed those few exhilarating seconds, Griffin had the awful premonition that they would be the last he would ever know of his command.

Chapter Fifteen

Jones reined in his horse. The two of them had just passed through the tiny hamlet of Swanborough and were on the Kingston road. It was less than three miles to Lewes, but every inch was uphill and he felt he had left Newhaven far enough behind to relax a little. The hedgerows had also given way to stone walls; far less useful for footpads or highwaymen to shelter behind, and only one stretch of forest cover remained before he entered the town.

His horse snorted and shook her head as she settled to the slower pace. The evening was drawing in, and her coat glistened and steamed from the miles of hard riding. She had no name; since Suzie had been shot from under him over six years ago Jones had not allowed himself to grow close to any of his official mounts even though this one, a chestnut piebald with a strong heart and tolerant nature, was fast becoming a favourite. The riding officer patted her neck, and whistled softly through his teeth as they went. It would be night before long and, as he had no reason to return to Newhaven, he felt he might stay in Lewes. He was considering this, and where he would eat, when the sound of approaching hooves broke into his thoughts.

Without pausing, he stirred the horse into movement. She responded well, as he had known she would, but was obviously tired, and it took a while for her to reach the gallop. Loose stones flew up behind, and the beast was breathing heavily once again, but still Jones could hear the sound of those approaching and kept the pressure up.

There were three of them following; or possibly four. It was not so unusual on a busy road; they may simply be keen for an evening's rest, just as he was. The package pressed inside his jacket was vitally important, however, and Jones was taking no chances as he bent forward over the horse's neck, urging her on under the darkening sky.

The road was straight for the next half mile, then began a long series of bends that ended just on the outskirts of Lewes. He looked back over his shoulder, and caught a glimpse of three mounted men riding hard about two hundred yards behind. It was impossible to identify them at such a distance; if they were members of the Horsebridge gang then it was likely they had made the same journey, and their horses would be just as tired. All he had to do was keep his head, and continue to make for the town.

They were approaching the bends now, which coincided with the last piece of forest, and Jones bent himself further as he noted the low boughs of the trees. But there was plenty of clearance, and the thick foliage muffled the sound of the oncoming horses. He told himself he was behaving like a child; that the events of the afternoon had simply made him over-sensitive, and his followers were nothing more than fellow travellers, keen to finish their journey before night finally descended.

A straight stretch appeared: it lasted no more than a hundred yards, but at the end Jones chanced another look behind. Nothing. He relaxed slightly, then the sound of hooves returned, and he glanced back once more.

It was the same group, and they had gained on him. More than that, the leading horse had a white patch across the eyes, so much like the one that Samuels rode. Jones slapped the free ends of the reins about the horse's neck and she snorted at his urging. The sound of something passing alarmingly close, followed by a distant crack, made her miss a step, and it was all Jones could do to keep the head from turning. That was long range for firearms, and whoever was chancing a shot would be doing so from the gallop, but at least there was no further doubt in his mind as to who they might be.

Another bend, followed by a straight of less than fifty yards. The horse took the corner badly; she stumbled, and this time he was nearly thrown. He patted her hard; she had already done more than enough for him that afternoon, but he needed just that little bit extra.

Now the next turn was almost upon them, and this time Jones did slow slightly; better by far to keep on the move than tumble and be taken. The sound of another shot came to him, just as the mare was accelerating into the straight, her powerful back legs digging deep into the loose surface of the road. Jones saw nothing of the bullet, but they were now close enough to hit him or the horse, and either would do the business. He tried to remember how far the town was. As soon as it came into sight he would be relatively safe, but there were at least two more tight bends, and one long straight before then. Again the horse stumbled; he was pressing her too hard, but there was no other option.

They approached another turn but it was a gentle one this time, and he did not slow as the following straight ran for over two hundred yards: more than enough space for them to take him. He glanced back; there were only two now: one had dropped back. Either the horse was exhausted or its rider had decided to reload, but the remaining two were closer than ever: less than fifty yards off and still coming at them like the wind.

The leather satchel in his jacket was digging into his chest, and its presence was every bit as encouraging to him as his spurs and constant urgings were to the horse. Should it fall into the hands of the Warrens, all of Newhaven would be rocked by the recriminations. It must not happen: he could not allow it, but his lead was fast running out, and the pair were gaining all the time.

The next bend was tighter, and rose slightly with the climb that would continue to increase until they reached Lewes. His horse snorted and coughed, but she carried him round well enough. The road grew steadily steeper; he could not keep her at the gallop, but neither was there time to relax in any way. He dug the spurs in, hating himself as he did, yet desperate for that slight increase in speed the action provoked. The horse was starting to lose her rhythm; she would stumble soon, or shy and try to throw him. He tensed further, willing her on; the next turn was the last before the town, and the dragoons were garrisoned within the bounds: he only needed a few hundred yards.

But it was more than she could give and, as they were approaching the corner, the old girl tripped, recovering briefly, before turning sideways across the track and venting her frustrations with a loud snort. Jones looked back at his pursuers, and was horrified to see them quite so close. There was a flash as one of them fired a pistol, and the horse seemed to fold up beneath him.

He struggled free as she slumped onto her belly. It was Suzie's death all over again; his mind was numbed with horror. The steaming carcass rolled to one side as Jones untangled himself from the stirrups and scrambled away. His body would not move fast enough: everything was happening far too slowly. Then he was clear and running, stiffly at first, for the safety of the nearby undergrowth.

There were shouts from the men, and he could hear the sound of their horses pulling up, but they would have to dismount, and he was already over the ditch and throwing himself through the dense thicket and brushwood that bordered the forest beyond.

A shot whined close by, but Jones did not look back. At that moment he was not totally certain if he was running to or from the town; it was enough that some distance was being put between him and his pursuers. Then he was amongst the trees and movement was easier, as much of the denser vegetation had been replaced by bracken. An animal started near to him, but he paid it no notice; there was what appeared to be a clearing ahead, and he made for it with all his energy.

It turned out to be a path, and quite a large one; there was even some evidence of a rough stone surface. It must lead to the town and was only a few paces away. Dragging his boots through the clinging undergrowth Jones tottered forward, his breath coming in short, shallow draughts. A low ditch ran by the track, and he was preparing to cross when, just as he braced himself, the ground below gave way.

There was a snap, the shock of cold pain, and his body, anchored by a suddenly immoveable leg, was thrown forward, landing him heavily against the far bank. Dirt filled his mouth, but still he cried out as the agony increased. Something had his leg in a vice-like grip, and seemed intent on biting the very limb in two. Jones looked back to see his boot held firmly in the steel jaws of a mantrap, and knew that there was nothing more he could do.

The sound of horses came to him; his pursuers must be closing. He tried to move, but the pain was intense. He could tell the horses were getting closer although the noise of their hooves kept being muffled by someone screaming in pain. The noise stopped quite suddenly as he realised it had been coming from him, and he blinked up in wonder at the line of mounted men that now stood above.

There were far too many for his pursuers and, even in his torment, Jones could sense the impression of security they emitted. He raised his hand, and tried to move, but the mantrap had him pinned. Two dismounted and approached, staring down at the torn creature lying by the road.

"Good God, Weston," one said, in a clear and cultured voice. "It's Jackie Jones, the riding officer."

His companion gave a sharp, harsh laugh. "Damn it, sir, if you ain't correct. And I'd have thought him the last person to be taken for a poacher."

* * *

They were closing on the brig at too great a speed. Griffin flashed a look at Davies.

"Be ready to spill just afore they are abeam."

The mate understood at once, and bellowed to the men at the sheets.

The brig was attempting to turn, but her larboard broadside would not reach them in time, and any progress she made in that direction would only make it harder for the starboard battery when the cutter had passed. Griffin folded his arms and waited; he knew he had her in almost exactly the right position and his feeling of confidence was now overpowering any ludicrous premonitions of impending doom.

The enemy had already been hit and badly damaged; with luck this next blow would prove terminal. Either that or the Warrens might accept that enough was enough, and be persuaded to strike. Should that occur he would take the brig back to Newhaven, he decided. There were other ports closer to hand, but to bring a major Horsebridge craft in as a prize would be a grand gesture indeed. It might not solve all the problems ashore, but could hardly do his standing any harm. Then, with a sudden sickening feeling, he remembered something to spoil all his foolish aspirations.

"They have chasers!" he said, his words unintentionally loud. Davies peered forward through the shrouds, then swore quietly to himself.

"Secure yourselves, men!"

All of the gun captains retained their position as well as those manning the lightweight swivels, although a few looked back at Griffin in apparent confusion. But others – the majority – threw themselves flat to the deck, gaining what shelter they could behind the bulwarks.

Griffin had forgotten about the two shots fired from the brig's prow earlier. They had been rushed and ill aimed but now the enemy would have all the time in the world. And here he was, presenting his vessel as the ideal target.

As he watched the brass barrel of a carriage gun came into closer focus. It was pointing forward: either the cannon had a limited traverse, or they were intending to hit *Bee* directly on her beam. It looked to be at least a nine pounder, and there would be another on the starboard side. Were they to be loaded with chain, the cutter could easily be dismasted; grape or canister would sweep the deck clear of her men, and a well-placed round shot must sink them for sure.

But there was no choice. They could not turn to starboard and risk the might of an entire broadside, whereas steering into the wind, and attempting to escape close hauled, would only see them raked on their vulnerable stern. No, he had placed them in such a position, and now had to take the punishment.

Griffin moved to the starboard side for a better view. The cutter's long bowsprit was crossing the enemy's now, it would be seconds before the ideal moment. He leaned out beyond the protection of the hammock-stuffed netting, before pressure on his shoulder alerted him to Davies' presence, and he allowed himself to be pulled back. Then, with a loud crack, the foremost of *Bee*'s guns fired. Almost immediately two more joined it, but then a larger double boom drowned out all further sound, and seemed to hang in the air as the enemy replied, and her shot bore down upon the cutter.

One struck her amidships; the starboard chains disintegrated, releasing shrouds and causing the main lower mast standing backstay to fly up. The second was aimed slightly higher, striking square on the jaws of the boom. The mainsail, being loose footed, allowed the heavy spar to crash to the deck, smashing a hatch cover and one of the hand pumps, while a good half-way up the luff, cringles and clews were ripped from the lining and the canvas ballooned out. Amazingly no one was hurt, but the cutter's mast was now unsupported on her lee side and they were effectively locked against the wind.

Davies shouted orders to take in sail, but even as men rushed to obey, Griffin knew the situation was hopeless. He might bring her closer to the wind, but to do so would risk losing the mast; neither could he turn to starboard for fear of the brig's full broadside, while to continue as he was only invited a sound raking. There was a further creak from forward, and he saw with rare clarity that the mast itself had been weakened and was flexing horribly at the break. Davies' party were working the windlass to lower the gaff, but it would not be in time and their efforts may even be exacerbating the damage. Then, as he looked, all ninety feet of *Bee*'s mast began to slowly topple.

It fell to larboard, wrenching the hull over to a steep list and covering most of the deck with canvas and line. There was a pause of no more than a second as the enormity of what had happened struck home, then the men reacted almost as one. Some started to hack at the lines with axes, while others manhandled the bulk of torn tophamper over the side. It was orderly and carried out with commendable efficiency, even if all knew the situation remained entirely hopeless.

"Starboard your helm!" Griffin commanded, as the last pieces of debris were jettisoned. The mast and spars had acted like a sea anchor, and brought *Bee* round to larboard. The brig's prow was too close upon the cutter's stern for further damage from the bow chasers, but she was still in imminent danger of her counter being run down by the larger vessel's stem. A chance remained, albeit a slim one, that they possessed enough momentum to continue the turn, then fire *Bee*'s larboard battery, although what good that might ultimately do was debatable.

"Should we strike?" he asked Davies, in a soft voice.

The mate shook his head. "Wouldn't give them the satisfaction, and even if you tried, the men wouldn't follow. There's plenty of fight in us yet."

"Very well," Griffin said, glad beyond measure that the decision had been taken from him. He drew breath. "Small arms, men: prepare for boarding!"

Davies took up the call and soon there was a veritable queue fighting for weapons at the arms chests.

"You'll take a sword, sir?" Davies asked, before beckoning Harry over. Soon both officers were equipped with crude but eminently serviceable boarding cutlasses. Griffin thanked the lad, before drawing the weapon, wrapping the leather lanyard about his wrist and throwing away the scabbard, while looking towards the advancing brig.

Bee had hardly turned, and the enemy would shortly run down on her taffrail. The men were filing aft, as if being organised for a regular exercise. Some were cursing, others dangerously silent but it was clear that every one of them was spoiling for a fight. Griffin looked at the faces, people he had known for so short a time, yet would never forget. Wooderson, the carpenter's mate, still wielding the axe he had used to clear wreckage, and now seemingly intent on adopting it as a weapon, while Calver was ready with a cutlass. Gadd made some remark that drew a laugh from a few and Fuller told him to hold his tongue, although it was obvious the comment had amused him also. This had been Griffin's first appointment as captain: if he never served as one again, or did and was forever disappointed in his crew at least he would know what a good one was like. Then the brig crashed into the cutter's hull, and *Bee* began to disintegrate beneath their feet.

* * *

"Over her prow, men!" Davies shouted, and clambered up onto the bulwark while the brig's stem bit deep into the revenue cutter's hull. Others followed, and Griffin found himself almost at the end of the line as he heaved himself over and onto the enemy's deck. There were the hated bow chasers, still smoking from their work, but the brass barrels lay unattended now. Ahead he could see his men laying into the crew of the brig, striking wildly and effectively at the smugglers who appeared to have been taken by surprise and were in the main unarmed. But what they lacked in weapons they made up for in number; there must have been forty or so on deck; the long, wide and unencumbered deck that seemed so remarkably spacious after *Bee*'s foreshortened lines.

Davies was by the brig's foremast, slugging it out with a seaman who was armed with a cannon ramrod. Griffin advanced with every intention of helping, but a burly fellow dressed in a blue jacket that looked almost like a uniform came at him with a belaying pin. He fended off the blow, then thrust his cutlass forward, impaling the man in the belly. The body, powered by momentum, fell past him, and he twisted his sword free. There was an unknown seaman with a musket; he was raising it to his shoulder, clearly with a target in mind, and had no eye for Griffin. The cutlass struck again, and both man and weapon dropped to the deck.

Screams and curses were flying all about him now, and someone was shouting his name, but Griffin paid scant attention. Forward, a smartly dressed dandy, his hair powdered and tied back in a queue, was carrying an ornate hanger and calling out orders. Griffin made for him, but was interrupted by a toothless oaf with arms the size of hams who leered at him as he advanced. One of the huge fists was swung in his direction; Griffin ducked, but still caught a blow on the side of his head. A swift swipe with his cutlass sliced the man across his chest, and Griffin followed up by hacking deep into the cleft between neck and shoulder. The body slumped down, almost tripping Griffin as he moved forward once more.

Now there were more smugglers coming from the brig's stern, and most were armed. A musket ball whined passed his ear, just as he heard his name screamed yet again. Griffin turned to see Davies, on the larboard side and slightly ahead, give a wave. He was in a group with Lamport and several others from the cutter, almost next to the brig's main mast.

"Make for the quarterdeck!" Griffin shouted, and received a nod in reply as another shot cracked out amid the carnage. He advanced, others following; Gadd and Wooderson had joined to either side, the latter still wielding his axe, and, glancing back, he saw Colclough, Fuller and Conway, along with the boy, Harry. The smugglers had re-grouped next to the wheel, and would be difficult to overcome. Many were armed with muskets and, even as Griffin's party advanced, Harry fell to a shot. But take them they must; there was no ship to retreat to, and capture was not an option to be considered.

"Come on!" Griffin yelled, raising his cutlass and charging forward. They moved as a body, and soon joined with those of Davies. But the smugglers heavily outnumbered them, and this was not going to be easy.

Chapter Sixteen

Night was falling quickly and the light from a dozen braziers started to gain importance, making the small town seem especially vulnerable. Surveying the scene from the first floor of the inn, Sophie realised she was not the only woman to be watching. Shadows from another uncurtained window in the bakery opposite showed where at least one other was looking out, while old Mrs Davey, who helped at the dame school, was standing boldly at her open front door with what looked like a rolling pin tucked under one arm. A cart had been turned on its side and lay across the street. Together with several piles of packing cases and two barrels, it acted as a barricade. Behind, a huddle of men sat quietly, their backs against the boards of the truck. Some smoked pipes and the red glowing bowls made the group appear sinister, although Sophie knew they were nothing more frightening than local tradesmen and neighbours. Most would not normally have chosen to scare a goose, and the weapons that were stacked in a line near to them were mainly agricultural implements, with fowling pieces and the occasional musket for variety.

That the Horsebridge gang would be coming was accepted by all. In the past there had been minor protests when the Warrens had pushed things a little too far, and retribution had always been swift. A year back John Musgrave, who farmed near Meeching, made a stand, refusing to lend a pair of horses for a landing. The gang had returned after the run and burned down both his stable and barn. There were other instances just as brutal and even some, like the occasional stolen sheep, or unexplained fall from a cliff, that might not have been the work of the Warren family at all. But such was their hold on the town that blame was duly apportioned and the fear increased.

This afternoon's incident would hardly be ignored. It was not the protest of one man or family, but a joint effort: the entire town had rebelled, and it was generally acknowledged that retaliation would be prompt and deadly.

Everyone knew of the efforts made at Goudhurst. There the villagers had stood up to a group not unlike those led by the Warrens, and had even proved victorious, killing three of the gang members and attracting so much attention and praise from the press and public that the ringleaders were arrested and later hanged. But that had been a long-planned battle; a campaign almost. Women and children were evacuated, and the defence was under the direction of a former army corporal. Arms had been catalogued and distributed equally about the defences, while a recognised chain of command ensured that no single area could be cut off, or overwhelmed; the men had been trained and were reasonably familiar with the techniques of street warfare.

There was no such leader in Newhaven; the closest they came to one was Jack Jones, and some were still uncertain as to where the riding officer's loyalties truly lay. And now even he had gone, having departed for Lewes several hours before, leaving the townsfolk to sort matters for themselves.

Perhaps if they were better organised: if some plan had been prepared, or even a commander elected before the afternoon's riot, they might fare well enough. As it was, there had been no time for discussion; everyone did what they thought logical, with little attempt at coordination or planning. A few groups were scattered about strategic areas in the town, but the only real strong point was the upturned cart and even Sophie could see that it would be easily overrun.

The Warrens could take it in a direct attack from the main street; if not, it would be a simple matter to send their men in small groups on foot. They could enter the town almost unnoticed and file silently through the streets, or come across the drawbridge and attack the barricade from behind.

Once that was achieved, and the Warrens had direct control, there was little knowing what they might do. Newhaven could be razed to the ground relatively easily, although she doubted they would stoop to such a measure when the town provided such a prime source of income and supplies. Far more likely that certain people would be seized, either as hostages against further protest or simply as a warning. Stories abounded of vengeance taken by other gangs in the area; several years ago, an elderly revenue officer and a civilian had been brutally murdered for daring to speak up against a bunch of extortionists who had also started as little more than free traders. The two were tortured for several days before one was thrown down a well and stoned to death, the other buried alive in a fox earth. At the time the newspapers had revelled in such devilment and the perpetrators were eventually executed, again to public acclaim. But nothing was done to protect against such a situation arising in the future, as the current problem proved only too well.

The local militia was an option, and one they had discussed for some time before deciding against calling them in. At least two of the officers were known to have associations with the Horsebridge gang, and many more were suspected of being members. They might put up a show, maybe win a few days' reprieve, but no Warrens would be arrested, and retribution would only be delayed. Eventually all agreed it better knowing when they were coming, so as to face them together, as a town. And whatever the outcome, if all ended in bloodshed or, in twelve hours' time, there was hardly a building left standing, the message would have been sent out, and whatever remained should at least be free from future intimidation.

* * *

Griffin was exhausted. His head hurt; there was an underlying sensation of nausea, and his right arm felt as if it had been wrenched from its socket. But their attack had been successful; whether this was down to the determination of *Bee*'s crew, or resignation on the part of the smugglers, the brig had been taken. He was still effectively on an enemy's deck, however, and knew there was no time to lose. They had control, but it could be lost with just a moment's inattention.

"Take them to the fo'c's'le," he snarled, and Lamport's team began to prod the beaten members of the brig's crew towards the forward hatchway. One protested, and tried to break away, only to be pushed roughly back by Conway, who was armed with a cannon handspike. The man struggled, apparently incensed at being included with the rest, and the mate, returning from attending the wounded in the great cabin, laughed.

"That looks like our friend Berkeley," he said, as he approached his captain. "He's put so many into custody in his time you'd think he'd be a touch more understanding his-self."

The name meant nothing to Griffin.

"Well known in these parts," Davies explained. "Justice of the peace from Bishopstone, and about as honest as a three-shilling coin. I hears he had an interest in that first smack we took, so he might have come along last night just to see us sunk."

The prisoners were starting to file down the companionway now, under the watchful eye of Lamport and the others. "If he's a magistrate, do you think we should separate him?" Griffin asked, but the mate shook his head.

"May as well put the sheep in with the goats," he replied. "I recognised at least one Warren amongst them, but reckon they'll be keepin' their heads down for a spell. Though if they think they're gonna get away with no one noticing them later they're in for a nasty surprise." He glanced at Griffin and seemed to relax. "Well, we took her, sir," he said. "Even if we did lose the barkie in the bargain."

"Yes," Griffin said thickly. "In that Mr Berkeley was not disappointed."

"Aye, but she died game," Davies agreed.

Griffin said nothing. He could remember with startling clarity the sound of the cutter's hull being crushed by the brig's stem, and felt a pang of loss at the thought that his precious command was no more. The brig had been captured, though, and it was a feat indeed considering the enemy's superiority in almost every aspect. His mind was not clear enough to consider all the ramifications, but registered it as good news, and he met the pleased expression of the mate with a lopsided smile.

"You did well, William," he said, unbending slightly, and Davies' expression deepened, gratified possibly as much from the use of his first name as any commendation.

Evening was falling fast but light enough remained for Griffin to inspect the brig, and the scene was of utter disorder. *Bee's* cannon had caused a great deal of damage; from where he stood the shattered quarterdeck could be seen, with the binnacle in ruins, and the taffrail almost non-existent. A deep scar ran along the deck showing where one of the cutter's round shot had dug deep and torn up the strakes, and there were dark stains in several places that Griffin realised, with something of a shock, must be blood.

He felt at his head: there was a large lump on one side, he must have been struck or received some sort of a blow, although he had no idea when. Actually, much of the fight remained a blur and now that it was over, and they had been victorious, he just wanted to rest. The sight and sounds of *Bee* being broken up were all too real, however, and he struggled hard to think of something else. Lamport returned from below, and seemed unusually animated.

"I've had all the fit ones placed for'ard, sir," he said, saluting smartly. "There are thirty-three altogether; less than we thought," he said, although Griffin's tired brain gave the impression that the words were not quite keeping pace with the petty officer's lip movements. "Colclough, Gadd and Calver are watching over them."

"You've put all the wounded together?" Griffin asked.

"Aye, sir," Davies interrupted. "There are more of theirs than ours and most are pretty cut about. None will be going anywhere for a while, but there's a guard on them just the same. We must have accounted for a fair few before we boarded. It were a damn fine show, sir, damn fine."

Griffin ignored the compliment; now was not the time to think about what had been achieved. There was still much to be done before they were safe, and he had the age-old fear of every captain of a prize crew. "You're quite sure there is no chance that any might get free?"

Lamport smirked. "No, sir. All our men are well armed and still spoiling for a fight; if any try they won't live long enough to regret it. Besides, they seem a pretty mournful lot," he added, oblivious to any irony. "Especially the Warrens."

"How many of them are aboard?" Griffin asked.

"Two brothers," the petty officer replied, with satisfaction. "They're nought but youngsters, but we got a couple; that's all that counts."

"What of our losses?" Griffin said, turning to the mate.

"Too soon to be totally sure." Davies' face had grown suddenly serious. "Nairn's dead. At least, we think so; no one's seen him since the mast fell. And Forsyth: he was killed by one of the scum after the rest had surrendered. Several more are wounded, though they're 'tended to, an' will keep 'til we raise Newhaven. Only young Harry's causing a worry; he stopped a musket bullet in his arm and will need to see a surgeon sharpish."

"I'd better set a course," Griffin said vaguely.

"You won't need to do that, sir," Davies chuckled, his spirits obviously rising, and he nodded to the north where the familiar outline of the Seven Sisters could just be made out. "With the wind in our favour, we might even be home afore the tide drops."

Griffin blinked. He supposed Newhaven was his home, although with *Bee* sunk and his lodgings destroyed there was precious little for him there; certainly not Sophie: that bridge was already burned. He had told Davies they had done well, which was true, no crew could have performed better. For a cutter to take a brig was a remarkable feat, and every man had the right to be proud. But the well-remembered feelings of despondency that Griffin often experienced after success were starting to make themselves known, and he had to fight to maintain his composure. Even if they did have two Warrens in custody, and one of their vessels to boot, there was no guarantee that Dobson or Dwyer would not find a way for them to be set free, probably implicating him into the bargain. But the mate was clearly expecting some sort of response, and he must be positive.

"Mr Davies, that is capital; you really have done magnificently. I can only thank you."

* * *

There was to be no shilly-shallying; the Horsebridge gang had arrived in force and were clearly preparing for an all-out assault. From her vantage point at the upstairs window, Sophie could see the dense crowd of men gathering at the top of the street, just out of musket range. There must have been forty of them; maybe more. She wondered how many were actually members of the gang, or had been hired for the evening's work: of one thing she was certain: none came from Newhaven.

Her father entered the room. She acknowledged him with a glance, before quickly returning to the window. He had left earlier to join the men. At the time she asked him not to go: pleaded almost. The old man had not listened, of course and, now that he had come back, Sophie could not be certain if she were pleased or sorry to see him.

Their inn was one of the larger buildings and main businesses of the town, and her father had much to lose if the Warrens decided to attack it. But then if he were hurt, and with Matthew in gaol, she would be left without any immediate family, and probably nowhere to live. He came and stood next to her, and she noticed he was carrying a musket.

"You're not joining the rest, then." It was more of a statement than a question, but her father shook his head.

"No, we decided to set a few men with guns in the houses, and I chanced I may as well stay in my own home." He stepped back from the window and placed the butt of the musket on the bed before starting to clean out the barrel with a rag tied to a piece of wire. She returned to the

264

window, and noticed that the crowd at the end of the street had moved forward slightly. The crack of a gun from below caught her attention. One of those at the barricade was chancing a shot; it was long range, however, and any bullet would do little damage even if it reached the Horsebridge mob. Sophie instinctively drew back, but there was no reaction from the crowd, and soon she was peering through the window once more. Movement from across the road caught her attention. A figure was standing in the alley that ran between the bakers and Mr Jackson's shop. She was watching it just as her father returned to her.

"By the butchers," she said quietly, her lips hardly moving. The man was cast in heavy shadows; he carried a gun, and was taking careful aim at the blockade. Her father nodded, and shouldered his own musket.

It fired with the usual double crack of pan and main charge, instantly filling the room with a smell of burning powder. Sophie instinctively brought her hands up to her ears, but it was too late to stop the ringing sound that remained for several seconds afterwards. There was a mournful cheer from the men below and, as the smoke cleared, a body could be seen lying prone on the road.

Her father retreated from the window and reached for the ramrod. "That's the first," he said.

* * *

Even with an intact rig, the brig's sailing abilities would have been disappointing when compared with their late lamented *Bee*. But damaged as she was she made extremely poor progress, despite the fact that the wind was with her. Almost as soon as they set off, every man on board realised it would be several hours before they made Newhaven, and when they finally did, her draught was too deep to clear the bar.

"Take a boat, and Lamport," Davies advised as they lay, hove to, in the deep water beyond the roadstead. "The prisoners are secure enough, an' you can organise things better ashore. Besides, young Harry's arm needs 'tending to."

Griffin glanced at the mate, drawing comfort from the steady blue eyes. "You're certain?"

"Certain I don't want to go, if that's what you mean," the older man laughed. "Tellin' Dobson's lot we've copped a Warren brig ain't going to go down at all well; I'd inform the militia first, were I you."

Davies had a point there; he should see to it that there were enough officials present when the brig finally tied up at the legal quay; the more who knew what had gone on, and the identity of the prisoners, the better. Griffin touched the lump on his head; it was still tender, but had ceased to hurt quite as much.

"How are the prisoners?" he asked Calver, who had just been relieved from his guard duties and was helping himself to water from the scuttlebutt.

"Quiet as mice, sir," the Londoner replied. "Skea, Mendy and Bennett are watchin' 'em now. All seem secure, though I don't think they'd make trouble even if we weren't lookin'," he said, before adding complacently, "we dusted 'em up proper."

"Very well then, I'll take five hands," Griffin said, switching his attention back to Davies. "That will still leave you with nearly twenty, and you may be better to keep Lamport. Calver, are you game for a run ashore?"

The seaman's face lit up.

"Good, then find four others and bring the lad up on deck, along with any of our wounded who can make the passage. We'll take the quarter boat."

* * *

In the town, things were moving on a pace. The group at the end of the street had edged forward, and were now at extreme musket range of the barricade. They had commandeered several barrels and a hand-cart, and formed a barrier of their own, and the whine of shots constantly filled the air as the two sides exchanged long-distance fire. But, to Sophie's mind at least, there seemed to be less of the Horsebridge gang than before. Peering from her vantage point, she could see fewer than twenty; a sizeable reduction on the original force.

"Warrens won't take kindly to being shot at," her father said, standing next to her with his musket once more loaded. "I'd judge we're in for an assault."

"Where will they come from?" she asked.

"Could be either side, or full on. I can take out any that come on their own, but if they move as a group the lads below will be overwhelmed in no time."

So far, the old man had accounted for just the one. There may have been others sheltering in the alley, but none had shown themselves. If there were to be a group gathering he could do little about it, and it was only a short run to the barricade.

"I could get a gun," Sophie told him. For a number of reasons it was the last thing she wanted, but the situation appeared desperate.

"No, that would hardly do good. We have little enough in the way of arms as it is. I reckon this will be settled below and it'll be down to cold steel." He suddenly thrust the musket at her. "You take mine, and I'll join them. Maybe they can find me a sickle with a decent edge," he added with a half-smile. She took the gun from her father; it was warm from the touch of his skin, and felt especially deadly as she weighed the thing experimentally in her hand.

"Take any shot that feels worthy," he said, already making for the door. "You've powder and ball a plenty on the bed. And if they come in a group, aim high and at the front, that way you may wound another should you miss." He was gone without waiting for a response, and the girl looked about the empty room, appalled at what she had been asked to do. Then she examined the musket more closely, eased back the hammer to full cock, and took up position at the window once more.

* * *

The west quay at Newhaven was unusually empty. Griffin guided the small boat in, the men banked and boated their oars without orders, and Wooderson made her fast.

"Can you hear something?" Calver asked, as they were seeing to the wounded Harry, who had accompanied them. The lad was comfortable enough, with his left arm bound tight against his body, but it would take some manoeuvring to get him out of the boat. They all paused for a moment, and the sound of distant gunfire became obvious.

"That will be the town," Colclough said. "There'll be a fight in progress."

"P'raps the French have landed?" Harry said. The men shook their heads.

"Warren trouble, more like," Wooderson stated with natural authority. "They'll have either taken control, or be trying to."

"A shame we are not better armed," Colclough grunted, and Griffin shared the sentiment with a trace of guilt. They all had cutlasses and two were carrying pistols but, had he known there were problems ashore, he would have brought more men and equipped them properly. For a moment he considered returning to the brig, but Davies also needed hands there and the loss of time might be vital.

"We have enough," Griffin said firmly, reaching up for the quay and hauling himself up.

"We have indeed, sir," Wooderson agreed. "'If God be for us, who can be against us?': Romans eight," he added, as if in explanation.

The men gently lifted Harry up and onto the harbour wall. "Can you walk, lad?" his captain asked.

The boy nodded. "Fine, sir. But I wouldn't be much use for fightin'."

Griffin gave a grin. "No, but you may go to Castle Hill. This part of town is out of sight from the shore battery and they might not be aware. Tell the commander there is trouble, and to send an armed party." He eyed the youngster carefully. "You sure you are fit?" The boy beamed back at him, his eyes bright, and Griffin relaxed.

"The rest of you men, group up; we'll make straight for the drawbridge," he said, before setting off at a moderate run, to be joined by the others close behind. It seemed like the obvious destination if the Warrens had attacked the town, and the fact that The Star, Sophie's home, was close by meant little to any of them.

* * *

The Horsebridge gang was coming. Sophie raised the musket a little awkwardly to her shoulder and rested the side of her face against her right hand as she took aim. The gun felt overly long, and was difficult to hold steady. She swung it down until the first man in the irregular group came into view. They were swarming towards the barricade, some holding torches, swords or clubs aloft while others brandished pistols and in one case what appeared to be a blunderbuss. The brass barrel caught her eye as it glinted in the light from the flames, and she focused on the man carrying it. He was close to the front, and seemed as good a target as any. The musket wobbled as she tried to keep a steady bead on the moving figure. She wondered if some allowance should be made for speed; after all, this was the first time she had fired a weapon of any sort, and was both worried and strangely excited. Then her father's words came back, and she raised the sights slightly, before half-closing her eyes and squeezing the trigger.

The flash in the pan made her jump and for a split second she thought the gun had failed to fire. A sudden jolt against her shoulder told her otherwise and the crack, surely so much louder than when father had fired it, almost made her ears burst.

She brought the weapon down, and stared through the smoke at the mob. They had just reached the barricade, and were clambering over. It was impossible to tell if her shot had caused any damage; there were a few bodies lying in the street, and one was staggering away from the fighting, but nowhere could she see a blunderbuss.

Her gaze returned to the blockade where a fierce battle was in progress. She could see her father wielding what looked like a garden fork against a man armed with a sword. He was fending off the cutlass blows as his assailant hacked at him. As she watched, the old man trapped the blade between the tines of his fork, wrenching the weapon free before leaning forward and calmly administering the coup de grâce.

The sight sickened her, but only for a second. More Horsebridge men had joined the fight, and soon it was obvious that the townsfolk were to be overpowered. She held her breath as Jackson, the butcher, fell to the sword of a brute who looked a good twenty stone. The man retrieved his weapon and glared about, looking for fresh prey, before deciding on her father. She watched, horrified, as the two were soon locked in deadly combat. Suddenly she remembered the musket, and stepped back from the window.

The powder lay in a cardboard pot, and there was a group of lead balls next to it, along with some cotton waste. Taking the tiny brass ladle, she measured out a scoop of raw explosive, and tipped it into the warm barrel. There had to be a wad, she knew that, but was uncertain if it came now or after the ball. Deciding on the latter, she dropped a lead shot down, and followed it with a piece of cotton, which she tamped down using the ramrod. The frizzen and hammer were stiff, but moved back under pressure, revealing the pan, which she filled with fine powder from the small, leather-covered priming flask. Returning to the window, she looked out. There was no sign of her father, nor the beast who had been fighting him, but another figure caught her attention.

Sophie took a sharp intake of breath when she realised it was Griffin, and he was leading several others. The group smacked into the fray like a damp cloth thrown against a wall, and now the battle was far more equal. She raised the musket. There was no clear target, all seemed to be a mass of fighting men, some friend, some enemy, and little to tell between the two. It was impossible to say which side was winning and soon she had lost sight of Griffin and his men. She lowered the gun, then rested it back on the window-sill. Really, there was little she could do save watch.

* * *

The men from the cutter were far more occupied; the battle became obvious as soon as they crossed the deserted drawbridge and, despite having already run from the quay, they increased their pace further. Griffin made for the first man he saw; a bearded lout who turned on him with a heavy sword. The journey from the wharf had all but exhausted the revenue officer and he drew breath with great gasps as the clumsy blows were blocked with the blade of his boarding cutlass. His opponent also appeared to be in poor shape, puffing and groaning loudly as they fought. Eventually, when the two men finally locked, Griffin was able to push him back against a pile of packing crates that had formed part of the blockade. The hairy man's eyes grew suddenly bright when a case momentarily checked his progress, then there was a deep-throated roar as Griffin gave one final shove, pushing him backwards into the pile of splintering wood. He fell heavily, his head cracking against the hard ground, and Griffin knew there would be no further problems from that quarter.

Other fights were in progress although, with very few exceptions, it was hard to define friend from enemy. A balding man and a youngster seemed to be taking alternate swings at each other with their fists but for the life of him Griffin could not tell who belonged to the town or the gang. He spotted Colclough apparently wrestling with a heavier adversary and was making his way to help when a far better dressed individual came from around the upturned truck, and advanced towards him. He was carrying a horse pistol along with an elegant sword, and Griffin guessed this to be another member of the Warren family.

The gun could not have been loaded, although its weight still made for a respectable weapon, and the man whipped the thin blade towards the revenue man's face with obvious skill. Griffin ducked, and parried the move, but the length of his adversary's sword prevented him from closing with his cutlass. Again he advanced, and once more Griffin was able to turn the weapon away, but could tell it would take little contact from such an edge to cut and wound him badly. The man spat an insult in his direction and Griffin smiled, before making his own attack.

With an audible hiss his opponent's sword swept up, and caught the sleeve of his jacket. The material parted as if by magic, but the weapon was slowed sufficiently to enable Griffin to raise his cutlass. He was too close to take a decent swing, but used the opportunity to slam the hilt downwards into the man's face. As a move it was unorthodox, and probably against all the gentlemanly rules of fighting, but Griffin cared little as it had bought him precious space and even a second or so of time. He briefly appraised his adversary, whose nose was starting to bleed, and who was clearly angry. Both were marks in Griffin's favour, although he also had problems of his own. For far too long his breath had been coming in snatched gasps, the wound to his head was beginning to ache once more: he was suddenly finding it harder to move, harder to think.

Once more the narrow blade sliced through the air. Griffin could almost feel its wind as he was forced to retreat, knowing there was scant space behind and he was in imminent danger of tripping. The blade flew again, this time connecting with the flesh of his cheek, and warm blood began to flow. Griffin brought his cutlass up, and pressed the sword arm away, before regaining a pace. He saw the pistol as it came across and ducked, barely missing the heavy metal barrel that swept above his head, but the action had also thrown his opponent off balance. Griffin seized the moment, taking another step forward and aiming a hearty left hook at the man's face.

His fist connected, and there was a shout of pain and surprise, but Griffin was now relying on pure fighting instinct and hardly noticed. Again he struck with the cutlass: this time the blade was caught by the guard of the sword and his opponent twisted it to one side. For a moment Griffin was undefended, and there was a look of victory on the other man's face as he swung his pistol up and smacked him hard under the chin with the heavy barrel. Griffin's head flew back and his world began to spin. The cutlass suddenly seemed incredibly heavy: he could not lift it, neither was he able to protect himself in any way, and he realised that it was now just a question of when and where he would be run through.

This was as far as it went. The Warrens had taken his girl, his home, his command and now he was about to lose his life. The sword moved again, drawing Griffin's eye, but it was the empty pistol that finally did for him. Coming from out of his line of sight, it landed firmly on the side of his head, and all began to grow dark. He knew the sword was being drawn back, but felt incapable of avoiding what had become inevitable. There was a stab of pain, but surprisingly from his right thigh, causing him to stumble just as the other man came forward at the lunge. Griffin allowed himself to reel to one side. He dodged the move and noticed the thin steel as it flashed uselessly past his left arm, but it was the last thing he did see.

His leg seemed no longer able to give support and with a cry he fell, hitting the ground and rolling, face down, onto the dirt. From far off he heard a girl's scream, but paid it no attention as, breathless and vulnerable, he crumbled into a heap. The pain in his head was steadily growing; soon it would become unbearable, and he sensed that consciousness would remain for only a few more seconds. There was nothing left to give. It had probably not been the finest of efforts, but surely no one could criticise him for not trying.

Chapter Seventeen

Light from the dragoons' blue flares mingled eerily with the yellow flame of the braziers and the more subtle glow of lamps and candles seen through uncurtained windows. Major Reynolds reined in his horse, which was foaming from the hard ride, and looked about. His men had arrived in the nick of time, or so it appeared. There were many wounded and not a few dead but a mob fight such as this could have easily ended in far greater bloodshed. In Ireland, he had frequently seen two sides all but wipe each other out in festivals of butchery that would never have been tolerated if either had been professional soldiers.

He turned his mount and made slowly for the barricade that seemed to have been the focal point of the battle. The animal picked its way carefully, avoiding the body of a wounded man who was waiting for medical attention but still held tightly to his cudgel. It was always the same with civilians; they knew no control. Fighting, for them, was an instinct, not a science, and their innate barbarism sickened him almost as much as the atrocities they so frequently carried out.

His men had stopped the combat within seconds; a proper force, well-governed and under military discipline, will usually staunch any amount of rioting, however small their number might be. Almost immediately afterwards they had been joined by troops from the nearby shore battery, and peace was restored. A group of civilians, still bickering in their misery, were now herded together at the side of the road, and would doubtless be separated into their appropriate clans in due course. Both sides had probably broken the law, but Reynolds was experienced in such matters and confident that a tidy report, one which made a clear distinction between good and bad, would finally emerge. From what the fellow Jones had told them, it might be more of a mess than was usual as several figures in authority were involved. Well, so much the better; Reynolds had little time for anything other than martial law. It would do no harm for a few petty officials to be taken down a peg or two, and if officers of the amateur militia were also embroiled, that would hardly sadden him. His adjutant appeared from the doorway of a nearby inn and approached.

"Are there any who may be considered responsible people, Weston?" Reynolds asked in a weary voice.

"A revenue officer, sir," the younger man replied. "From the maritime service, by all accounts. He's wounded, but seems to have a story of some sort to tell, 'though it seems a touch confusing to my mind."

"Very well," the major said, dismounting and handing the reins across. "Look after Shannon; he could do with some water. And see if you can get those artillery johnnies to take charge of the prisoners."

"Do we keep them together, sir?" the adjutant asked. "I mean, all in one group?"

"Unless you can tell one from the other," the major replied, with a wry smile. "They all look the same to me, but no doubt we will discover a difference eventually."

* * *

Davies eased himself into Griffin's tiny ground-floor room at The Star. The mate's face appeared ruddier than usual, and he was slightly out of breath. But then he seemed to have spent the last few days constantly on his feet and, after two nights with hardly any sleep, was almost exhausted. It was not his first visit; he had called several times before, but on each occasion the commander had been sound asleep, and this time appeared to be no different. Then, as he was about to turn and go, Griffin's eyes finally did open.

"How is it with you, sir?" Davies asked, noticing the movement. Griffin looked about the room, before focusing on his visitor. "You look a mite better than earlier," the mate added.

Griffin smiled, and reached up to the bandage that felt strange about his head, before easing himself more upright in the bed. "Well enough, thanking you," he said, unconsciously using the Sussex phrase. The army surgeon who removed the musket ball from his thigh three days back had also inspected his skull. It was fractured, but not depressed, and Griffin had been prescribed laudanum. A deep sleep followed, and had pretty much lasted until that morning. Even now he was finding it hard to shake off the sensation of inner peace; it was a feeling that had been notably lacking since he first set foot in Newhaven.

But seeing Davies effectively brought him back to the real world. There were a myriad questions that needed answering, and he was still uncertain as to where he was, or who had been looking after him.

"What word is there of the town?" he asked, pulling himself further up the bed and wincing only slightly when his wounds objected to the movement.

Davies pulled up a chair and sat down heavily, making the frame creak under his weight.

"Dobson and Dwyer are taken," he said, giving the most important news first.

"Indeed?" Griffin said, stopping half-way through a stretch; he had not expected such a development.

The mate nodded. "Dragoons marched them out yesterday morning, as well as a couple more from Custom House. What with the Warrens they're holding, those they picked up on the night and them in the brig, I'd say Lewes Gaol must be pretty well up to the gunnels by now."

The mate was probably right, although Griffin wondered quite how long such a situation might remain; somehow he could not see either of the revenue officials spending long in a prison cell. Both were artful talkers, and doubtless knew a good few in high places who would listen to their story. And the Warrens were not without influence; there must be lawyers, politicians and petty officials by the score who had benefited from their dealings in the past, and would be keen to see them back in business.

He settled back on his pillow as the thoughts ran through his tender head. In the last few weeks he had grown cynical about government methods of administration. It seemed to need only the right word in the right place, and perhaps a nominal fine, then that blind eye would be turned, and everything could continue as normal.

"Oh, and Jackie Jones is up and about," Davies continued.

"He was wounded?" Griffin asked.

"Ran into a mantrap in the woods south of Lewes, but he's sorted right enough. Indeed, I have seldom known him better," Davies grunted. "Bone wasn't broken and the leg's stitched up proper. He's been charging about the town like a two year old. Why, I saw him just a moment back; he's dining here in the inn – shall I send for him?"

Griffin was about to answer when a loud rap at the door made them both turn. Davies stood as the door opened, admitting the riding officer. He wore uniform, with shoes, rather than boots and his right leg was thick with bandage. He also appeared every bit as tired as the mate, although his face still bore the well-remembered smile.

"Well, there's lucky," he said, on seeing Griffin. "The girl said she could hear talking: I'm glad to see you awake, sir."

"Glad to see you also, Jackie," Griffin told him.

"I was just filling in the Commander," Davies explained. "It was Jackie what brought William Bourne in from Lewes."

"Bourne?" Griffin exclaimed. "The excise surveyor? He's here, in Newhaven?"

"Oh no," the riding officer protested. "You're not pinning that one on me. It was Colonel Douglas' idea, though I'll admit the old sod has played a fair enough hand."

"Well, whoever it was, it sounds like an act of genius," Griffin said, genuinely impressed. For William Bourne to become involved meant that little, if anything, would be covered up. As excise surveyor he was officially the area head of a rival organisation, one that collected tax on dutiable goods manufactured on land. Rather than cooperate, however, the two forces were daggers drawn, and if anyone was going to weed out corruption and dishonesty in the customs service, it would be him.

"All those arrested are being sent to London for trial," Jones continued. "Bourne's clerk told me it was his way, not trusting the local magistrates."

Griffin relaxed; that was far beyond anything he had hoped for, and might indeed see the end to corruption at Custom House as well as the tyranny of the Warrens.

"And they've found the *Bee*," Davies said, instantly recalling Griffin's attention. "What's left of her hull washed up on the Cuckmere yesterday evening. There's precious little to salvage," he added hastily. "We'll go down and set her alight afore so very long."

"I should like to see her again before you do," Griffin said quietly, and the mate seemed to understand.

"Reckon we'll be getting a new barkie in time," Davies reflected. "Along with fresh faces at Custom House. And

Newhaven itself will be a different place, you can be assured of that."

Griffin nodded. Things had certainly turned out better than he could have wished, even if there still remained a number of unanswered questions.

One was his room; he knew he was in The Star, but it was a very different place to that given him when he first arrived. This was more delicately furnished, almost with a feminine touch, and he was fairly certain it was on the ground floor. That made sense; he had been brought in with a wounded leg, after all; it would have been foolish to have carried him upstairs. But what of Sophie? Had she been responsible for placing him here? And he needed to know about the brig, and the men from the cutter. He closed his eyes as the thoughts began to swim about his brain, and by the time Davies and Jones closed the door, he was snoring softly once again.

* * *

Sophie did not come until later that day. It was evening, in fact and Griffin had eaten a good meal, brought to him by the landlord. The man sported a bandage to his right arm and a large patch of diachylon plaster across his cheek, although he still seemed about ten years younger. He had been eager to tell of his part in the fight, and how he had come about his injuries. Now Griffin was exhausted, and lay back on the bed contemplating another night's sleep with a desire that was bordering on lust. But even from the knock at the door, he knew it to be her, and all traces of tiredness vanished as she stepped inside.

"How is it with you?" she asked softly, and Griffin smiled.

"It is a question that has been posed often today," he said. "In truth, I am well enough, and am thanking you, and your family, for the hospitality."

"It is the least we could have done," the girl replied, before seeming to stop herself from saying more. She had not admitted to being the one who had shot Griffin in the leg and, thus far, no one had guessed. Or at least, so she thought; the one person who might be aware was lying in the bed before her. "You have done much for us," she added, rather lamely.

"Your brother is in gaol," he reminded her. "I hardly think that constitutes help of any kind."

"I know now that you probably saved his life, and that of another of his crew," she replied quickly, seating herself on the small chair that Davies had almost wrecked earlier. "Besides, he will not be there for long."

"They are sending him to London?"

She shook her head. "No, he is to be released."

Griffin's expression hardened. If this was due to some underhand dealings, then all their efforts had been wasted. "How so?" he asked.

"He is to volunteer for the Navy," she said simply. "He may be tried, and then given the option, but Mr Jones believes the court will accept his offer and waive charges without such bother."

It was a common enough method for smugglers to avoid prosecution; they would forgo any bounty, and be tied to the service for a minimum of five years, while the Navy gained a much needed skilled seaman. Such a course was considered the better alternative to any penalty faced in court, although the option was usually only open to members of a gang. Sophie's brother was about as small an operator as could be imagined, but he still had a crew and the law must consider him a ringleader.

"Surely Matthew is the boat's owner?" he asked hesitantly.

"He has a two-third share," Sophie replied. "Nothing official, of course; that's not how we do things hereabouts. Jamie Nettle, the man who was killed, had the other third."

Griffin waited.

"Matt will make over his portion to Nettle's widow," she explained. "The boat took quite a drubbing, but there'll be enough in salvage to pay off any fine that Pete Romsey, the other crew member, is given, and still leave enough to tide her over."

Griffin lay back on the bed and considered for a moment. The solution was logical, but hardly within the letter of the law, and he wondered if he really could approve.

"Joe Lamport will be joining as well," she continued, unaware of any debate on his part. "It seems he feels guilty for what happened to Matt, although none of us can see why."

It was late, and he needed sleep, but Griffin's thoughts swung from one quandary to the next. Mention of Lamport's name struck a chord; as a revenue man he had been excluded from any suspicion of informing on them and yet, now that the possibility was brought to his attention, the petty officer's involvement seemed all too likely. He felt his face colour: it had been far easier to blame the girl. At the time there had been no doubt in his mind, but now he knew he was mistaken. Griffin drew a deep sigh; it was not his first mistake since moving to Newhaven.

"Do they wish for the Navy?" he asked, temporising.

"Oh yes." Sophie was quite positive. "In truth Joe is keener than Matt, but I think they will both fare well. And Joe's wife, Emma is equally eager; she sees it as a way to stop herself having children, even if it might not prove to be so very effective. After all, sailors cannot spend all their time afloat."

Her eyes sought Griffin's as if for confirmation then, realising what she had said, she blushed and went to tidy her hair back from her face. But Griffin felt that she could not have looked lovelier, and reached out his hand.

"So, will you be remaining in Newhaven?" she asked, taking it in hers as if she had done so a thousand times before.

"I have no command," he replied. "And nowhere to stay."

"You will always have a place here," she said simply.

Her words also found a home, and he was deeply reassured, but the Ward problem, coupled with guilt from his own private failure, had taxed his weary brain to exhaustion, and all he really wanted was peace. Whoever had thought of the ruse, and both Davies and Jones were equally capable, it was clear that a trick had been pulled to set the lad in the Navy, rather than at the end of a rope. Well, so be it, Griffin was scarcely in a position to judge; not only had he missed Lamport as the informant, but blamed Sophie in his place. It had hardly been the act of an honourable man, or a trusting lover.

In the light from the single candle her face looked especially endearing, and suddenly there was no argument left in his mind. Right or wrong, he knew that any allowance was fully earned, although a strange desire to allow not one modicum of doubt to come between them remained.

"I had considered it to be you," he said, finally. She looked at him, and her face tempered slightly, although she retained hold of his hand.

"Me?"

Griffin nodded. "As the informer, the one who told the Warrens we would be off that beach near Brighthelmstone."

Sophie started to play with his fingers as if they were pieces of an intricate puzzle, before saying simply: "I would never have done so."

"No, I can see that now," he replied. "And I am sorry. But I wanted to tell you. I wanted, most of all, that there be nothing unknown between us. Can you understand that?"

"Yes," she said. "Though there was no need; not on my part, at least. And it was difficult, living under the Warrens," she continued, speaking more to the hand than the person. "Everything we did became distorted, or had a cast to it, as if viewed through a piece of coloured glass." Now she was holding his hand quite tightly. "But the future looks better; they are gone and we will be sure are not replaced. And nothing else, known or unknown, can come between us."

"I'll never mistrust you again," he said.

"Nor I you," she replied frankly, her gaze returning to his face once more. "Nor hurt you in any way: you may be certain."

"I am." He smiled, before adding: "Though perhaps, in the future, we should keep you from any muskets."

Author's note

For several years, a romanticised image of the smuggler has been popular in many forms of entertainment. These 'free traders' are frequently depicted as carrying out deeds of bravery and guile, much to the chagrin of the revenue service. They have even been likened to latter day Robin Hoods, and their activities as nothing more than bringing high-taxed luxuries into the reach of the oppressed working man, although it was a business not without more sinister consequences.

Some indeed were courageous, and the ingenuity and cunning necessary to defeat the preventive men cannot be disputed. Such qualities were sadly misplaced, however, and in reality the majority of the smuggling community were hardened criminals with little care for anything other than their own welfare.

During what has become known as the 'Golden Age of Smuggling' (roughly 1750-1830), Britain became involved in a number of wars and, in the time that this book is set (autumn 1801), Addington's government was actively suing for peace with France. Despite this, numerous gangs and independent operators were prevalent, not only on the south coast, but throughout most of the country, and even as far afield as the Isle of Man. They made high profits from trading with the enemy, with a subsequent and significant loss to the Treasury, although their activities were also damaging in other ways.

Besides importing much that would normally be taxed, the smugglers were also exporters and, throughout the Revolutionary and Napoleonic Wars, they cultivated a thriving market in the very countries that were threatening their homeland. These supplies mainly consisted of wool, then a major and much needed commodity, and gold. The latter had become increasingly scarce in France from 1798, and yet it is estimated that over £10,000 of coin or bullion was regularly shipped from British shores each week. Towards the end of the French wars the smugglers were effectively helping to clothe and finance Napoleon's armies, while much of the general's information came courtesy of a fisherman based in Bexhill-on-Sea, who regularly supplied his offices with military intelligence.

The proliferation of free trading during a time of war had other detrimental effects. Smugglers were said to make lazy drunkards of honest working men. Without doubt a labourer could earn more helping with a landing in one night than during an entire week in the fields, and finding a workforce large enough to bring in the harvest was often a major problem.

Living outside the law as they did, it was not uncommon for smugglers to look for other nefarious means to raise their income, and organised crime proliferated. Gangs, such as that depicted in this book, were relatively common, and could rise to such a prominence that they effectively administered the law. Instances of civil population rebelling against such tyranny, as was seen in Cranbrook and latterly Goudhurst, were heroic, but unusual; the majority accepted that their lives, already harsh from living through almost continuous war, were to be made harder still by the gangs' activities and bore this with misplaced resilience.

The main force used to combat the smugglers was insubstantial, and often consisted of older men unsuitable for military service. The life of a land-based revenue officer was hard and not particularly well rewarded. At sea they fared better, and a relatively lucrative career could be made either as an officer or a simple mariner. The latter benefited from a better wage than his opposite number in the Royal Navy, with the added advantage of being able to maintain a passably normal home life. Officers also drew reasonable pay for their duties, although prospects of advanced promotion were limited. Additionally both enjoyed a good share of seizure money, and the sums could be substantial, even if it was often said that a smuggler was in greater danger from storm or shipwreck than arrest by a preventive man.

With the vast rewards that might be involved in one single run, the smugglers were not adverse to offering bribes, and many Treasury officers succumbed, to the extent that some ports were all but run by the gangs. Instances abound of revenue men and smugglers co-operating to such a degree that the former would actually assist in a landing and it was not uncommon for the proceeds of a particularly fruitful haul to be paraded openly through the streets, to the approval of the local populace. This level of corruption is not surprising, being common in many other industries and government sectors at that time. The following year, Lord St Vincent began a major crusade to eradicate a similar problem with the Royal Dockyards. It was a fight that lasted many years and, even with such a stalwart campaigner to lead it, was not wholly successful.

Alaric Bond
Herstmonceux, 2013

Glossary

Able Seaman	One who can hand, reef and steer and is well-acquainted with the duties of a seaman.
Anker	Cask holding from six to nine gallons. See half-anker and tub.
Back	Wind change; anticlockwise.
Backed sail	One set in the direction for the opposite tack to slow a ship.
Backstays	Similar to shrouds in function, except that they run from the hounds of the topmast, or topgallant, all the way to the deck. Serve to support the mast against any forces forward; for example, when the ship is tacking. (Also a useful/spectacular way to return to deck for topmen.)
Backstays, (running)	A less permanent backstay, rigged with a tackle to allow it to be slacked to clear a gaff or boom.
Barkie	(*Slang*) Seamen's affectionate name for their vessel.
Bat	Smuggler's weapon, usually of ash and up to six feet long.
Batsman	Smuggler armed with a bat to defend a landing.
Belaying pins	Pins set into racks at the side of a ship. Lines are secured to these, allowing instant release by their removal.
Binnacle	Cabinet on the quarterdeck that houses compasses, the log, traverse board, lead lines, telescope and speaking trumpet.
Bishop	(*Slang*) A mixture of wine and water flavoured with a roasted orange. Often warmed.

Bitts	Stout horizontal pieces of timber, supported by strong verticals, that extend deep into the ship. These hold the anchor cable when the ship is at anchor.
Blab	(Slang) A gossip.
Blind Eye	At the battle of Copenhagen (2nd April 1801) Vice-Admiral Nelson led the main attack under Admiral Hyde Parker, who was in overall command. During the action, Nelson is reputed to have disobeyed his superior's order to withdraw by holding the telescope to his blind eye when viewing the signal. The fact Parker had not ordered, but merely given *permission* for Nelson to withdraw (at his discretion) is often ignored, and the idiom 'turning a blind eye' was swiftly incorporated into everyday speech.
Block	Article of rigging that allows pressure to be diverted or, when used with others, increased. Consists of a pulley wheel, made of *lignum vitae*, encased in a wooden shell. Blocks can be single, double (fiddle block), triple or quadruple. The main suppliers were Taylors, of Southampton.
Board	Before being promoted to lieutenant, midshipmen would be tested for competence by a board of post captains. Should they prove able they will be known as passed midshipmen, but not assume the rank of lieutenant until they are appointed as such.
Boat fall	Line that raises or lowers a ship's boat.
Boatswain	(*Pronounced Bosun*) The officer who superintends the sails, rigging, canvas, colours, anchors, cables and cordage, committed to his charge.
Boom	Lower spar to which the bottom of a gaff sail is attached.

Box the Compass	Officially the act of reciting all 32 points of the compass both clockwise and anticlockwise, but often used to describe a full 360-degree turn.
Braces	Lines used to adjust the angle between the yards, and the fore and aft line of the ship. Mizzen braces, and braces of a brig lead forward.
Brig	Two-masted vessel, square-rigged on both masts.
Broach	When running down-wind, to round up into the wind, out of control, usually due to carrying too much canvas.
Bulkhead	A wall or partition within the hull of a ship.
Bulwark	The planking or wood-work about a vessel above her deck.
Canister	Type of shot, also known as case. Small iron balls packed into a cylindrical case.
Cannonade	A shorter cannon used by the HEIC. (Not to be confused with the more effective carronade.)
Carronade	Short cannon firing a heavy shot. Invented by Melville, Gascoigne and Miller in late 1770's and adopted in 1779. Often used on the upper deck of larger ships, or as the main armament of smaller.
Cascabel	Part of the breach of a cannon.
Caulk	(Slang) To sleep. Also caulking, a process to seal the seams between strakes.
Channel	Projecting ledge that holds deadeyes from shrouds and backstays, originally chain-whales.
Chit	(Slang) An infant or baby.
Chub	(Slang) A fool; from the fish that is supposedly easily taken.
Cleat	A retaining piece for lines attached to yards, etc.
Close hauled	Sailing as near as possible into the wind.
Coaming	A ridged frame about hatches to prevent water on deck from getting below.

Collector (of customs)	Chief customs officer responsible for a port or sector.
Companionway	A staircase or passageway.
Comptroller	Customs officer subordinate to the collector, and responsible for checking the collector's accounts.
Counter	The lower part of a vessel's stern.
Course	A large square lower sail, hung from a yard, with sheets controlling and securing it.
Crop	A cargo of contraband.
Crowling gin	(Slang) Smuggled gin.
Crows of iron	Crow bars used to move a gun or heavy object.
Cruiser	(Slang) a revenue cutter.
Cutter	Fast, small, single-masted vessel with a sloop rig. Also a seaworthy ship's boat.
Deadeyes	A round, flattish wooden block with three holes through which a lanyard is reeved. Used to tension shrouds and backstays.
Ditty bag	(Slang) A seaman's bag. Derives its name from the dittis or 'Manchester stuff' of which it was once made.
Driver	Large sail set on the mizzen in light winds. The foot is extended by means of a boom.
Dry goods	Literally non-liquid contraband.
Dunnage	Officially the packaging around cargo. Also (slang) seaman's baggage or possessions.
Diachylon plaster	An early form of sticking plaster.
Factor	Master merchant in the HEIC.
Fall	The free end of a lifting tackle on which the men haul.
Fetch	To arrive at, or reach a destination. Also the distance the wind blows across the water. The longer the fetch the bigger the waves.
Flasker	(Slang) One who smuggles liquor.
Fleet (Prison)	Notable prison in London, first built in 1197.
Forereach	To gain upon, or pass by another ship when sailing in a similar direction.

Forestay	Stay supporting the masts running forward, serving the opposite function of the backstay. Runs from each mast at an angle of about 45 degrees to meet another mast, the deck or the bowsprit.
Free trader	Popular euphemism for a smuggler.
Glass	Telescope. Also, hourglass: an instrument for measuring time. Also a barometer.
Go-about	To alter course, changing from one tack to the other.
Gobbler	*(Slang)* Smuggler's euphemism for a revenue official.
Grappling-iron	Small anchor, fitted with four or five flukes or claws, often used to hold two ships together for boarding.
Half-anker	Cask holding about four gallons; often referred to as a tub.
Halyards	Lines which raise yards, sails, signals etc.
Hanger	A fighting sword, similar to a cutlass.
Hawse	Area in bows where holes are cut to allow the anchor cables to pass through. Also used as general term for bows.
Hawser	Heavy cable used for hauling, towing or mooring.
Headway	The amount a vessel is moved forward (rather than leeway: the amount a vessel is moved sideways) when the wind is not directly behind.
Heave to	Keeping a ship relatively stationary by backing certain sails in a seaway.
HEIC	Honourable East India Company.
Hide	Safe place for concealing contraband.
Holystone	*(Slang)* Block of sandstone roughly the size and shape of a family bible. Used to clean and smooth decks. Originally salvaged from the ruins of a church on the Isle of Wright.
Hulled	It is said of a ship that when fired upon the shot passes right through the hull.

Interest	Backing from a superior officer or one in authority, useful when looking for promotion.
Jape	*(Slang)* Joke.
Jib-boom	Boom run out from the extremity of the bowsprit, braced by means of a martingale stay, which passes through the dolphin striker.
Jibe	To change tack with the wind coming from astern. Also to wear, a term more commonly used in square-rigged vessels.
Jigger	*(Slang)* Mizzen mast.
John Company	*(Slang)* The East India Company.
Junk	Old line used to make wads, etc.
Jury mast/rig	Temporary measure used to restore a vessel's sailing ability.
Kerseymere	Woollen cloth.
Landshark	*(Slang)* Popular smuggler's euphemism for land-based revenue officers.
Landsman	The rating of one who has no experience at sea.
Landwaiter	Revenue officer responsible for recording imported goods or contraband.
Lanthorn	Lantern.
Larboard	Left side of the ship when facing forward. Later replaced by 'port', which had previously been used for helm orders.
Leeward	The downwind side of a vessel.
Leeway	The amount a vessel is pushed sideways by the wind (as opposed to headway, the forward movement, when the wind is directly behind).
Let down (to)	The act of diluting over-proof spirit.
Linstock	The holder of slow match which the gun captain uses to fire his piece when the flintlock mechanism is not working/present.
Lubberly/lubber	*(Slang)* Unseamanlike behaviour; as a landsman.
Luff	Intentionally sail closer to the wind, perhaps to allow work aloft. Also the flapping of sails when brought too close to the wind. The side of a fore and aft sail laced to the mast.

Main tack	Line leading forward from a sheave in the hull, allowing the clew of the main course to be held forward when the ship is sailing close to the wind.
Martingale stay	Line that braces the jib-boom, passing from the end through the dolphin striker to the ship.
Militia	Local military force, usually non-professional, employed when needed.
Owler	(Slang) One who smuggles wool.
Pandle	Sussex term for shrimp.
Peach	(Slang) To betray or reveal; from impeach.
Pipe	Cask holding 105 gallons.
Pitch Cap	Form of torture used by British forces during the Irish Rebellion of 1798.
Pox	(Slang) Venereal disease.
Prigger	(Slang) A criminal, usually a thief.
Privateer	Privately owned vessel fitted out as a warship, and licensed to capture enemy vessels. The licence allows a greater number of guns to be fitted.
Protection	A legal document that gives the owner protection against impressment.
Quarterdeck	In larger ships the deck forward of the poop, but at a lower level. The preserve of officers.
Queue	A pigtail. Often tied by a seaman's best friend (his tie mate).
Rascal	A rogue or villain. A hunting term, originally meaning a stag at the time of changing his antlers.
Ratlines	Lighter lines, untarred and tied horizontally across the shrouds at regular intervals, to act as rungs and allow men to climb aloft.
Reef	A portion of sail that can be taken in to reduce the size of the whole.
Reefing points	Light line on large sails, which can be tied to reduce sail in heavy weather.

Reefing tackle	Line that leads from the end of the yard to the reefing cringles set in the edges of the sail. It is used to haul up the upper part of the sail when reefing.
Riding officer	Shore-based customs officer, usually mounted, detailed to search for smugglers and hidden or abandoned contraband.
Rigging	Tophamper; made up of standing (static) and running (moveable) rigging, blocks etc. (*Slang*) Clothes.
Rondey	(*Slang*) The *Rendezvous*: where a press is based and organised.
Rummage	To search.
Running	Sailing before the wind.
Schooner	Small craft with two masts.
Scran	(*Slang*) Food.
Scot-free	(*Slang*) Originally from sceot, the Old English word for tax, referring to anyone who had been able to avoid payment.
Scupper	Waterway that allows deck drainage.
Seizer Money	An allowance given to revenue men for confiscating contraband goods.
Seven Sisters	A series of chalk cliffs between Seaford and Eastbourne.
Sheet	A line that controls the foot of a sail.
Shrouds	Lines supporting the masts athwart ship (from side to side) which run from the hounds (just below the top) to the channels on the side of the hull.
Smack	Vessel similar to a cutter in rig.
Snow	Type of brig, with an extra trysail mast stepped behind the main.
Spring	Hawser attached to a fixed object that can be tensioned to move the position of a ship fore and aft along a dock, often when setting out to sea. Breast lines control position perpendicular to the dock.

Sprit sail	A square sail hung from the bowsprit yards, less used by 1793 as the function had been taken over by the jibs although the rigging of their yards helps to brace the bowsprit against sideways pressure.
Square heads	*(Slang)* Dutchmen.
Stag	*(Slang)* To turn against your own.
Stay sail	A quadrilateral or triangular sail with parallel lines, usually hung from under a stay.
Stern sheets	Part of a ship's boat between the stern and the first rowing thwart, used for passengers.
Stingo	*(Slang)* Beer.
Strake	A plank.
Suds (in the)	*(Slang)* To be in trouble.
Tack	To turn a ship, moving her bows through the wind. Also a leg of a journey relating to the direction of the wind. If from starboard, a ship is on the starboard tack. Also the part of a fore and aft loose-footed sail where the sheet is attached, or a line leading forward on a square course to hold the lower part of the sail forward.
Taffrail	Rail around the stern of a vessel.
Tattletale	*(Slang)* Gossip.
Tide waiter	Officer responsible for searching any newly arrived, or impounded vessel.
Tight ship	In good order: watertight.
Tophamper	Literally any unnecessary weight either on a ship's decks or about her tops and rigging, but often used loosely to refer to spars and rigging.
Trick	*(Slang)* Period of duty.
Tub	A small cask, or half-anker, the main purpose of which was for smuggling.
Tub man	Smuggler employed to carry tubs inland, usually about the neck, one in front and one behind.
Turnpike	A toll road; the user pays for the upkeep. Usually major roads.

Veer	Wind change, clockwise.
Waist	Area of main deck between the quarterdeck and forecastle.
Watch	Period of four (or in case of dog watch, two) hour duty. Also describes the two or three divisions of a crew.
Watch list	List of men and stations, usually carried by lieutenants and divisional officers.
Wearing	To change the direction of a ship across the wind by putting its stern through the eye of the wind. Also jibe – more common in a fore and aft rig.
Windward	The side of a ship exposed to the wind.

About the author

Alaric Bond was born in Surrey, and now lives in Herstmonceux, East Sussex. He has been writing professionally for over twenty years.

His interests include the British Navy, 1793-1815, and the RNVR during WWII. He is also a keen collector of old or unusual musical instruments, and 78 rpm records.

Alaric Bond is a member of various historical societies and regularly gives talks to groups and organisations.

www.alaricbond.com

About Old Salt Press

Old Salt Press is an independent press catering to those who love books about ships and the sea. We are an association of writers working together to produce the very best of nautical and maritime fiction and non-fiction. We invite you to join us as we go down to the sea in books.

More Great Reading from Old Salt Press:

The Beckoning Ice

A fifth Wiki Coffin mystery

"Combining historical and nautical accuracy with a fast paced mystery thriller has produced a marvellous book which is highly recommended."
— David Hayes, Historic Naval Fiction

The Beckoning Ice finds the U. S. Exploring Expedition off Cape Horn, a grim outpost made still more threatening by the report of a corpse on a drifting iceberg, closely followed by a gruesome death on board. Was it suicide, or a particularly brutal murder? Wiki investigates, only to find himself fighting desperately for his own life.

Hell Around the Horn

Thrilling yarn from the last days of the square-riggers

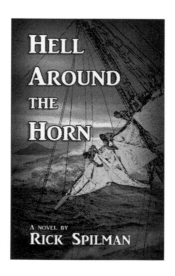

In 1905, a young ship's captain and his family set sail on the windjammer, Lady Rebecca, from Cardiff, Wales with a cargo of coal bound for Chile, by way of Cape Horn. Before they reach the Southern Ocean, the cargo catches fire, the mate threatens mutiny and one of the crew may be going mad. The greatest challenge, however, will prove to be surviving the vicious westerly winds and mountainous seas of the worst Cape Horn winter in memory. Told from the perspective of the Captain, his wife, a first year apprentice and an American sailor before the mast, *Hell Around the Horn* is a story of survival and the human spirit in the last days of the great age of sail.

Captain Blackwell's Prize

A romantic adventure from the days of wooden ships and iron men

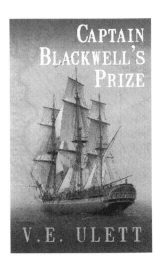

A small, audacious British frigate does battle against a large but ungainly Spanish ship. British Captain James Blackwell intercepts the Spanish *La Trinidad*, outmanoeuvres and outguns the treasure ship and boards her. Fighting alongside the Spanish captain, sword in hand, is a beautiful woman. The battle is quickly over. The Spanish captain is killed in the fray and his ship damaged beyond repair. Its survivors and treasure are taken aboard the British ship, *Inconstant*.

Captain Blackwell's Prize features sword fights and sea battles alongside the manners, ideas, and prejudices of men and women from the time of Nelson and Napoleon.